DANRITE

a

THE YELLOW SNOW

Best the

To Enzo

Best W[ishes]

8/June/24

The 1st signed.

STEFAN JAKUBOWSKI

Published in 2024
by
Zygmunt Stanley

ISBN 978-0-9574625-3-3

©2024 Stefan Jakubowski

Cover designed by Zygmunt Stanley
Pages designed and typeset by Zygmunt Stanley

Bound and Printed by Biddles Books Limited

Titles
by
Stefan Jakubowski

*

Supernatural comedy

STRANGE RELATIONS
DEAD PECULIAR

Fantasy comedy nonsense

MISCREATION

Time travel comedy with Tom Tyme

ONCE UPON A TYME
TYME AND TIME AGAIN
SOME OTHER TYME

Comedy tales of the short kind

NOT JUST FOR CHRISTMAS

Magical comedy

DANRITE WILLOCKY
DANRITE WILLOCKY and THE YELLOW SNOW

*

THE AUTHOR

Originally from Reading,
Stefan moved to Wales in the latter part of the last century.
(He wishes to point out he is not as old as that makes him sound!)
(Nia, his wife, wishes to point out: 'Oh yes, he is!')
He lives with Nia somewhere in Carmarthenshire.

For

The things that make you smile

It is written that if myth, fantasy, and make-believe should ever threaten to fade from the earth, to become but shadowy memories on its surface, a champion will arise, a hero who will face the dark and lead the creatures of the fantastic from its depths, and back into the world of the light.

Well, that happened, sort of, not all of it. For one thing, they spelled Earth with a lowercase e. How are you supposed to know what on earth is going on if they do that? Which earth/Earth do they mean? The big one or dirt?

Anyway, they got over that and are now heading to another Otherworld. One that is shadowy and dangerous.

Danrite, Jose, Salor, Vlad, and Twinkle have a new mission. Oh, and now Frida. And Basil. To seek out and destroy the Evil. The mastermind behind everything bad. Well, not everything. Not tummy upsets. Shoelaces breaking. That sort of thing. But certain things bad enough that needs our heroes to go seek it out and destroy it. The Evil.

Wish them luck. They are going to need it. There's yellow snow, for goodness' sake!

Oh, dearie me.

CHAPTER 1

'Blimey,' said Vlad.

'With you there,' said Twinkle.

'Ditto,' said Danrite and Frida as one. They stared at each other.

'Ay caramba, with knobs on,' said Jose.

'Oof,' said Salor, falling forward.

Basil said nothing. He was just happy he'd had such a soft landing.

'Blimey,' said Vlad.

CHAPTER 2

Four faces looked up as one.

'What was that?' asked a face.

'You sensed that too?' said another.

'Sí,' said another.

'Grief,' exclaimed the fourth, 'you don't think…?'

'Sí,' said the one that had already said sí.

'Sí to what?' asked the first face that had spoken. 'Sí, you sensed it or sí, you don't think?'

'Sí to both,' said Pablo, who owned the frowning face that had said sí. He thought it a stupid question. He whispered something under his breath.

'What did you just say?' growled Wrinkle, the owner of the glowering face that had asked the question. And who was also the face that had first spoken.

'Sí,' said Pablo, all innocent-like.

Wrinkle glowered some more but said nothing.

'Then we should make plans,' suggested Wazzock, who owned the face that had also sensed it.

'Fat lot of good that did us the last time,' said Wrinkle.

'But there wasn't a last time to plan for,' said Von Vlod, who claimed ownership of the fourth face. 'We *were* the last time.'

As usual, where these four faces were concerned, things were getting a little confusing.

'Whatever,' sighed Wazzock. 'But I do feel we should go take a look, though. Just in case. It might be our way out.'

Wrinkle, Von Vlod and Pablo exchanged worried glances.

CHAPTER 3

'Oh-no!' exclaimed a creature, his black eyes filled with sudden dread. 'No-no-no! Flipping soggy snowballs, no!'

It had been a fair while since someone new had entered the world he existed in. The world he was stuck in. They would be looking, hunting, and he would be the prey.

He had been expecting it. Had hoped he was wrong. He had tried not to think about such things. But now he had to. Think about such things. And the first thought, when thinking upon it, was that he had to hide. Make with the skedaddle. Vamoose. Make like a ghost and disappear. He also had to stop thinking about it and do it. He had a habit of dithering when frightened. Not a good habit to have. Not when danger was about. So, go, he thought.

The creature, his name not important, started to move. Began to wobble to the left. Wobble to the right. Wobbling as fast as he could. He needed to get to his hiding place and fast. Toot-sweet. Pronto. Today, not tomorrow. Just go, he thought, go!

CHAPTER 4

'They've arrived,' whispered a hooded figure into a talky-walky.

'Good. Keep a close eye on them,' came a reply. 'All of them.'

'You mean the others?'

'Of course, I mean the others,' snapped an irritated response. 'Use your brain for once; that's why you're there.' There was a heavy pause as the irritated one thought about what they had just said. He was most definitely not there to use his brain, goodness forbid. 'Just do what you're there to do.'

'But what if they try to interfere? It might all go wrong again,' whimpered the hooded figure. He hated it when the boss was angry with him. Which was most of the time.

'Then tell me,' said the irritated one, who was sounding even more irritated than before.

'But last time.'

'Forget last time,' snapped the irritated one, who was the hooded figure's boss but preferred to be called Master. 'And forget about all the other times as well. This time is different. This time, the real hero is there.'

'But the other others.' The hooded figure was fixated on disaster.

'They know nothing,' snapped Master. 'Just do your job!'

'Yes, Master,' said the hooded figure, wilting as he suddenly realised the disaster he was fixated on might well be his own. 'I will, Master.'

'And you know what has to happen when they find him?'

'Yes.'

'Good. Now, why are you still talking? Be off with you. You lose them, and I lose you, got it?'

'Ye—,' started the hooded figure before thinking better of it. He quickly turned the talky-walky off.

On the other end of the talky-walky, someone wondered if they were doing the right thing. Sending more idiots to do a job that would be better served if they did it themselves. But what if it did go wrong? No, it wouldn't, not this time. But if it did? Then better to send the idiots to do it. They're expendable.

CHAPTER 5

'What the?' wailed a winded Salor as he twisted beneath Basil, who had knocked him over and was now sitting on his back. Salor half turned and pushed at him. 'Get off me.' Basil, who had landed on Salor when coming through the portal, was duly pushed off.

'Oof,' groaned Basil as he landed on his bottom. He immediately started to get to his feet, using the still prostrate Salor's back to push on. Salor groaned. 'Sorry, I'm sure.' Which was doubtful, as it wasn't his fault to his mind. Now upright, he brushed himself down.

'What the what?' said Twinkle, bending to give Salor a hand up.

'What?' said Salor, taking Twinkle's hand.

'You said what the,' said Twinkle. 'What the, what?'

'Did I?' puzzled Salor, forgetting he had.

'Yes, we all heard you.'

'Oh,' said Salor, 'then I must have.'

Twinkle rolled her eyes. 'Never mind, I doubt it was important. But talking of what the, what the heck is going on?'

'What do you mean?' asked Salor, the only one yet to take in the surroundings.

'This.' Twinkle did a sweep of her hand. 'We haven't gone anywhere.'

'Sí,' agreed Pablo, 'she is being right in what she is saying.'

'Nonsense,' said Salor, who was faffing with his tie, 'we went through the portal.'

'Did we?' questioned Twinkle.

'Perhaps we returned without realising it,' reasoned Danrite.

'That or the portal didn't work for some reason,' suggested Frida.

Salor, who had finished with his faffing, finally looked and took note. 'Ye gads!' he exclaimed when he did. He then just stared and joined the others in wondering what the heck was going on.

Were they victims of some devious deed? Someone's idea of a prank? Had they just imagined it all, walking through the portal? Or were they actually somewhere else, but the somewhere else was the same as where they were when they were somewhere else other than here? Thankfully, before everyone started to get headaches from thinking too much, Basil came to their aid.

5

'Of course, we've travelled,' Basil assured them.

'Then,' said Salor, sweeping his arm out before him, though with a more theatrical air than Twinkle had, 'how do you account for this?'

'This what?'

Twinkle scowled at the little man. 'This,' she said, using both hands this time.

'Sí, this,' said Jose, just before he fell on his face. The sweeping of three limbs was a limb too far.

'They have a point,' said Danrite, as he knelt to see if Jose was okay. He was.

'They do.' Frida, hands on hips, wondered if the little man was being purposely awkward.

'Oh,' said Basil, 'you mean the castle roof.'

'Yes, we mean the castle roof,' snarled Twinkle.

Basil suddenly realised they were serious; they hadn't noticed. He wanted to laugh, but seeing the look in both Twinkle and Frida's eyes, Basil decided it might be best not to and own up to what he knew for his own safety. 'It's a different roof,' he said, whilst skipping over the obvious clue to their being somewhere else. He couldn't help himself.

'Explain,' demanded Twinkle.

'How do you know it's a different one?' asked Danrite.

'How do you know we've travelled?' asked Salor.

But enough fun, he had a job to do. They all did. Basil told how he knew they had travelled. He then finished arranging his rucksack to his liking – the Font had packed it – and hefted it onto his back. He hadn't wanted to be there. But there he was. And to get back to where he really wanted to be, he would just have to put up with the way it was until it was all over. He sighed. Such was life. He looked at the circle of dumbfounded, uncomprehending faces. Time to go. He made for the door that led to the stairs that led to the exit. He knew where he was going because this castle was an exact copy of the one they had just left.

At the door, Basil turned and gave one last look. They were still staring at each other like gormless numpties, but he was sure they would soon follow once they got over the shock. He shut the door behind him.

CHAPTER 6

'Better had,' said Wazzock.

'Better had not,' argued Wrinkle.

'Sí,' agreed Pablo, 'I am with her.'

'But if we find them, we might be able to help them.' said Von Vlod.

'Vlod's right,' said Wazzock, 'it might be a chance to escape.'

'How long have we been here?' asked Wrinkle, knowing full well just how long it had been.

'Too long,' said Von Vlod, glumly.

'Your point?' groaned Wazzock, knowing full well Wrinkle knew just how long.

'My point is,' said Wrinkle, widening her stance as if readying for a brawl, 'is that we have survived thus far, so why put ourselves in pointless danger?' She turned and looked towards the cave they called home; something or someone, half hidden, was standing in the gloomy entrance and staring back at her.

'But what if this is our last chance?' whispered Von Vlod. 'Shouldn't we at least have a look?'

Wrinkle turned on Von Vlod. 'Who said it was our last chance?' she growled. But it wasn't anger that had her acting as she was; it was fear. Fear of the unknown. A fear Wrinkle wouldn't admit to.

'I agree with Vlod,' said Wazzock, ignoring Wrinkle's posturing. 'If, by chance, this is indeed our way out, shouldn't we take it?' He, too, then looked towards the cave. 'Do you really want to end up like them?'

'Oi!' came a voice scratching from within that cave. 'We can hear you, you know.' It was an extremely scratchy voice.

The stance Wrinkle was taking suddenly weakened. She shivered. What was she doing? Wrinkle glanced at the cave. At the figure, half hidden, who had spoken. No, she didn't want to end up like them. Wrinkle shivered again.

'Well?' said Wazzock.

'Drat,' said Wrinkle.

'Then it is decided,' declared Wazzock.

'When do we go?' said Von Vlod.

'As soon as we are ready.'

Something growled. It was an indignant Pablo. 'Am I not having a saying in things?' he asked.

'Unanimous decision,' said Wazzock, who turned and headed for the cave before Pablo could argue.

Pablo wasn't happy and stamped a paw. He was frowning and began to mutter quietly. 'When I am finding you, you younanny mouse who had been choosing for me, I will be having the many words with you. Sí, the many strong words.' He stooped and sniffed. He could not catch the scent of the younanny mouse, but he would find him. He would find him. Or her.

Or not.

CHAPTER 7

Wobble. Wibble. Slither.

CHAPTER 8

'What did he mean?' asked Salor, puzzled by Basil's words. 'No colour?' He lifted his tie and stared at it.

Twinkle, though, was a step ahead. Her first reaction had been to look at her hands. 'Agh!' she wailed as she saw them. They were grey.

And then, like dominoes, they all began to notice. They looked here, looked there, looked at each other. There was no colour anywhere. Everything was black, white, or grey. The scene around them was like those seen on the screen of an early black and white television set.

'Flipping 'eck,' cried Danrite.

'What the heck?' said Frida.

'My beautiful tie!' wailed Salor.

But not all were upset by their newly found situation.

'Look,' enthused Jose, a large fang-filled grin across his face. 'My coat, it is black.' He had always fancied himself in a black coat. One he could look broody in. He swished his tail. A black sword of a tail. Broody was swiftly forgotten. His eyes widened with delight. 'I am being a knight like of old.' He swished his tail again. 'I am being a black knight.' He did a little twirl so all could get a good look.

'Yeah,' muttered Twinkle, 'and one that will soon be seeing stars if he doesn't shut up.' She was in a grump because her tutu was no longer leafy but more your ashy camouflage, just right if you wanted to merge into the background of a long, cold bonfire.

'I am only saying,' pouted a crestfallen Jose, his feelings hurt.

'It's okay,' said Frida, 'she's only jealous. You cut quite the figure.'

'Sí,' smiled a now happier Jose, 'it is what I am thinking.' He swished his tail for good measure.

Twinkle wrinkled her nose, mumbled something to no one in particular and turned her attention to the next object of her ire: Basil. She wanted a word with him.

'What do we do now?' groaned Salor, still staring at his tie. The moons no longer silver. The stars no longer gold.

'Perhaps we should have a word with Basil,' suggested Danrite. 'He might know what's going on.'

'Good idea,' said Frida, eyeing the space he was no longer in. 'But, where is he?'

'Good question,' growled Twinkle, disappointed her new target was nowhere to be seen.

'I am thinking I am seeing him that way,' said Jose, swishing his tail in the direction of the door Basil had left the roof through. At the time, Jose had been the only one with his wits about him.

'Did he now?' snarled Twinkle, still with the angry. Fists clenched, she headed towards it with the intention of shaking what Basil knew, if anything, out of him.

Frida quickly got in step. 'What are you going to do?' she asked, hoping there was going to be something left of Basil they could talk to.

'I don't know, but I'll have fun finding out,' Twinkle growled. She really wasn't a happy bunny.

Twinkle strode across the roof with purpose. Frida, trying to keep up beside her. A worried-looking Danrite followed. Behind him, Salor, who was still staring at his beloved tie in dismay, was being tugged along by his robe by a beaming black knight, his tail wagging happily.

CHAPTER 9

The hooded figure was nervous. His master had said the real hero was here this time. But wasn't the last hero real? Or the one before that? What made his master say that? But it wasn't for him to question the Master. His was to do. Follow orders. But the hooded figure wanted to go home. Too long for comfort in this place, he felt. The real hero, though. What did that mean? It worried him.

The hooded figure sighed heavily as he emerged from his hiding place. Do the job. Don't think. Thinking gets you into trouble. But when would it all end? And would all be all right when it did? No. Stop it. Don't think. Do the job. The hooded figure picked up his pace. Didn't want to lose them. More than his life was worth if he did. If it mattered in the end. Stop it!

CHAPTER 10

They reached the main hall. Strangely, it only seemed a moment ago that they were last there. But of course, they were, in a way. Even stranger, perhaps because of the lack of colour, it also felt a lifetime ago. A weird feeling. The room also looked bigger. The lack of colour? And colder. No one felt any colder, but it hadn't stopped them from shivering when they entered it. It just looked colder. No colour to warm it? And across the room, waiting for them, was Basil. He was seated on the only piece of furniture, the only thing, other than them, in the room. The Fonts chair, or throne, as Basil liked to think of it. His feet were dangling. He appeared to be enjoying the moment, his little legs swinging back and forth.

'Oi,' shouted Twinkle as soon as she saw him, shattering Basil's moment, 'I want a word with you.'

A startled Basil jumped and then half-fell, half-scrambled from the throne. He had all but forgotten about them as he had enjoyed his moment. He glanced once and quickly at Twinkle before heading just as quickly towards the door that would take him from there to outside. Outside, yes; out of Twinkle's clutches, no. Pointless then. But a survival instinct had kicked in.

'Not so fast,' yelled Twinkle, who, for her size, was surprisingly nimble and quick.

Still going but not knowing quite why, Basil was still skedaddling for all he was worth when a fist, the size of a large one, grabbed him by the collar. The next moment, his feet were no longer touching the floor. A dangling, helpless Basil, held aloft like a prize turnip, sighed and sagged.

'We need answers,' demanded Twinkle.

'Yes,' said Frida.

'With them,' said Danrite.

'Sí,' mumbled Jose, though a mouthful of robe.

'My tie,' wailed Salor.

CHAPTER 11

Wibble. Wobble. Slither. Slip!

CHAPTER 12

Wazzock led the way. Striding forth with purpose. This could be their chance; he didn't want to miss it.

Behind him, Von Vlod. Striding with equal purpose. Desperately wanting to get back to before. Away from this shadow of Von Vlod's former self.

Wrinkle kept up with hardly any purpose at all. She had gathered as much enthusiasm as she could muster to spur her along, but it wasn't much. She wanted, as much as the others did, to get back to the worlds they had left behind; she just wasn't holding out much in the way of hope of it happening. She hoped she was wrong.

With no purpose whatsoever, Pablo dawdled behind. He dawdled because he was in no hurry. He was in no hurry because they had all day. All week. All year. The rest of their lifetimes. Because others had seen it all before. Because they were still here, those others. Because once upon a time, he, Wazzock, Von Vlod and Wrinkle had been their hope, and look how that had turned out.

Pablo dwelt for a moment at that thought and looked behind him. They were there. They were following.

CHAPTER 13

'Let me down,' wailed Basil, who was now hanging upside down by a foot. A scowling Twinkle had hold of it.

'Shouldn't we just ask him what he knows?' suggested Danrite. 'He is supposed to be on our side.'

'He's right,' agreed Frida.

'I suppose,' sighed Twinkle. 'Just one more little shake though.'

'No!' yelled Danrite and Frida as one. Both frowned as they looked at each other. They would have to get used to it.

Twinkle went to release her grip on Basil's ankle.

'Whoa!' said Frida. There was a drop of at least a metre between the floor and Basil's head. 'Perhaps you should put him down. He's no good to us with a broken head.'

'Fank ou,' stammered a relieved but dizzy Basil as he was lowered, but not too gently, but lowered all the same, onto the floor.

Basil quickly got up. A little too quickly, it appeared, as he instantly lost balance, stumbled, and promptly fell backwards, landing on his bottom with a thump. His head now started to swell, and his eyes began to spin weirdly. His face, which would have been bright red had there been colour, was now taking on a more purpled hue. If there had been colour.

'That's weird,' observed Danrite. 'Look at his eyes. I've never seen eyes swivel like that before.'

'Sí,' agreed Jose. 'It is being crazy, loco.'

'I always thought he was a bit weird,' said Twinkle, chipping in.

'I expect your eyes would be swivelling too if you had been hanging upside down for five or so minutes,' said Frida, who wasn't actually looking at Basil as her attention had turned to Salor, who was still staring at his tie. 'Salor?'

'Only if I was in a cartoon,' said Danrite.

Frida gently removed Salor's tie from between his fingers and made eye contact. 'Salor?'

'Sí,' said Jose. 'If he is being in a cartoon, that is being weird.'

Making sure Salor appeared to be stable, Frida turned to have a look at what Danrite and Jose were going on about. 'Grief!' she said when she saw Basil's eyes for herself. 'That's not normal.'

Removed from his tie, Salor suddenly became Salor again and decided he wanted to know what was going on. He pushed between Danrite and Frida and confronted Basil. 'So,' he demanded, ignoring Basil's predicament, 'how about you telling us what you know.' It was as if his tie no longer existed.

'Yes. And right now,' demanded Twinkle, thinking enough was enough. If the little man's head was going to explode, then they needed to gather as much info as they could before it did.

'Give him a chance,' pleaded Frida.

'Well,' muttered Twinkle.

'Five minutes,' said Salor.

If his head lasts that long, thought Twinkle.

They waited, and after a minute or so, Basil's eyes began to slow their swivelling. His head was also returning to its original size, and his face its original shade of greyscale. Until finally, he resembled – apart from some blotches and the pupils of his eyes being almost as large as his eyeballs – his normal self. He was now able to focus on and look at the expectant faces that were staring at him, and as he did, he wondered if they would believe him whatever he told them, truth or not. Not that he knew much. Only one way to find out, he decided.

'Osay,' slurred Basil. So, not all was quite back to how it was.

'What did he say?' said Twinkle, already thinking the little man was trying to pull a fast one.

'Give him a chance,' said Frida. She didn't like the look of Basil's eyes one little bit. Perhaps he won't be able to tell us anything now, she thought.

Basil took a deep breath and tried again. 'Solly.' He coughed. He tried again. This time, with more success. 'Sorry.' Things were looking up. 'Okay,' he managed. 'What can I tell you that you'll believe?' Basil wasn't big on creating trust.

'The truth,' suggested Danrite.

'Sí,' said Jose.

'The whole truth and nothing but the truth,' said Salor.

'Well?' barked Twinkle, who could scare paint into drying.

'Basil?' urged Frida.

'We're at the castle,' said Basil. 'Kind of.'

17

Twinkle growled. 'We gathered that.'

'Basil!' Frida's tone now a mite sterner.

'Okay,' said Basil, knowing when to give in. But what could he tell them when what he knew could fit in a thimble? And most of that thimbleful of knowledge was on a strict need-to-know basis. There was also the television to think of. The threat of not having one if he were to say too much. He wanted a television. It was his dream. He didn't want to chance losing the chance of having one. The Font had told him he could have one if he were good. Did his job well. But she had said that before, and what did he have to show for it? An empty TV stand and a copy of the Radio Times gathering dust beside it. That's what. But there was always the chance. But he had to tell them something. He glanced at Frida. But not just anything. He felt she would know if he was lying. He thought again of the empty TV stand and suddenly felt alone. As usual, the Font had left him out on a limb. He decided he would tell the truth, tell them what he knew. He then thought of the television again. But perhaps not all he knew.

'He's up to something,' said Salor when Basil's silence grew.

'Maybe he needs help remembering,' threatened Twinkle.

'What?' sputtered Basil as Twinkle loomed over him. He hadn't realised how long he'd been taking working things through his mind. 'No, what I mean is it's complicated. I was just trying to remember everything. You know, after my episode.'

'That's reasonable,' said Frida.

A wary Twinkle backed off a little. 'I suppose.'

'And?' said Salor.

Okay, thought Basil, here goes. 'We *are* in the Otherside, in the darkest of the Othersides.' And now the thimble was empty. Or at least the part of it Basil thought he could share.

'That's all the Font told you?' asked a sceptical Salor.

'That, and that we have to save imagination,' added Basil. 'Oh, and to keep an eye on you all.'

'And what's that supposed to mean?' demanded Twinkle.

'To look after you and keep you safe, I suppose,' said Basil.

'You?' said Twinkle with a smirk.

Basil managed to look embarrassed. 'Yes,' he said. He wasn't lying. The Font had told him to keep an eye on them.

'So, what happens now?' said Danrite. They all knew they had to save imagination. That's why they were where they were. But the Font hadn't actually said how they were going to do that. They had all assumed Basil would fill them in with details when they arrived.

'I want to know why this Otherworld?' said Frida.

'Yes,' said Salor. 'Why this one? And why is it the darkest?'

'And why is there no colour?' asked Twinkle.

'And I am thinking, why is it the castle is being here?' puzzled Jose. He was also wondering where the nearest tree might be.

Basil took on a worried look. They were all good questions. One he didn't have the answer to, but the others he did. However, he had to be careful what he said if he did answer them. So should he? He decided he could. No harm if he was careful. So he answered them. 'We're here because the Font thinks this is where everything started. The lack of colour here because it needs imagination, which I suppose is why it's the darkest. That's all I know.' It wasn't.

'What about the castle?' said Wazzock.

'Sí,' said Jose. 'The castle.'

'I don't know,' said Basil. 'It was as much a surprise for me as it was for you.'

'You didn't look surprised,' said Twinkle.

'What can I say? I've worked for the Font for years,' said Basil wistfully. 'Nothing much she does throws me anymore.'

'You haven't answered my question,' said Danrite.

'Your question?' said Basil.

'What do we do now?'

This was another question Basil could answer, but it was the one he would have to be most careful with when he did. He didn't want to give too much away.

'You have to find the evil that wants to destroy imagination and stop it,' Basil explained. 'The Font believes it lives here.' His mouth was suddenly dry. Had he said too much? Was his dream of a television no more? No, he thought, it is why they are here. No damage done. But he knew if he told them what they had to do once they found that evil, there would be a revolt. No one would do it. Could do it. He knew he wouldn't be able to. The plan was to find the evil and then thrust it upon them. So they had no time to think about it. Kid gloves and then a knee-jerk reaction. The Font said it was the only way. Grief, he thought, television or no television, I wish I was home.

'Then we are going,' said Jose, brandishing his tail like a sword. He swished it. 'We go to fight evil!'

'I suppose,' said Frida.

'Then let's get to it,' enthused Salor. It would be nice to have his tie back to its wonderful, colourful self.

'Ahead of you,' said Danrite, reaching for a door handle.

'Not that door,' warned Basil as Danrite went to open it. 'That's the broom cupboard. This way.'

Twinkle gave Frida a worried glance. Frida returned it.

'He's not telling us everything, is he?' said Twinkle as they also headed for the door Basil was making a bee-line for.

'No,' said Frida. 'But for the moment, I think it's best to go with the flow.'

Twinkle nodded and then went to help Danrite – who had opened the door to the broom cupboard anyway – disentangle himself from one of its occupants.

Basil meantime, had opened the right door and had stepped outside. Closely followed by Salor and Jose.

'So,' said Salor, staring at the colourless scenery that met them. 'Which way?'

'I don't know,' said Basil. He wasn't lying.

CHAPTER 14

The slithering had stopped. The wibbling and wobbling had stopped. The slip had been dealt with. A rest for the moment. The slope had been steep. The summit had been reached. And now home. Or not.

'Fiddlesticks.'

The creature with the unimportant name squinted down to whence he had started from. There it was, back at the bottom of the steep slope. An eye. His eye. It looked back at him. He would have to get it. At the bottom of the slope, the eye watched and waited.

With a tentative wobble. And then a careful wibble. The now one-eyed creature with the unimportant name started to slither. Easy now. Not too quickly. Don't want to slip.

'Agh!'

At the bottom of the slope again, his descent a smidgeon quicker than intended, the creature with the unimportant name wobbled to a stop. Once steady, he picked up his wayward eye and popped it back where it belonged.

With two eyes again, the creature with the unimportant name once more looked to the task at hand. He sighed. It wasn't going to be easy; it wasn't the first time. So, to make sure there wouldn't be a third time, he pushed all that protruded firmly into place.

Right. All secure. He hoped. He set off up the slope again.

Wibble. Wobble. Slither.

CHAPTER 15

'Do you remember the way?' asked Wrinkle.

'Yes,' said Wazzock, who was walking just ahead.

'Are you sure?'

'Yes.'

'Perhaps I should lead,' suggested Von Vlod. 'I am considered a count, you know.'

Wrinkle hated it when Von Vlod went all hoity-toity. 'A count for nothing more like.' It was said in jest.

'Harsh,' Von Vlod retorted. 'Pablo, what do you think?'

Pablo was a little way behind them. 'I think I am smelling stinky,' he answered as he frowned at something dark and nasty that may have been brown if it were in colour. Perhaps it was the younanny mouse? A younanny mouse would be stinky, he decided.

'Leave it alone,' warned Wrinkle. In her experience, sniffing at things that looked unpleasant could prove to be unpleasant. Or, in this Otherworld, downright dangerous.

'Agh!' wailed Pablo as the not brown, black thing suddenly sprouted four eyes and a number of spindly legs. It then scooted away, blowing a raspberry as it went. It disappeared into a hole. 'I think the stinky thing it did not like me calling it stinky.'

'Stay close, Pablo,' cautioned Von Vlod, 'Wrinkle's right. You don't know what's about. That thing might be a baby.'

The thought of the stinky thing, perhaps a younanny mouse, having larger family members sent a shiver down Pablo's spine. 'Sí,' he said, 'I am being close.' He hurried closer, the younanny mouse shoved from his thoughts.

'Will you lot hush,' said Wazzock, 'I'm trying to concentrate.'

'He means he's no idea where he's going,' chuckled Wrinkle.

'I do,' said Wazzock.

'He's lost,' smiled Von Vlod, winking at Wrinkle.

'I am not,' snapped Wazzock.

'Perhaps I am smelling the way,' offered Pablo.

'No!' Was the younanny mouse answer to that.

CHAPTER 16

'Master, do you copy? Over.'

Nothing. No, not nothing, static. The hooded figure shook the talky-walky. Still nothing. No, still static.

This wasn't good. He needed to ask the master something. No, two somethings. Why he hadn't thought to ask before was beyond him. Which, when he thought about it, was probably why. Most things, sadly, were beyond him. Sometimes, he wondered if that's why he had been given this job. But that didn't make sense. Why trust him with the job if the Master thought it was beyond him? He had no idea. It was beyond him. Never mind, he thought. He tried the talky-walky again.

'Master? Do you copy? Over.'

Nothing. No, not nothing. Static.

CHAPTER 17

They looked left, they looked right, they looked left again. Twinkle then gave Basil a nudge.

'I've told you,' said Basil, moving out of nudge distance. 'I've never been here before.' He was telling the truth. 'I have no idea where we'll find the evil.'

'Perhaps we should split up,' suggested Danrite. 'We could cover more ground.'

Salor was aghast. 'What! We can't do that. We'll leave ourselves vulnerable.'

'Vulnerable to what?' asked Twinkle. 'We don't know what we're up against yet.'

'To the unknown,' said Salor.

'Well,' said Frida, 'I, for one, don't think us arguing about it is going to help. We need to make a decision. We're here to find evil before it destroys imagination and us with it.' She had nearly said some of us. She doubted she or Danrite would be affected, except for making their lives incredibly dull, but the others; she had already noticed a slight change here and there, subtle ones. Salor's hat had got slightly smaller. Perhaps it was just arriving in this Otherworld that had done it. She hoped so. But whatever, time didn't appear to be on their side.

'She's right,' said Twinkle. 'Who's got a coin?'

'Sí,' said Jose, 'I am having one.'

Faces turned to the little chihuahua.

'You do?' said Salor.

'You,' said Twinkle slowly, 'have... a... coin?'

'Coin? Ah, no,' said Jose. 'I am thinking you saying, who is having a sword?' He swished his tail. 'See, I am having one.'

'Give me strength,' said Twinkle. 'And what's he up to?'

Assuming all faces had turned from him to look at Jose, Basil had taken the opportunity to have a quick rummage in his rucksack. Sadly for him, Twinkle had only trained one eye on Jose, the other never leaving Basil. She wasn't going to let him out of her sight.

'Basil?' said Frida, who had turned in time to see him acting suspiciously.

24

'What?' said Basil, all innocent-as-a-lamb-like. He had thought no one would notice him as they chatted inanely amongst themselves. But he had been caught and now had to think quickly. A coin, that's it, he thought. 'I was looking for a coin. You said you wanted one.'

'Find one?' queried a suspicious Twinkle.

'Sadly, no,' said Basil, smiling weakly. 'As poor as a church mouse, me.'

'He is having something in his hand,' said Jose. He was being on his guard, as a good knight should do. Always on the lookout. He was hoping it might be a chew toy. A ball. They are for good boys. He was a good boy. 'Perhaps it is being squeaky?'

'Has he now?' said Twinkle.

'Squeaky?' said a frowning Danrite.

Basil swiftly put his hand behind his back. Not a good move.

'Don't want us to see it, eh?' said Salor.

'I think it best if you show us,' said Frida, not liking the way Basil was acting.

'Here,' said Twinkle, putting out a hand.

'It's nothing,' said Basil. Grief, he thought, what do I do now? He gripped harder on whatever it was in his hand. He could feel the chance of a television set drifting away.

Frida quickly stepped sideways to get a better look at Basil's hand. 'Then why are your knuckles getting so white?' she said, noticing how tight Basil was holding nothing. 'Hand it over.'

'I am with the first dibs if it is being a sausage,' said Jose. Food trumped squeaky where Jose was concerned.

This time, Danrite ignored Jose; he was more interested in seeing what Basil had in his hand.

Basil, as usual, knew when he was beaten. He would have to tell them. He slowly opened his hand to reveal…

'A compass,' said Danrite.

'Give it here,' said Twinkle, snatching it from Basil's outstretched hand. She turned it over in hers. 'What is it?'

'As Danrite said,' said Basil, 'it's a compass.'

'I think Percy had one just like it,' said Danrite. Percy was his uncle until he fell off a roof.

'Percy?' said Frida.

'Yes,' said Danrite. 'Our uncle. I told you about him.'

'Ah,' said Frida. 'The one that looked after you.'

'That's him.'

'It's not like any compass I've ever seen,' said Salor, 'it hasn't got a North, South or West.' Meaning it hadn't got an N, S, or W on it. He looked at Twinkle, looked at the compass, but before he could do what he was planning to do, Twinkle's hand snapped shut. 'I was only looking,' he said.

'Of course, you were,' said Twinkle, who knew precisely what Salor had had in mind. 'And then you were taking.'

'May I have a look, please?' asked Frida.

'Sí, me also,' said Jose, jumping up and down on his back legs. He hadn't yet given up on the idea that the compass thingy might be edible. Or at least throwable.

Twinkle smiled at Salor as she handed the compass to Frida. 'She said the magic word.'

'As if you know one,' said Salor.

'Magic word?' said Danrite, slow on the uptake.

'Please,' said Frida. She smiled at him. 'Do keep up.'

'Oh,' said Danrite, colouring a slightly darker grey.

'A compass?' said Frida. She looked Basil straight in the eye. 'As Salor said, it's not like a normal one.' It did have a needle, though. That and the letter E. She handed the compass to Danrite. 'You said Percy had one?'

In the background, Salor was jigging on the spot, so desperate was he to get his hands on it.

Danrite examined it. It was exactly the same. 'It's exactly like the one Percy had,' he said. He looked accusingly at Basil.

Big breath in time for Basil. 'It's an Evil detector.' He glanced at Danrite. 'I was given it.' Bang goes the television for sure now, he thought. Big breath out. Followed by sagging shoulders.

'And when were you going to tell us about it?' demanded Twinkle. 'Not that we can trust you to tell us the truth.'

Basil shrank back as more accusing eyes turned on him.

'Let me see it,' cried a certain someone.

'Ay caramba,' said Jose, dodging the jigging Salor. 'I am thinking Salor, he will be doing a mischief to himself soon.'

'Here,' said Frida, frowning as she gave the compass to Salor.

Salor gratefully took it. He had felt a cramp coming on. 'Thank you,' he said, remembering another magic word.

'So,' said Frida, attention back on Basil, 'can we trust you?'

Basil now found himself between another rock and a hard place. The television had gone, but the wrath of the Font would be waiting for him sometime. Something he wasn't looking forward to. But to do that, feel the wrath, he had to get home in one piece. So, to do that, what he didn't want to do was to feel the nearer wrath of Twinkle. He would have to tell the truth. At least the compass truth. If he wanted to get home in one piece. And a transistor radio wasn't that bad. Was it?

'He's hesitating,' snarled Twinkle.

'Yes,' said Basil at last, 'you can trust me.'

Twinkle didn't believe him one little bit. She edged closer to Frida and whispered in her ear. 'Can we believe him?'

'What choice do we have?' A shrugging, Frida whispered back.

No choice but to was the only option, but they would be watching him like hawks.

Salor, on the other hand, only had eyes for the compass. 'How does it work?' he asked after numerous prods and pokes had revealed not a hint of a secret compartment anywhere. Or what the purpose of it was. 'And what does the E mean?'

'East?' suggested Danrite. Though why would a compass only have East on it?

'Sí, East,' said Jose, eager to join in, even though he was the only one not to have seen it yet. 'I am, too, thinking it is East.'

'Basil,' said Frida. 'Perhaps you can tell us what the E's for?'

'Evil?' suggested Basil, raising an eyebrow. No wonder the Font wanted an eye kept on them, he thought.

'They have compasses for that?' said Danrite. He then started to wonder why Percy would have had one.

'So it would seem,' said Frida, feeling a tad silly. What else would the E on an evil detector stand for? Perhaps we do need someone keeping an eye on us? 'It's how we find the evil, isn't it?'

'Yes,' said Basil.

'Then why didn't you tell us you had it?' said Danrite.

'Because it was my job to keep it safe,' said Basil. 'The Font didn't want it falling into the wrong hands.'

'Ah,' said Jose, 'she is not meaning me, I am having no hands for it to fall into.' He pushed home his point by waving his front paws at everyone.

'But surely we're not thought of as the wrong hands,' said a flabbergasted Salor, ignoring Jose.

'Exactly,' said Twinkle, making it one of those rare occasions when she and Salor agreed on something. 'How can we be the wrong hands?'

'That doesn't make sense,' said Frida, trying to work out why the Font would think they couldn't be trusted with the compass. It was they, after all, that had to find the evil and stop it. 'She knows she can trust us.'

'Maybe, maybe not,' said Basil. 'She never said who the wrong hands were, just don't let it fall into them, so I decided it best to keep it to myself.'

'He has a fair point,' said Danrite. 'If the Font didn't say who the wrong hands were, I'd have done the same.'

'I suppose so,' said Frida. 'To tell the truth, thinking about it, I would have done the same as well.' Doesn't mean I trust you, though, she thought, looking at Basil.

'See,' said Basil, who was pleasantly surprised and more than a tad relieved by their reaction.

'Still don't trust you,' said Twinkle, unknowingly voicing Frida's thoughts and bringing Basil back down to earth again.

'So how does it work?' said Salor, who suddenly wasn't sure if he wanted to hold on to it any longer. What if it attracted evil in some way? 'Here,' he said, shoving it towards Twinkle, who gave him a curious look, 'share and share alike.'

Strange, thought Twinkle. But as strange was undoubtedly one of Salor's middle names, she took it and stuck it under Basil's nose. 'Answer the man then,' she said.

'As I've already said, it's an Evil detector,' said Basil. Then, when Twinkle growled and her hot breath got uncomfortably closer, he decided more explaining was needed. He pointed at the needle. 'When the needle points to the E, that's the direction evil lies.'

'Show me,' said Twinkle, handing the compass back to Basil.

'Nothing to show, really,' said Basil. 'It does what it says on the tin.'

'What tin?' said Salor. 'I see no tin.'

'There is no tin,' said Basil.

'Then why mention one?' said a scowling Twinkle.

'What he means,' said Danrite, in an attempt to explain, 'is that it does what it's supposed to do.'

'Then why mention a tin?' said Salor. 'It's confusing the issue.'

'Just show them,' said Frida, trying not to laugh.

'Okay,' said Basil, wondering why it was so hard to understand. 'You just hold it in your hand, like so.' He placed it on his open palm. 'And when the needle and the E meet, it's pointing in the direction of the evil. Then we follow.' He looked at the compass as the needle began to move. 'See,' said Basil, 'it is pointing that way. The evil is that way.' Because not everyone could see where the needle was pointing, he pointed a finger. At Salor.

'Ah-ha!' yelled Jose, his eyes narrowing, his tail swishing. 'It is as I am thinking. Salor is the evil!'

'No, I'm not,' said Salor, backing away.

'It is what I am being saying if I am being the evil. Which I am not,' said Jose, now baring his teeth.

'Oh, for goodness sake,' cried Salor. 'Show him the compass before he does a mischief.'

'I am not being the mischief. You are.' Tail swishing faster, Jose advanced on Salor.

Frida quickly grabbed the compass and lowered it for Jose to see. 'See,' she said, 'it's not pointing at Salor.' As she showed Jose the compass, she waved her other hand at Salor for him to move aside.

Jose looked and then looked ahead again. The needle now pointed at a tree directly behind where Salor had been standing.

'Ah-ha!' said Jose, teeth still showing. 'Please be standing back, the tree, it is being evil.'

'Oh, for goodness sake,' said Twinkle, who didn't know whether to laugh or cry. 'It's just pointing in the direction of evil, not at it.'

Jose let Twinkle's words sink in. Then, deciding the compass thingy made no sense, he set off to the tree anyway, intent on showing it who was boss by giving it a one-legged salute.

'But could it be the tree?' worried Danrite as Jose headed towards it.

'No,' said Frida, no longer holding back a smile.

'But how do we know?' Danrite persisted. 'The compass was pointing at it. How do we know it isn't the evil we're looking for?'

'He's got something there,' said Twinkle. 'For all we know, it could be the tree.'

Frida now eyed the tree in a new light.

Salor took a step or two away from it.

'I doubt it's the tree,' said Basil.

'How do you know?' said Twinkle.

'I don't, but I'm thinking that if it were, we would have known about it by now,' said Basil. But that didn't stop those watching the tree from wondering when it would make its move.

'Someone should do something,' said Twinkle.

'Before it's too late,' said Salor.

Neither of whom moved. No one moved. No one knew why.

'There,' said Basil. 'Not an evil tree.' Jose had reached the tree and was now happily watering it. 'Do you think an evil tree would allow that?'

No one did, which was a relief – especially for Jose. A relief that brought questions with it.

'Which means, and correct me if I'm wrong,' said Frida, 'you're saying we follow the compass until evil basically jumps out on us?'

'I suppose,' said Basil, who hadn't really thought about it like that until now, and now he did, wasn't at all comfortable with the idea.

'So, no warning?' said Twinkle.

'Not as such,' said Basil. Not comfortable at all.

'And it could be anything we are looking at?' said Salor.

Not comfortable at all. But there was one bright spot. When the evil appeared, they would have no choice but to deal with it. All he needed to do was stay back out of harm's way. Basil allowed a small smile to form on his lips. He may get back in one piece after all.

'We'll just have to keep our eyes open,' said Frida, not as confident as she sounded. She glanced at the compass and supposed it was too late to worry now. Onwards and upwards, it is then, she thought. 'This way.' To the tree and around it.

'Blimey,' said Danrite, 'looks like we're off to find the evil.'

'Grief,' said Salor, who hadn't had time to argue. He started to follow. He wasn't going to be left behind.

Twinkle waited for Basil to gather his rucksack and then walked with him. She wasn't going to let him out of her sight. She was sure the little man wasn't telling them everything.

They reached the tree, where Jose joined them, and made their way around it.

To whatever lay ahead.

To whatever waited for them.

CHAPTER 18

Wibble. Wobble. Slither. Stop.

The creature with the unimportant name took a cautious look around. He had thought he had heard something. Something like something bumping into a tree. But as there were no trees in sight.

Wibble. He would be glad to get back to his safe place. Wobble. Why had he ever left it? Because otherwise, he would have gone stir-crazy, that's why. Holed up like a bear with insomnia trying to hibernate. But at least there, he would be safe. But would he?

'And here we go again,' moaned the creature with the unimportant name. 'With the worrying about nothing, something and everything.' He groaned. 'Next, I'll be talking to my—.'

The creature with the unimportant name sagged as low as he could get. Perhaps, he thought, I should just let them get me. It would be easier than hiding and worrying all the time.

But the creature was not a defeatist by nature. He shook his head. Which wobbled. He would go on. He had not been defeated yet. To the hideout, then.

With renewed spirit, the creature with the unimportant name continued on his way.

Wibble. Wobble. Slither.

CHAPTER 19

'What do you think we'll find?' Danrite asked his sister.

'Something not good, I'll be bound,' she answered grimly. She was watching Salor, who, for some reason only known to him, had decided to take back the compass and was now leading the way. 'Do you think he knows what he's doing?'

'I've known him for years,' said Twinkle, walking beside them, 'and I wouldn't bet on it.' She smiled. 'If he did, he wouldn't have taken the compass.'

'Why did you let him take it?' asked Danrite.

'Because I'm not stupid,' smiled Frida. 'I want to be ready when we meet the evil, whatever it is, not be the first it eats.'

'Eats?' Danrite stopped in his tracks.

'Well,' laughed Frida, 'whatever it might do to the first one that stumbles upon it.'

'Oh,' whispered a relieved Danrite. 'Perhaps he shouldn't get too far ahead then. He might need our help.'

It was Twinkle's turn to laugh. 'Oh, he will,' she said, 'don't you worry about that.'

'Sí,' said Jose, only half listening, so involved in his tail was he, 'and I am being ready with my sword.' He gave his tail a mighty swish, nearly taking his tiny back legs from under him.

'He knows it's still a tail, right?' said Frida.

'Who knows?' joked Twinkle, grinning down at Jose, the black knight, who had just caught the swish of his tail from the corner of his eye. Something to be chased.

'I will get you,' snarled Jose as he started to chase it. 'You are daring to be creeping up on me. You are mine!'

Their task was forgotten for a moment as laughter was shared at the expense of the crazy chihuahua. Even Basil managed a chuckle. The four of them. Salor too far ahead. Four?

'You not laughing, Vlad?' said Twinkle. No Answer. 'Vlad?'

Everyone stopped. Apart from Salor, who was in his own little world and wandering merrily ahead into the jaws of whatever might be waiting for them. He was ignored. Something was up.

'Vlad?'

CHAPTER 20

'Blimey!' exclaimed Vlad for the fourth time.

The first blimey had been when he, like the others, had arrived on the roof of the castle.

The second blimey had been uttered when he then landed in the middle of what appeared to be the Disenchanted Forest, in a clearing similar to the one they had all landed in when meeting Basil for the first time.

The third blimey had been spoken when he noticed his surroundings had no colour.

The fourth blimey had been when he realised he was on his own.

CHAPTER 21

'Do you copy, Master? Over,' said the hooded figure into his talky-walky.

It had been a while since he had made contact. Still nothing but static on the other end of the talky-walky.

There were questions he wanted to ask. Two from before and now a new one. Though, in truth, with all the static toing and froing, and the worrying, and the static, he couldn't remember what the first two were. So only one question now. And an observation. And the observation was important. He had to let his master know.

But what if there was no answer? What did he do then? Did he stay, or did he go?

'Stupid, stupid, stupid,' shouted the hooded figure quite suddenly. 'So stupid. Of course, I have to go.' He looked at the talky-walky. 'Stupid useless thing.' He was tempted to throw it on the ground and stamp on it, but that would be stupid. 'Grr,' he growled. Everything was stupid. He now pouted. 'Stupid,' he whispered. He calmed a little.

'Stupid.' This one was said even quieter and aimed at himself. A ticking-off. Did he want them to know they were being followed? That chihuahua had ears like a hawk. Was it a hawk? Never mind, whatever, the dog would hear him if he weren't careful.

The hooded figure peered from his hiding place. All seemed okay. Should he follow? He shook his head. What else should he do? So stupid, he thought. He quietly made a move to follow. Then again.

CHAPTER 22

At last, they came upon something familiar. A broken wizard's staff. Wazzocks. They were going the right way. It had taken a while. Though Wazzock insisted he hadn't got lost.

'See,' beamed Wazzock, 'I told you I knew the way.' The sad thing was he believed it.

'Dumb luck,' said Wrinkle.

'Sí,' agreed Pablo. 'The luck of the dumb.'

Von Vlod tittered.

'Whatever,' said Wazzock, kicking at the pieces of staff. He had broken it when he discovered the magic had left it. When hope had left.

'Shouldn't do that,' warned Wrinkle. 'What if there's some magic left in it?'

'If there was, do you think I would have broken it?' To make his point, he picked a piece up and threw it as far as he could.

Pablo immediately ran after it.

'Oh, for goodness' sake,' groaned Wrinkle. 'Pablo, come back.' The last thing they wanted was a lost Pablo.

Thankfully, the stick – because that was what it was to Pablo – had only travelled a couple of metres. Such was the power of the great Wazzock.

Pablo trotted back with his trophy gripped firmly between his teeth.

'Drop,' commanded Wrinkle.

Cocking his head to one side, Pablo gave Wrinkle an "are you being serious" look. What did she think he was, a dog? Besides, he wasn't giving up his prize for anyone.

'Okay,' said Wrinkle, backing off, 'but if your teeth drop out, don't come whining to me.'

Pablo cocked his head the other way. And who did she think she was, his mother?

'Don't you take any notice,' whispered Von Vlod, 'you keep your toy.'

Wrinkle huffed and stepped after Wazzock, who had already

started walking.

Von Vlod and Pablo fell into line a couple of paces behind.

Behind them – more than a few paces behind – came the sound of snickering and a couple of louder tee-hees.

CHAPTER 23

There was more than a tad of confusion going on with the discovery of the lack of a Vlad.

'Vlad!' called Frida through cupped hands. She had retraced their steps a fair distance in her search for him.

With her was Danrite, sword in hand. The compass had been pointing the other way when they had realised Vlad was missing, but who knew what dangers might be lurking, waiting to pounce, in the shadows of this colourless Otherside.

'Any luck?' yelled Twinkle, who was far enough away from the brother and sister for the need to shout.

'Nothing yet,' Frida yelled back.

'I think we might have to go back to the castle,' said Danrite.

'Looks like,' said Frida. She waved for Twinkle to join them.

Twinkle joined them, Basil, by her side, Jose at her ankles. But Salor was nowhere in sight. Twinkle reckoned he had either not heard her calling him or had ignored her. She suspected the latter. Whichever it was, it appeared he was still going where the compass led him.

'Should we go after him?' asked Danrite.

'He'll be all right,' Twinkle assured him. 'He'll turn around and come running once he realises he's on his own.'

'Sí, when there is being no one to be in charge of,' added Jose.

'Then we go back,' said Frida.

'It's a mistake,' said Basil, unhappy at the delay in the plan. 'We need to keep going.' Twinkle glowered at him. 'But of course, finding your friend comes first.'

It was decided. They would go back to the castle to see if Vlad was still there for some reason. An eye being kept open for him as they travelled.

CHAPTER 24

The way ahead was daunting to look at. Ice, snow, and frost. All permanent. Cold looking trees. Sinister shadows. Treacherous ground to navigate. And amongst all this, in the distance, a cave. Its mouth as black as a pirate's heart and just as welcoming. Anyone with an ounce of sense would never venture forth. Do not enter, sang the scene. Go back, it warned.

But it was more than that to the creature with the unimportant name. It was home. It was why he was still there. No one had looked for him here. No one in their right mind would. It was a sanctuary from those who might want to hunt him. So why had he left it? The creature didn't know.

Didn't know? It did. It was lonely. It was fed up living in a cave. It wanted to go home. But for now, until something good happened to change the way things were, the creature with the unimportant name would have to keep on hiding.

Wobble. Wibble. Slither. Slip. Slip. Slip.

CHAPTER 25

Drat, thought the hooded figure, as the main part of the group headed back towards the castle. Now, what did he do?

Earlier, he had decided to follow. Follow because there was no point in staying where he was. Why had he even thought that? But now the follow had just become complicated. Did he follow the one with the compass, or did he follow the rest?

The hooded figure decided to try the talky-walky again. If he managed to contact the Master, he would have to decide for him. Made sense. Did it? He would try anyway.

'Do you copy, Master? Over.'

Static.

'Master, do you copy?'

Static.

Drat-drat-drat, thought the hooded figure as he watched the group start to move off. He would try one last time. Then, if still no contact, he would have to decide. The compass or the missing Vlad? At least he knew he couldn't stay.

'Master, it's me. Do you copy?' Drat, he thought, of course, it's me. Who else would it be?

Something.

At last, thought the hooded figure, relief flowing through him. 'Master?'

'This is Southern Radio, bringing you all you want in Country and Western music,' announced the talky-walky.

The hooded figure stared at the talky-walky as if the thing had suddenly come alive in his hand. 'What?' he managed to utter as he gaped at it. 'Master?' he ventured. But the static returned midway through a jingle. The hooded figure was at a loss. He was even flummoxed. What was that all about? But as much as he stared at the talky-walky, it wasn't going to tell him.

So, he was back at square one. 'Drat,' muttered the hooded figure. But he knew he had only two choices. Follow the one with the compass, the hapless-looking wizard who looked capable of finding all sorts of trouble? Or follow the group with the so-called hero in it? Follow a chinless wonder or the one that is here to destroy the evil? And when he thought about it like that...

The hooded figure quickly packed the talky-walky away and scurried after those heading back to the castle.

CHAPTER 26

'Hello!' It was a half-hearted attempt. And Vlad's last. He had shouted for a while now but to no avail. It was time to stop. Time to admit it. There was no one else around.

Vlad had stayed in the confines of the clearing since he had arrived. Wondering where the others were. Wondering what had happened. Wondering where he was. And in between all that wondering, he had almost shouted himself hoarse, calling to anyone who might hear him. But now was the time to think about what he did next.

One thing he knew for sure was he couldn't stay here forever. He needed to find his friends. But would it be better to stay where he was? Wouldn't they be looking for him? No, he decided he needed to move. Perhaps they would bump into each other as they searched. Maybe.

Vlad headed to the edge of the clearing. There, he stopped and looked at the surrounding forest. He didn't like the look of it. The trees had a sinister look to them. He wondered if the forest was the same one they had wandered through when searching for the Font. That one had been sinister enough. It looked the same. Apart from the lack of colour. But if he wanted to leave the clearing, that's where he would have to go.

No, the forest looked too menacing in that direction, so he went to the other side of the clearing. It looked no different.

'I don't know what to do?' he suddenly wailed.

'I do,' exclaimed a cheery voice from nowhere.

Vlad jumped so high his cloak acted like a parachute on the way down.

'Who's there?' he asked when he landed. He looked this way and that, but he couldn't see the owner of the voice. Then, directly in front of him, a shape detached itself from the cover of the trees and stepped into the open. Vlad couldn't believe his eyes. Vlad blinked. And blinked again. It couldn't be. Could it? 'Percy?'

CHAPTER 27

Slide. Glide. Slide. Glide. And relax.

CHAPTER 28

'How far is it now?' asked Wrinkle, who doubted Wazzock knew but was keen to get to the castle before the others caught up. It wasn't that she didn't like them, more that they were odd. Some very odd. Some very, very odd. Goodness knows how long some had been trapped here.

'Can't be far now,' guessed Wazzock.

'Is it me,' said Twinkle to Von Vlod, 'or are the others getting closer?'

'They are most certainly catching us up,' said Von Vlod, glancing behind.

'Knew it,' groaned Wrinkle. 'It's Wazzock's fault. Keep getting us lost.'

'I have not got us lost,' argued Wazzock.

'Perhaps we should have let Pablo sniff the way there,' said Von Vlod.

'And if there's a tree? Or something shiny? Or anything?' said Wrinkle.

'Sí,' agreed Pablo through the stick clenched between his teeth, 'she is perhaps the being right.' His face took on a downcast look.

'And what if they do catch up?' said Wazzock. 'It's their chance as much as ours.'

'Says the wizard who wouldn't have anything to do with them because he felt it was beneath him,' said Wrinkle.

'I was young and foolish back then,' said Wazzock.

'Deluded more like,' whispered Wrinkle to no one in particular. She doubted he was ever young. Foolish, yes. Besides, he hadn't changed since they'd arrived. Not in age or foolishness, at least.

Von Vlod, who had heard Wrinkle's remark, smiled.

'There!' yelled an excited Wazzock, pointing ahead.

Everyone looked to see what he was getting so excited about. It was the castle. Still a distance away. Looking small enough to fit in a pocket. But the castle, all the same.

'I told you I knew where I was going,' crowed Wazzock. He began to pick up his pace and strode briskly towards it.

'Well, I'll be,' declared Wrinkle.

'We shouldn't just rush in though,' cautioned Von Vlod, but walking quicker anyway.

Behind them, Pablo wagged his tail with excitement and sank his teeth deeper into his stick. So deep that what hair he had suddenly stood on end and did a Mexican wave right to the end of his tail. 'Ay-yi-yi!' he yowled, his eyes wide. 'I am being like electric!' He then shot off like a rocket after the others.

Behind him, the other others, those that could, exchanged looks. Some were worried. Some were confused. Some picked up the ones they had dropped. What had just happened to the animal? A discussion ensued. Some giggled. Some tripped over. But it was eventually decided they didn't know, and they didn't really care. But they would show caution, so slowed a little.

The hooded figure watched from the shadows of a large bush as Frida, followed by the rest of the group, entered the castle.

There was nothing else he could do now but wait. And possibly try the talky-walky again.

The search for Vlad had so far been a fruitless one. They had even looked in the broom cupboard. Danrite's idea. But no, just the same broom Danrite had had a tangle with. So now they stood on the roof of the castle. It had been the last chance. But again, there was no sign of Vlad.

'Well,' exclaimed Twinkle, 'that's that. He's not here.'

'Shall we go then?' said Basil, eager for a return to the search for evil.

'Hush,' hushed Twinkle, making the word sound strangely sinister. Basil hushed. But she had to admit the little man was right. There was no point hanging about now. The castle had been scoured from top to bottom.

'Do you know?' Pondered Danrite. 'I'm sure I saw him here, with us, when we arrived.'

'Me too,' said Frida. 'But what could have happened to him?'

'He more than likely followed us and got lost somewhere,' said Twinkle. 'He could be anywhere.'

'So, no point standing around here then,' said Basil.

Twinkle gave him a black look but nothing more.

'Sí,' agreed Jose, 'I am thinking the Basil man is being right.'

They all knew he was, but Vlad was their friend. They couldn't just leave him. Perhaps another sweep of the castle first?

And they were about to do just that – as pointless as they knew it would be – when Frida had a lightbulb moment. She turned to Jose.

'How are you at tracking scents?' asked Frida. She was thinking that if Vlad wasn't at the castle, then they might be able to track where he went after they had left it.

Jose wagged his sword. 'Sí, I am being like a hound of blood,'

This caused Twinkle to scowl at the little dog. 'If you can do that, why haven't you done it already?'

Frida hadn't thought of that.

'I am not being asked,' said Jose.

'Give me strength,' muttered Twinkle.

'But you must have smelt him by now?' said Basil.

'If he had been here,' said Danrite, coming to Jose's rescue. It was obvious if Vlad had been at the castle, Jose would have detected his scent.

'No,' admitted Jose, batting Danrite's rescue for six. 'I am just not turning it on yet. I am first looking.'

'Turning it on yet?' said an incredulous Twinkle.

'Sí,' said Jose, 'it is being an art. It is not to being using nilly-willy.'

Twinkle's face began to resemble a thundercloud.

'Okay,' said Frida, stepping in before the situation became more complicated. 'How about you doing your stuff, I mean your art, now?'

'Sí,' said Jose, 'I do it.' He sniffed. 'No.' he said.

'What do you mean no?' said Frida.

'I am not smelling him,' said Jose.

Frida sighed. Bang went her lightbulb moment.

'I knew we were wasting our time,' moaned Basil, turning for the door down from the roof, but stopped from doing so by a meaty fist grabbing his shoulder.

'When we go, we go together,' warned Twinkle.

'Wait,' said Frida, 'I have an idea.'

'Another one?' said Twinkle, raising an eyebrow.

'We saw Vlad, right?'

'I did,' said Danrite.

'I might have,' said Twinkle, unwilling to commit to Frida's growing madness.

'But where did we see him?' Frida looked excited.

'Here?' said Danrite.

'You, all right?' asked Twinkle.

'Fine,' smiled Frida. 'Which means if Jose isn't able to smell him on the roof, then he never came with us. So, he can't be lost somewhere outside the castle.'

'And?' said Twinkle, wondering if perhaps she should take charge of the group. They did it on ships sometimes when the captain went mad, right? At least something like that.

'Which means, even though we saw Vlad, he never touched the floor?' continued Frida. Blank looks all around. 'Which means

48

something must have happened to stop him?'

One of the blank faces suddenly changed and filled with understanding. Surprisingly, or not, it was Basil's face. 'Are you thinking he may have gone into another portal?'

'Exactly what I'm thinking,' said Frida. 'What other explanation could there be?' And before anyone could say anything else, she stooped down, grabbed Jose, and raised him into the air. 'Sniff now,' she said.

'Ay caramba!' wailed Jose, his eyes wide as he suddenly left terra firma behind him. His eyes then grew even wider. 'I am smelling him. I am smelling Vlad!' Frida lowered him. 'And now I am not!' Frida raised him again. 'And now I am!'

Well, I never, thought Twinkle.

'See,' said Frida, 'Vlad was here, but he never touched the ground.' She put Jose down, who then staggered for a moment.

Blimey, thought Danrite, no wonder she's a hero.

'So where did he go?' said Twinkle, now willing to be sucked into Frida's craziness.

'Good question.' Frida stared into the nothing that Vlad had once been in. 'I have no idea.'

'I smell him,' said Jose, who had just jumped as high as he could. 'He is being there.'

'Where?' asked Danrite, half expecting to see Vlad.

'Not there,' said Jose as he landed. He looked at Danrite. 'Somewhere.'

In a world of his own, Salor, oblivious to the drama unfolding behind him, had wandered far from the others.

'A-ha!' yelled Salor as he skirted a hole in the ground. 'Trying to catch me out, are you?' He was talking to the compass.

'I won't be caught out as easily as that,' cried Salor. 'A true leader is always vigilant. Aware of everything around him.' Because that was what Salor was. 'Don't you agree?' he threw behind him to anyone who might be listening. But no one was.

The lack of an answer didn't bother him. He put it down to one of two things. Awe, at his leadership skills. Or, sadly, the jealousy because of them. He smiled to himself.

'And brave,' he spouted. The smile grew wider. 'One needs to be brave to face the evil the compass is leading us to.'

And Salor was brave. Brave in the knowledge that if something did happen – when they met the evil they were hunting for – there would be safety in numbers. He could also run a lot faster than some of them. He wouldn't tell them, though. No. He wanted the glory of finding the evil for himself. What happened after, when he had thrown the compass and had legged it, didn't matter. It was about who found the evil. Once the enemy was discovered, great leaders left the dirty work to others. His smile grew even wider.

'Cat got your tongues?' he bellowed.

Again, there was no answer, but Salor didn't care about that. Obviously, they had come to realise he was the leader. In fact, the silence had been most pleasant. Not a chiding remark for ages now. Salor felt chuffed. Not even Twinkle had let fly with one of hers.

Not even Twinkle. Salor's step suddenly faltered. He slowed. Why not? No one had said anything for ages when he came to think about it. Jealousy, of course. He took another step. But this time, it didn't wash. Surely, someone would have said something by now. Since they had set out with the compass.

Suddenly, the little world Salor had been living in for the past hour or so started to fail. To think of it, he hadn't even heard Jose say something ridiculous. Which he did all the time. Salor stopped.

He slowly turned.

There was no one there. Salor went white.

'Twinkle?' he ventured. 'Jose?' But no answer. Because he was on his own. On his own with a compass that was seeking evil. And the thought made his legs go weak at the knees. But he rallied. He would have to find them, he thought, that's what good leaders did. It was also what certain wizards did when they found they were on their own and in the firing line of something evil.

With a pounding heart, he started back the way he had come. His eyes set on the compass. His mind dealing with the situation like a certain wizards did. There's no point in me hogging all the glory, he now thought. There's no I in team, after all. His footsteps quickened. Besides, they could be in trouble.

'Fear not, friends,' cried Salor, his quickened steps now turning into a full-blown run. 'I, Salor, will save you!'

CHAPTER 32

Percy was Danrite and Frida's uncle.

Eccentric is how Danrite described him after looking the word up in a dictionary. And eccentric he was. But for all his strange ways, Percy had raised Danrite from small after Danrite's parents had mysteriously disappeared.

As for Frida, it isn't known what contact Percy had had with her while she was growing up, her being a secret and all. And if he had, it would have been in secret, and Frida most certainly wouldn't have known about it.

And it is doubtful anyone will ever know. Sadly, Percy is no longer with us, you see. Him having tragically fallen from the roof of the house one day where he lived with Danrite. A sad day for all.

But then, if Percy is no longer with us, how is it Vlad is seeing and hearing him at that very moment?

'Good grief!' exclaimed Vlad, as the detached shape he had seen coming out of the forest spoke to him. It *was* Percy.

'Hi, Vlad,' said Percy, waving. Percy knew Vlad. He knew that cloak anywhere. He also knew Twinkle and Salor. They were old friends from way back.

'But-but-' stuttered Vlad, 'you're not—'

'Alive?' said a smiling Percy, guessing what Vlad was trying to say. 'No. And you are?'

'Yeah, but…' said Vlad, who couldn't argue with that; he was a vampire. But that was not what he was going to say. 'True,' said Vlad. 'But you—'

'Are really here,' said Percy. 'I am. I know. Weird right? But I'm not a vampire, just your common or garden ghost.' He went to hug Vlad, but Vlad backed away.

Vlad hadn't been going to say, you're not alive; he had been going to say, not real. At least, that is what the Font had told everyone back at the castle. Never real; just an avatar, the Font had said. A thing conjured up from her imagination. But now, here he was, and saying he was a ghost.

Mind scrambled from all that had already happened to him, Vlad was on the verge of having it served up on toast. A ghost? What was going on?

'You okay?' said Percy, wondering what was up with his old friend. He couldn't see him, but he knew him.

'What?' said Vlad, startled. He had been on another planet for a moment. But, now back in the here and now, Vlad came to a decision. Ghost or imagination, Percy's or the Font's version, he would go along with whatever. Percy had said he knew what to do, and that meant he was here to help. So, help, he would let him. He had little choice anyway, it seemed. Alone with no idea what had happened or where he was, he needed help. So, for the moment, questions regarding Percy's existence would be put to one side, and any help Percy could offer, he would take. That said, there were other questions. He asked one. 'How did you get here?' asked Vlad.

'Long story,' said Percy, 'but I'll tell you on the way.'

'Way?'

'Come on.' Percy started to walk back to where he had appeared. 'We've got imagination to save.' His stride lengthened, causing Vlad to hurry alongside him. 'And while we're about it, I'll tell you how you got here. In the clearing.'

Vlad was all ears.

CHAPTER 33

'Home sweet home,' sighed the creature with the unimportant name as he settled in familiar and safe surroundings. But for how long? he wondered.

He had sensed something different about these latest arrivals to enter his world. Something more dangerous than the others before them. Why? He didn't know. He just felt it.

The creature with the unimportant name stared miserably from the depths of his cave at the frozen, colourless world outside. He wondered when they would come. For he was sure they would. These new hunters. He was sure. He felt it.

CHAPTER 34

The flummoxed feeling they had the last time they were on the roof was nothing compared to the flummoxed feeling they were feeling now. Vlad had been there, not there, now somewhere. But where?

'Right,' said Twinkle, 'let's get this straight. He was here, then he wasn't. And you and Basil think he popped into another portal just after we landed.'

'That's the gist of it.' Frida shrugged. 'What else could have happened?'

Twinkle glanced towards the castle's parapet, but she didn't like what she was thinking. It had to be said, though, however horrible it sounded. 'Perhaps he fell off,' she said.

'Fell off?' Danrite was horrified.

'Over the parapet.' Twinkle pointed to the wall surrounding the castle roof.

'Oh,' said Danrite.

'Sí, oh,' echoed Jose.

'Someone had better go look,' said Danrite.

Everyone looked at Basil.

'Why me?' said Basil.

'I'll go,' Frida volunteered.

'We'll all go,' said Twinkle.

So they did. And they found nothing. No cloak, at least, which was all they would have seen. But it was a relief. But just to double-check, after Basil had pointed out the cloak might have blown away, they asked Jose to have a sniff. Nothing. Vlad hadn't been there. More relief. And when Basil suggested that maybe Vlad had blown away, Twinkle shut him up by proposing they see if that was a possibility by dropping him off the roof. Basil shut up.

'What now?' asked Danrite.

'Sí,' said Jose, 'what is it that we are doing now?'

Everyone looked at Frida, who shrugged again. Vlad could be anywhere. In another Otherworld for all she knew. But they couldn't stand at the foot of the castle wall wondering forever. 'Only one thing we can do, I suppose,' she said after a moment or two. 'We follow the compass and hope we meet Vlad somewhere along the way. Other than that, I have no idea.'

It wasn't the best of plans, but it was their only one. Now, all they had to do was find Salor.

CHAPTER 35

The hooded figure was still watching from the shadows when the group, now led by Basil, left the castle.

At last, he thought. He was getting a cramp. But, to his surprise, they didn't continue back the way they had come. Where were they going? Instead, they were walking around the outside of the castle.

As quickly and as quietly as he could, the hooded figure followed. He stopped when they did and sidled up as close as he dared to try and find out what was happening. He could hear them talking. He saw the little dog sniffing. They were trying to find out where the other one went. Which reminded him that he had better try to contact the Master again. But not yet; he didn't want Southern Radio to suddenly blurt out and give him away. He would wait. But the Master needed to know what was going on and soon. He waited.

At last, just as a new pang of cramp threatened him, the group set off again, this time back on the path that had led them to the castle. Heading back the way they had come.

Thanking goodness for that, the hooded figure stealthily left his latest hiding place and began following yet again.

CHAPTER 36

The castle would no longer fit into a pocket as it loomed large ahead of them.

'We're here then,' stated Wrinkle with a side of sarcasm.

'Looks like,' said Wazzock, ignoring it.

'So,' asked Von Vlod, 'what's the plan?'

Pablo said nothing. He would leave it to them. Which could take a while. He lay down and chewed on his new toy.

'Plan?' puzzled Wazzock.

'Yeah,' said Wrinkle. 'Plan.'

'Plan?' repeated Wazzock. What plan? He was confused. He had never mentioned a plan. But now Wrinkle mentioned it...

'We can't just go up to whoever it is and say hello,' said Von Vlod. 'We need a plan. They could be dangerous.'

Plan, thought Pablo, that would be a first. He continued chewing.

'And we have those.' Wrinkle waved her thumb behind her at those following.

Grief, thought Wazzock. 'We need a plan.'

Or, thought Pablo, we are just blundering our way in as we are always doing.

And so three heads came together. And there was much discussion. And there followed a decision. If one could call it that.

They would play it by ear. Wing it. Hope for the best. But first, as they had to start somewhere, they would look in the castle.

'The entrance is on the other side if my memory serves me right,' said Wazzock.

'We need to be careful,' Von Vlod reminded them.

Wrinkle agreed, so she voted Von Vlod to go first.

'Why me?'

'You'll merge in,' said Wrinkle.

'She's right,' agreed Wazzock.

And Von Vlod had to agree. Being the only one able to slip in without being seen, it made sense. That didn't mean Von Vlod liked the idea. 'And you follow me in?'

Pablo looked up.

'When it's safe to do so,' said Wrinkle.

'So, you are just going to wait here and see what happens?' said Von Vlod.

'Just until you let us know how the land lies inside,' said Wazzock. 'We don't want to walk into a trap. If there is one.'

This is making sense, thought Pablo. He looked down again.

'But it's okay for me to go in there on my own?' said Von Vlod.

'As I said, you can blend in,' said Wrinkle.

Von Vlod could.

'And if it's all clear, signal to us from the roof,' said Wazzock.

'But you might not be able to see me,' Von Vlod pointed out.

'Wave something,' suggested Wrinkle.

'But what if whoever came through sees it?' asked Von Vlod.

Pablo looked up again. He had listened enough. He didn't want to get involved; he was quite happy to chew on his toy and let them make the decisions, but they were taking forever. And besides, those behind were slowly creeping closer. He dropped his stick. 'I will go.'

'But Von Vlod is going,' said Wrinkle.

'I go with.'

'You will?' said Von Vlod, quietly pleased.

'Sí,' said Pablo. 'I will sneak with you. I am small. I am good at sneaking.' No one could argue with that; the second part. 'And when you are seeing no one, you will be waving to me as I am waiting at the bottom of the wall. I am then being running the swiftly back to here.'

'Good plan,' praised Wazzock.

'Are you sure?' asked Wrinkle. 'You're not as small as you think.'

'I am sneaking in the shadows.'

'That's settled then,' said Wazzock, eager to get on.

Pablo picked up his toy. Nodded to Von Vlod. And together, they set off for the castle.

And as Von Vlod and Pablo set off, the other others, those behind, who had gained ground while Wazzock, Wrinkle and Von Vlod had bickered, stopped in their tracks and watched.

CHAPTER 37

The creature with the unimportant name suddenly stopped what he was doing. Which was nothing. Nothing important. But what had made him suddenly stop might be. Just for a second. A very short second. The creature with the unimportant name had felt something. Something he thought no longer existed.

'It couldn't be,' murmured the creature with the unimportant name. But he had felt it. He was sure of it. But no, it couldn't have been. He was just on edge. It doesn't exist anymore. He had imagined it.

The creature with the unimportant name shook his head. Carefully. And carried on doing nothing important.

CHAPTER 38

Percy's pace didn't let up. Behind him, Vlad was struggling to keep up.

'Wait!' shouted Vlad when it seemed likely he would lose sight of Percy in the forest. 'I can't keep up.'

Percy stopped and turned. 'We need to keep moving,' he said. 'It's urgent we do.'

'I get that,' said Vlad, 'but I'm out of puff.'

'I didn't think vampires had puff.' Percy frowned.

'Well, whatever it's called,' wheezed Vlad, 'I'm out of it.'

'Very well then,' said Percy. He walked back to Vlad, who was now sitting on a handy tree stump.

'Lack of energy, that's all,' said Vlad. 'But you were fairly haring along, to be honest.'

'Sorry,' said Percy. 'Didn't think. Got a job to do and not much time to do it in.'

'Just give me a moment.'

'Will do,' said Percy. He had an idea. 'And while we have a moment, why don't I tell you everything I know while you get your puff or whatever it is back?'

The path the compass had taken Salor on was not a path in the sense of a clear way leading to somewhere but more a pathway in the sense of an overgrown obstacle course trying hard to get you nowhere.

Salor was going full pelt now. Even though he was heading away from where the compass indicated the evil was, his limited imagination was working overtime, imagining all sorts were out to get him.

'Ouch!' he wailed as yet another piece of grey greenery snatched at him. Another piece of grey greenery that wanted to drag him into the undergrowth, never to be seen again.

Where are they? he thought, still with the notion that the only reason he was running so fast was because he was on a mission to save them.

And then, from out of nowhere, a shape appeared in front of him. He screamed. Tripped. And hurtled head-first into the undergrowth he had been so desperate to avoid. Never to be seen again. Was what went through his mind as he disappeared amongst it. In truth, he wasn't seen again for at least a minute or so.

CHAPTER 40

After searching the castle and finding no one, Von Vlod went to the roof. Once there, Von Vlod moved to the parapet to signal to Pablo that all was clear. Von Vlod and Pablo had agreed that a wave or a shout as a signal was not a good idea as Pablo might not be able to see it, or someone might hear them, so instead, they decided on a stick dropped over the side, a heavy one so that it would come straight down. Von Vlod dropped the stick over the side.

'Ay-yi-yi!' cried Pablo as the stick brushed one of his ears.

'Shush,' floated down from above. Followed by a whispered apology. 'Sorry.'

'You are being trying to break my head,' moaned Pablo.

'Shush!' whispered Von Vlod. 'I just wanted to make sure you saw it.'

'Perhaps then you are throwing it so it is not hitting my head,' growled Pablo.

Von Vlod was just about to whisper down to Pablo again, then realised it was pointless as the noise Pablo was making would have already alerted anyone within listening distance to their presence. Instead, Von Vlod shouted to Pablo to get the others.

'Shush,' said Pablo, looking around. Shouting like that could alert anyone listening to their presence. He looked up. 'The others, or the other others?' he asked.

'Our others,' said a dispairing Von Vlod.

Pablo trotted off.

A little while later, Pablo, Wazzock and Wrinkle joined Von Vlod on the roof of the castle.

'So, no one here,' said Wazzock, stating the obvious.

'But was there?' asked Wrinkle. She wanted to know if the recent arrivals if they existed, had entered this Otherworld the same way they had. In another lifetime, the castle roof was where they had arrived, when it was their job to find the evil. They had failed.

Von Vlod admitted not being sure, so suggested they use the talents of Pablo, his nose.

'Sí,' said Pablo, 'I am with honour to do the honour.'

'Go on then,' urged Wazzock.

Pablo gave him a dirty look. 'It is being an art,' he said. 'I am not being rushed.'

'You've only got to sniff,' said Wazzock, drawing another dirty look.

'You are being sniffing, and you are having a runny nose,' said Pablo. 'When I am being sniffing, I am being arty.' He started to sniff.

'Well!' cried Wazzock as he was put in his place.

'Well?' said Wrinkle, eager to know.

'Give him a moment,' said Von Vlod.

'Sí,' said Pablo, 'I am having a moment.'

'Yes, you are,' smirked Wazzock.

'Take your time,' said Von Vlod, staring daggers at the wizard.

'I am having it,' announced Pablo suddenly. He was sniffing here, there, in the air. Everywhere.

'And?' asked Wrinkle.

'I am smelling four,' said Pablo.

'I thought so,' cried Wazzock. 'A group of four, just like us.'

A waft of excitement drifted over the other others, who had followed but at a distance.

'No, five,' said Pablo.

'Not like us,' said Von Vlod.

'No, six,' said Pablo. 'No, seven, no six.'

The other others, who had followed the others up to the roof and were mostly huddled around the door to it, were now puzzled and amazed and, in some cases, just plain befuddled. Which mostly matched the feelings of Wazzock, Wrinkle and Von Vlod.

'So how many are there?' asked Wrinkle.

More sniffing by Pablo. 'I am thinking seven. But then I am thinking six. I know not why.' He was now as puzzled as the rest of them were.

'Does it matter?' asked Wazzock. 'Someone was here, and now they're not. We should follow them.' He headed for the door that led down. The other others, seeing him coming, quickly disappeared through it. Not stopping until they were outside the castle.

'It might do.' Von Vlod was thinking.

'Why?' said Wrinkle.

'Because I think there were seven, but only six actually landed on the roof.' Was what Von Vlod thought.

'How do you know that?'

'Because when Pablo counted six, he was sniffing at the floor,' said Von Vlod, 'but when he counted seven, he was sniffing at the air.'

'So, what does that mean?' asked Wrinkle, more confused than she had been.

'I don't know,' admitted Von Vlod.

'Then no point worrying about it,' said Wrinkle. 'Come on, before Wazzock gets lost again.' She shrugged and then headed after Wazzock.

'What do you think?' Von Vlod asked Pablo.

'I am not knowing also,' Pablo admitted. 'Perhaps it is being the best.'

'You could be right,' said Von Vlod. But deep down, Von Vlod couldn't help but wonder.

CHAPTER 41

Salor was pulled unceremoniously from the grey undergrowth.

Earlier, at least a minute or so earlier, Twinkle had wailed, "What the!" as something suddenly appeared in front of her and then, after screaming a scream, disappeared again, just as suddenly.

'You idiot,' stormed Twinkle as she pulled Salor upright, 'you scared the living bejiggles right out of me.'

Salor, covered in twigs and things that looked wet and perhaps alive, didn't know what that meant. But what he did know, now he was on the verge of not shaking, was that he was safe and in the clutches of one of his best friends. But he wasn't about to tell her that. He was also not going to tell anyone the real reason he had been running so fast towards them. He would instead stick to the delusion he had been under as to why he had been running. He didn't want to look like an idiot again. Especially in front of witnesses. 'Ah-ha!' he exclaimed, brushing a wet thing off his shoulder. 'You're safe. I thought I might be too late to save you.'

'We are?' asked Twinkle. 'And from what?'

Deep breaths. 'Things,' said Salor, unable to come up with anything specific.

'Things?' said Danrite.

'Precisely,' said Salor, puffing out his pigeon chest. 'And such is why I came back as fast as I did. To save you. When I realised you had somehow lost your way. Straight away. No hesitation.'

Of course, no one believed him. Basil included, who was in the process of taking the chance, while everyone's attention was elsewhere, to sidle off.

'He is realising he is being all alone,' whispered Jose.

Danrite and Frida both smiled.

'The man doth protest too much, methinks,' spouted Frida. A tad of Shakespeare that went straight over everyone's head.

'Of course you did,' said Twinkle, talking to Salor whilst frowning at Frida. 'And just in time.'

'Just in time?' said Salor, giving the surroundings a nervous glance. 'For what?'

'Just in time to turn around and head back the way you've come.' Twinkle was turning him as she spoke.

'Back?' said Salor. He looked bewildered. But it did make sense. It was the way they had been heading. It was just taking Salor a while to think straight after his fright. 'Okay.' He turned around.

'And as we go,' said Twinkle, 'I'll fill you in on the Vlad situation.'

'Vlad?'

'Oh, and while I think about it.' Twinkle held out a hand. 'The compass, if you will. I think a real hero should take charge of it from now on.'

Another time, Salor would have been reluctant too, begrudging the idea, but after his recent mishaps, he decided it might be for the better. Besides, a good leader knows when to delegate. He handed the compass to Frida, who took it and immediately started down the path Salor had helpfully gouged.

'Well done,' said Twinkle. 'Now,' taking Salor by the arm, 'about Vlad.' Salor was about to be double bewildered.

And so they set off. To search for the evil and to look for Vlad. Except for Basil, that is.

Hanging back as everyone headed along the track from which Salor had appeared, Basil opened his rucksack and reached inside. He pulled out his talky-walky. It was the first chance he'd had to use it since arriving in this greyish Otherworld. He glanced at the track. They were almost out of sight. He would have to be quick.

'Font? Do you copy?' whispered Basil into the talky-walky. 'It's Basil, I have news.' Nothing.

He tried again. Still nothing. He tried again. But the same result: no answer.

'Drat,' dratted Basil.

He went to try again, but he heard Danrite calling for him before he could. Double drat, he thought. He quickly stowed the talky-walky away. 'Coming.'

The talky-walky stowed, the rucksack on his back, Basil headed for the track, numerous excuses for why he wasn't with them going through his mind. 'On my way,' he yelled. Contacting the Font would have to wait for now.

67

CHAPTER 42

The appearance of Salor had almost frightened the hooded figure as much as it had Twinkle. Thankfully, he had been quick-witted enough to stifle the scream that would have given him away.

Hand now taken from mouth, the hooded figure watched on amazed as the shaking Salor talked himself into believing he had just rescued them all. From what, the hooded figure did not know. The man was obviously a fool. Which then led to worry about what would happen if the wizard continued to lead the way. Because, if he did, the hooded figure doubted the evil would be destroyed anytime soon. If at all. Oh woe.

But then, as he watched, relief as the compass was passed to someone else. Someone, to his mind, who looked more capable of doing the job. The real hero? Maybe? It's what the Master had said.

The hooded figure readied himself to follow as Frida started down the path Salor had made. The rest following. No, not all following. The hooded figure checked his movement and wondered at what he was seeing. The one called Basil had stayed where he was and was now opening his rucksack. The hooded figure watched as Basil pulled something from it.

Well, I never, thought the hooded figure. He's got a talky-walky. Something else he would have to report. He allowed himself a small smile. Perhaps he would be in the Master's good books for once. He allowed the thought to linger. A good thought for him was rare. But it didn't last long as a yell from down the track brought the hooded figure back to reality.

The hooded figure nestled deeper into his shadowy hiding place and watched. He saw Basil quickly put the talky-walky back. Heard Basil answer the yell. Watched as Basil headed in the direction of the yell. He then wondered who the one called Basil had been trying to talk to. With that in mind, the hooded figure decided it was high time he used his own talky-walky.

The hooded figure looked at it. He had urgent things to report. But his mind wandered for a moment. His face clouded. He suddenly doubted his earlier thought about him being in the Master's good books. He doubted he would ever be in his master's good books. He doubted his master even owned a good book. Or even a book. He sighed. Such is life. His life. He spoke into the talky-walky. He didn't expect an answer. Perhaps a radio station. A jingle. What he got was a shock.

'Yes?' said the Master.

CHAPTER 43

The tale Percy told Vlad was unbelievable. So much so that Percy had to swear on numerous things so Vlad would believe him. But to believe Percy or not was neither here nor there, as Percy was there, standing before Vlad, telling it. Telling his unbelievable tale.

The tale had started with Percy wandering about wherever it was you believed you went after passing off your mortal coil. When, then, blammo! Percy's words. He was no longer there.

'Where were you?' asked Vlad, who was still taking the whole ghost thing with a large pinch of salt.
    'I'm getting to that,' said Percy.

While wondering why he was no longer wandering and wondering where he was wandering now, Percy suddenly came face to face with his worst nightmare. Which, to be honest, when told, as nightmares go, wasn't that bad. But each to their own.

'You were asleep?' Vlad wondered why a ghost should need to sleep.
    'No,' said Percy.

Standing before Percy was another Percy. A Percy who was standing in a large galvanised tub, the type your great, great grandmother might have used to wash clothes in. His trousers were rolled up to his knees, his feet hidden in mucky-looking water. In one hand, he held a half-peeled potato. In the other, an old-fashioned potato peeler – a knife.

Vlad was taken aback. But not too far. 'That's your worst nightmare? Really?'
    'What can I say?' shrugged Percy, 'I hate peeling spuds.'

'Don't be afraid,' announced the potato-wielding nightmare. 'I am here to help.'

'He wanted to help you peel spuds?'

'Let me finish.'

'Sorry.'

And as Percy didn't know he needed help, he asked the nightmare what he meant. The nightmare then proceeded to tell Percy a tale. A tale that, as the tale went on, appeared to show that Percy's nightmare and the other nightmares who had sent him knew very little about what was going on. So, as help went, it wasn't looking very helpful. But they did know that imagination was disappearing and everything imaginary disappearing with it. And that they needed to save it. To stop it happening. And that was why they had reached out to Percy.

'But you knew that, didn't you?'

'That's what I thought,' said Percy. 'But then…'

Percy's nightmare had then continued with what he perhaps should have started with.

It had been discovered that somewhere in the Otherworld, where imagination had first started to disappear and where it had been thought imagination now no longer existed, something had survived. Had been overlooked. So, had remained. A small piece of imagination still existing in some form or another. Stopping imagination from totally disappearing. A small piece of imagination existing in a glimmer of colour. The only colour left in an otherwise grey Otherworld.

It had to be saved. How? No one was sure, but one theory went that if it were mixed with magic, then it might be possible.

And then, once imagination was saved, the nightmares had an idea of how they could help return it to those who had lost it. Return it by absorbing the imagination and spreading it, with help, to all as they slept.

'Do they mean this world?' Vlad taken aback a little further this time.

'Yes,' confirmed Percy. 'That's why I'm here.'

'Then we're in luck,' declared Vlad, his mind a whirr. 'Salor has his staff. All the magic we might need is here.'

'Sadly, no,' said Percy.

'No?'

'Magic no longer works here. And besides, you and the others were sent here to destroy it, not save it.'

So, to cut a long story short.

The nightmares have an idea to save imagination. To do that, the last bit of imagination in this Otherworld has to be saved.

Danrite, Frida, and the others, on the other hand, are there to destroy what the nightmares believe will save imagination. Because they believe it to be evil, which is why they have the evil compass. Which means they need to be stopped.

And the only ones that can do that are Percy and Vlad.

'Lots of ifs and buts.'

'There is,' answered Percy, 'But if the nightmares idea works?'

'Another if,' Vlad pointed out. He wasn't convinced by it all.

'True,' agreed Percy. 'But, if it weren't for the fact that I'm here talking to you right now, I'd be having the same doubts as you. But I am here, so that must count for something.'

'I suppose,' said Vlad. 'But how do we stop anyone from destroying the colour when we don't know where anyone is? And on top of that, we haven't got a clue where this colour is either.'

'Ah, but we have this.' Percy took something from a pocket and showed it to Vlad. It was a compass. He had been using it earlier.

'A broken compass?'

'No,' said Percy, 'a compass that points to evil.' It was the one Danrite had seen when Percy was alive. A ghostly version.

Vlad frowned. 'And that helps us, how?' he asked. 'Surely, we're looking for something that isn't evil.'

'That's true,' admitted Percy. 'But if we thought it was evil, then the compass would point the way. It's all in the way you look at things.'

Again, Vlad wasn't convinced, but what other choice did they have? Wander aimlessly until they no longer had the imagination left to wonder what they were doing? Or use what imagination they had left and imagine the non-evil thing as being evil? And suddenly, just like that, Vlad could imagine it working.

'Right,' yelled Vlad, jumping up from the tree stump he had been sitting on. 'What are we waiting for? Let's open a portal and go save the day.'

'Portal?' puzzled Percy.

'That's how I got here, isn't it?' said Vlad. 'And, I take it, you as well?'

'Yes,' said Percy, realising he hadn't told Vlad everything yet. 'But portals only work to get you in here. They don't work here.'

'But how did I get from the castle to here?'

'The nightmares hijacked the portal you arrived in by piggybacking another one to it, the one I arrived in,' explained Percy. 'We then ended up here.'

'Why here?' Vlad, thinking, wouldn't it have been easier to just go to the colour? He said this to Percy.

'What can I say,' said Percy, shrugging. 'Other than it was a nightmare getting us here.' He looked at the compass. 'Come on, this way.' And off he went.

Grief, thought Vlad, here we go again. But as he tagged along behind, he had another, more serious thought come to mind. If the portals didn't work in here, then how were they going to get out again? No, he then thought, not now. He would file it with the others like, for example, why him? No, he would worry later. In the meantime, he would just concentrate on keeping up with Percy. 'Wait up,' he yelled.

CHAPTER 44

He couldn't relax. Since that very short second when he had felt something that no longer existed, he had felt increasingly uneasy.

The creature with the unimportant name wibbled. He had never done that before, in the cave, in all the time he had hidden there. Wobble, yes. Wibble, no. That was something for outside. When he frequently wibble wobbled. He wibbled again. The unease was getting to him. He wobbled. Wibbled. Oh dear, he thought and quickly held onto his head. The last thing he needed was for it to fall off. Things were happening, and it wasn't the time to lose your head. Literally!

CHAPTER 45

Wazzock, Wrinkle, Pablo and Von Vlod, and the other others had left the building. They now milled around outside the castle as Pablo, with the others and the other others looking on, picked up the scent of whoever it was that had come through the portal.

The scents were faint, to begin with. 'They go this way,' said Pablo. Then grew stronger when Pablo latched on to individual scents. 'Phewie,' he muttered, his nose wrinkling. 'The werewolf, he is being stinky strong with his smell.'

'Werewolf!' exclaimed an alarmed Wazzock. He didn't like the sound of that. 'You never said anything about a werewolf when we were on the roof.'

'No one is being asking me.'

'Well,' said Wrinkle, 'perhaps you should have mentioned it anyway.'

Pablo stood his ground. 'You are asking me if someone is coming through,' he said. 'You are not asking me who.'

But that was now beside the point, so Von Vlod asked Pablo about the rest that had come through. A werewolf was dangerous enough unless it was friendly. But what if it wasn't? What if the rest were worse? An ogre. Or a hobgoblin. Or even a politician? Von Vlod shuddered at the thought. Von Vlod asked. Pablo sniffed.

'Now I am with the smelling humans,' said Pablo. 'There is being the two.'

'Humans!' exclaimed Von Vlod, concerns over politicians now spilling over.

'Can't trust humans,' said Wrinkle.

'Some you can,' said Wazzock, who, though a wizard, was in theory a human, albeit a magical one.

'Not politicians,' said Von Vlod.

'Politicians?' said Wrinkle, wondering where that had come from.

'Some you can, I think,' said Wazzock, giving Von Vlod a quizzical glance.

'But at least they're not ogres,' said Von Vlod.

'Can't trust ogres,' agreed Wazzock.

'Ogres?' said Wrinkle, now wondering if Von Vlod was feeling all right.

'Never mind,' said Von Vlod.

'Now it is the smell of a wizard,' said Pablo.

'Can't trust wizards,' said Wrinkle.

'Oi!' cried Wazzock. 'Some you can.'

'And now I am smelling a fairy,' said Pablo, who was ignoring the others and concentrating on his art.

'Can't trust... What did he just say?' said Wrinkle.

'He is smelling a fairy,' said Wazzock. 'You can't trust them, you know.'

Wrinkle glared.

Von Vlod smiled.

'There.' Pablo, looked up. A tiny twig stuck to his nose. 'I am being finished. I am smelling six.'

Von Vlod reached down and brushed the twig away.

'Gracias,' said Pablo, who then sneezed.

'You're welcome,' smiled Von Vlod.

'So, six of them,' said Wazzock, counting on his fingers. 'And correct me if I'm wrong, a wizard, a fairy, a werewolf, and two humans.' He now got to his sixth finger. He stared at it. He looked puzzled. He turned to Pablo. 'What did you say number six was?'

'I am not being saying.'

'Why not?'

'Because I am not knowing.'

'Not knowing?'

'Sí,' said Pablo. 'But also, I am smelling the humans. They are being different with it.'

'Different?' said Wrinkle. 'What do you mean, different?'

'They are not being normal to the smelling,' said Pablo.

'And what does that mean?' asked Wrinkle.

But Pablo didn't answer. He was heading to a tree that was calling to his nostrils.

'Could mean anything,' reasoned Wazzock.

'I suggest we ask him then,' suggested Von Vlod. 'Though I have the feeling he's in the dark as much as we are.' Von Vlod walked after Pablo.

'Perhaps,' said Wrinkle, 'but we should ask him anyway.' She did the same.

'Yes,' said Wazzock, who was ahead of the other two. 'We need to know what we are dealing with.' So, caught up with Pablo before they did. 'Pablo?' And wished he hadn't. 'Yuk,' he said, averting his eyes.

'Sí,' said Pablo, one leg in the air.

'When you've finished,' said Von Vlod.

A little shake of the leg later, and Pablo was among them again. 'What is it you are wanting?' he asked.

'We want to know what you meant when you said the humans were different,' said Wrinkle.

Pablo shrugged. 'It is as I am saying, they are not smelling as other humans.'

'Yes,' sighed Wazzock, shaking his head, 'we gathered that, but in what way different?'

'I am smelling them as magic,' said Pablo, who then put his nose to the ground and sniffed. 'Ah, they are going there.' He nodded towards the tree he had just christened and set off towards it, nose down.

'What!' exclaimed Wrinkle. 'Wait, what do you mean? Magic?'

Pablo shrugged again. 'I am not knowing. I am just smelling.'

Worried glances were exchanged by the others.

The other others did the same. But without the worry. Most were excited glances. Some were blank. And the ones who hadn't been taking any notice at all were wondering why they were being glanced at.

'Told you,' said Von Vlod, 'he has no idea either.'

'I don't like it,' said Wrinkle.

'You never do,' said Wazzock.

Wrinkle glared.

Wazzock turned away.

'Perhaps we should follow Pablo and find out,' said Von Vlod. 'It's the only way we'll know for sure what it is he is or isn't smelling.'

'I suppose,' said Wrinkle doubtfully.

'If we must.' A worried-looking Wazzock wasn't overly keen.

'Pablo,' called Von Vlod.

'Si,' said Pablo, who was back at the tree.

'Lead on.'

'I am being on it.' Pablo put nose back to ground and followed it around the tree, being careful to dodge the small puddle that lay at the foot of it.

'Come on,' said Von Vlod.

Wrinkle grunted and moved.

Wazzock worried and did likewise.

The other others stirred. Went to follow. Stopped. Made sure all were heading in the same direction. Then followed.

CHAPTER 46

The hooded figure almost dropped the talky-walky when the voice of his master brought it to life.

'Master?' whimpered the hooded figure, staring at the talky-walky with a mixture of surprise and dread.

'Who were you expecting,' quizzed the Master, 'the talking clock?'

The hooded figure was now in a tizz. What was the talking clock? He didn't know a talking clock. Why should he have been expecting a call from it? Perhaps it was a trick question. Oh, misery, he thought, as he overthought things. 'I...well,' he sputtered. Then, something he had half expected to hear came to mind. He mentioned it. Why not? 'Southern Radio?'

A pause on the other end of the line for a moment. 'You heard that?' said the Master.

'Yes-no-a bit,' admitted the hooded figure, not sure whether to admit to it or not, but doing it anyway.

Strange, thought the Master. The talky-walky then went quiet again for a couple of moments. Time enough for the hooded figure to grow anxious. Then, abruptly. 'What have you to report?'

The suddenness of the question caught the nervous hooded figure off guard. He faltered. He regrouped. He then prattled on like there was going to be no tomorrow. Something that was wholly possible for him should the Master be inclined.

Thankfully for the hooded figure, the lack of a tomorrow for him wasn't on the Master's mind. 'Slow down!' snapped the Master. The words were short and sharp and as good as a slap across the face. And to the hooded figure, it felt like one. His babbling instantly stopped. 'Now, repeat all you just told me, but slowly. And start with the news about the one called Vlad.'

CHAPTER 47

'From the roof?' said Salor, still bewildered by the news Vlad was missing.

'Another portal,' Twinkle explained. 'At least that's what we think happened.'

'But where did he go?'

'That's the question,' said Danrite.

'Sí,' said Jose, 'it is being the question.'

'But I don't understand,' said Salor, 'I was sure he was with us.'

'We all were,' said Frida as she dodged a rather nasty-looking prickly bush in the path the compass was leading her. How Salor had missed that in his panic to get back, she didn't know. Perhaps he hadn't. 'Watch that.' She walked on.

'It's all the excitement,' reasoned Danrite, dodging the bush. As did most of them.

'What excitement?' asked Twinkle, who hadn't noticed any.

'Of being here,' said Danrite.

'Danrite's right,' said Frida, stopping and turning around. 'We've been so caught up in what's been going on, we've not seen further than our own noses.'

Jose went cross-eyed, looking at his.

'Valid point,' agreed Twinkle, nodding sagely while making a big thing of looking at Salor's nose. Now, she thought, if ever there was a nose that never got looked farther than.

'Oi,' grumbled Salor, wondering what was going on with her.

Frida saw what Twinkle was doing and smiled but felt perhaps they needed to be taking things a little more seriously. Especially if they wanted to leave this Otherworld in one piece. She suggested it. Do the job they were here for. Keep their wits about them. And then, if Vlad still hadn't turned up, they find him.

All agreed. Especially Basil, especially the wits bit, as he walked into the prickly bush everyone else had dodged. 'Ow-ow-ow!'

The journey continued. And a fair distance was covered.

'I still can't help but wonder if Vlad's okay,' said Danrite, who was now walking alongside his sister.

'As we all are,' said Frida, watching the compass.

Danrite hesitated but said what was on his mind. 'How far do you think it is?' he asked. 'You know, the evil.'

'As the little man said,' said Twinkle, meaning Basil. 'We'll know when we know.' They were all keeping close.

'So, we get there when we get there,' said Danrite.

'Flipping flippings,' moaned Salor. 'We'll see it when we see it! We'll get there when we get there! We'll find Vlad when we find him!' He was having a bit of a meltdown and was looking older than he had ever done. 'Is nothing straightforward in this flipping place?'

'Do you really want an answer to that?' asked Twinkle.

'No, I suppose not,' said Salor, his shoulders slumping. 'But I just wish we had something concrete to work with.'

'Like that?' Frida stopped so suddenly she caused a concertina effect behind her.

Frowns in abundance, everyone untangled and peered to see what Frida was talking about.

Mouths then dropped open. Eyes widened. Questions began forming.

CHAPTER 48

'But why me?' Vlad asked after a while of trying to keep up with Percy. The question had been nagging at him. Other questions had as well, but he didn't want to ask them. He didn't think he would like some of the answers.

'Why you what?' said Percy, not breaking his stride.

'Why was I chosen?' said Vlad, suspecting it was because of one of his talents.

'Chosen?'

'For this.'

'For this?'

Grief, thought Vlad, getting annoyed. Annoyed enough to suddenly call a halt. 'Stop!' he cried.

Percy stopped, turned, and gave Vlad a look that was a mix of worry and puzzlement.

'What's wrong?' asked Percy.

'I want to know why I was chosen to help you.'

'Oh,' said Percy. 'Is that all?'

'Yes,' said Vlad. He was irked. Is that all? he thought.

'You weren't,' said Percy, not noticing Vlad had become a little hot under the collar.

'What?' said Vlad, in reply to the answer he wasn't expecting.

'You weren't,' Percy repeated. 'It was just a case of pot luck, and you were the nearest pot. You just happened to be closest to my portal when it opened. The lucky pot if you like.'

Vlad didn't like. He had expected something more. Though what, he wasn't sure. Perhaps he wanted to be a hero? 'So, I wasn't chosen.'

'No,' said Percy. If he noticed that Vlad was a little upset, he didn't show it.

'Oh.'

Percy shuffled his feet. They needed to be somewhere else. 'Shall we go?'

'Suppose so,' said Vlad.

Without another word, Percy about turned and continued on his merry way.

A miffed Vlad followed and wished he hadn't asked. There was no way he was going to ask any more questions. For the moment. But he would think about them. And worry a little.

CHAPTER 49

Led by a nose to the ground, Pablo, the others, and the other others had started along the path Salor had made, and which Frida was at that moment following, being led herself by the compass.

'We've been travelling for hours now, and still no sign of them,' whined Wazzock.

'Twenty minutes since we left the castle, by my reckoning,' said Wrinkle.

Wazzock tutted. 'Seems like hours.'

'No patience, that's your trouble.'

'And fairies have?' said Wazzock, knowing fairies are well known for their lack of the quality.

'That's different,' defended Wrinkle, 'it's a part of who we are. Something you know full well.'

'That's it,' snapped Von Vlod, 'will you two please stop bickering.' They had been at it since they left the castle, and Von Vlod had had enough. Twenty minutes of it. Or hours by Wazzock's reckoning. Von Vlod had to agree with Wazzock. It certainly felt like hours having to listen to them go on and on. 'We'll catch up with when we do.'

'Sí,' said Pablo, from up ahead. His stick still between his teeth. 'We are finding them when we are finding them.' He lifted his head and sniffed. 'And I am still with the sniffing.'

'Well done,' said Von Vlod. At least someone had their mind on the job.

'See,' said Wrinkle, 'even Pablo has more sense than you.'

Wazzock sniffed and mumbled something under his breath that no one took any notice of.

Behind them, the other others had stopped for a picnic.

CHAPTER 50

The hooded figure took a deep breath and started again. He had told his master about the missing Vlad. The compass, belonging to the one called Basil, who had given it to the one called Frida. And that Basil had a talky-walky.

The hooded figure now waited as his master mulled over what he had told him.

Half an hour later.

'And nothing else?' asked the Master as if no time had passed.

'Er-what? Ow,' groaned the hooded figure.

The hooded figure, who had managed to nod off while resting his head on an arm that had rested on a knee, awoke with a start. His arm slipped from the knee as his head slipped from the arm. Thus, his nose and knee had a brief encounter.

'I said,' said the Master, with all the patience of a fairy, or a whining wizard, or someone who didn't have any, 'and nothing else?'

'Oh,' said the hooded figure dabbing at his nose.

'Oh?'

'Oh-no.'

'No?'

'Yes,' said the hooded figure. 'No.'

A sharp intake of breath on the other side of the talky-walky had an instantly sobering effect on the hooded figure.

'No, Master,' said the hooded figure quickly. Or was there? He desperately tried to remember if there was. No. Maybe. What did the Master know that he didn't? Or did the Master know nothing? No, possibly, just to be on the safe side. Fingers crossed. 'Nothing else.'

'Umm,' said the Master, in such a way it made the hooded figure's skin crawl. Especially as it continued.

The hooded figure waited. The umm was still going. He was sure he had missed something. He started to sweat. The umm stopped.

'Good,' said the Master, catching the hooded figure by surprise.

'Good?' The hooded figure wasn't sure if he had heard right.

'Yes,' confirmed the Master. 'Keep tracking and report anything else I should know about immediately.'

'Good?' repeated the hooded figure, dicing with never look a gift horse in the mouth.

'Yes,' repeated the Master. 'Your report was most revealing.'

This delighted the hooded figure in the same way someone might be delighted when finding a cuddly bear cub in the woods while ignoring the growly noises behind you. A dangerous thing to do.

'Thank you, Master,' gushed the pleased hooded figure into the talky-walky. 'I'm…Master?' He shook the talky-walky. 'Master? I'm…' Deluded was a word that would come to him later.

And while the hooded figure figured that out, his master was thinking how wise it had been to have a plan to speed things along a little if needed. And how wise it was to have already put it in motion. Especially now because of the changes in circumstances. Nothing would come between the Master and the plan.

As for the circumstances, the Vlad disappearing was a slight concern. Someone was poking their noses in where they didn't belong. The evil compass and the one called Basil – why did that name ring a bell – with the talky-walky was of little matter; in fact, the compass could only help.

And then there were the others, and the other others, whom the minion had failed to mention. Words would be had. They, again, were of little concern. Unless. Unless it was they that had taken the Vlad. Why though? For what reason? A slight concern had suddenly changed to a slightly larger concern. A question needed to be asked. The Master clicked the on button on the talky-walky.

CHAPTER 51

The creature with the unimportant name had finally lost it. His head. He knew he would. That's why he had held onto it so tightly. Problem was the creature with the unimportant name had held onto it so tight it had popped off.

The creature with the unimportant name now searched for it. It could be anywhere. It might have rolled out of the cave. The thought made him panic. What if it had? But then reason stepped in, and the panic was over. Silly me, thought the creature with the unimportant name, I'd see if it had.

You see, the creature with the unimportant name could still see, even with his head detached. Unless it was broken. Another panic of what ifs. Then calm. No, he could see shapes. Dark shapes, as in the cave. Not lighter ones, as in outside. His head was in the cave.

But there was still a problem. The creature with the unimportant name couldn't see his head to find it. He needed his head to see his body. Once that happened, his head could guide his body over to wherever it lay. And once his body had found his head, it was just a case of popping it back on, and hey presto, all was right again. Until then, the creature with the unimportant name would have to stumble in the dark.

Wibble. Wobble. Stumble. Bump. Repeat.

CHAPTER 52

'Blimey,' said Danrite.

'Is that what I think it is?' said Twinkle.

'If it is, then I must be dreaming,' said Salor.

'Ay caramba!' exclaimed Jose. 'I am with the thinking that I am thinking that it cannot be what I am thinking.'

'That's exactly what I thought,' said Frida.

And the wonderment continued as they slowly moved forward. Downward. Together. To get a closer look at what they saw. No one leading the way. No one following the compass. No one sure what to think. Apart from Jose, who was still thinking that what he was thinking couldn't be what he was thinking.

Slowly, they went. Then slower as they got nearer. Slow. Stop. They gathered and stared. There were now less than twenty metres between them and what they couldn't believe they were seeing.

But not all had travelled down the slope to where the thing they couldn't believe they were seeing was. Basil, who himself had wondered what the goodness, when he had seen it, had wasted no time saying what he thought out loud and had then retreated, quick, quicker, to a safe distance away where he could use the talky-walky without being seen. And by the look that had been on the faces of the others, he doubted he would be missed or disturbed anytime soon. But just in case that wasn't the case, he disappeared into the cover of a large grey hedge.

'Hello,' whispered Basil, 'Do you copy? Over.'

Nothing for a moment. Then, something that made Basil frown. And then...

'Font here, over.'

The hooded figure was still looking at the talky-walky when it took him by surprise by clicking back into life. He just managed to catch it before it hit the ground.

'You there?' said the Master.

And before the hooded figure had a chance to not answer, he did. 'Yes, Master.'

'The others?' The Master need say no more for the hooded figure to break out in a cold sweat.

Drat! thought the hooded figure. He knew there was something else. He had forgotten all about them. What did he do now? Lie. It was the obvious choice. But what if the Master knew he had forgotten? Why else would the Master ask him about them?

'Well?' The Master's tone had icicles hanging from it.

'In their cave,' said the hooded figure. Not a lie then, unless they weren't. He crossed his fingers. Everyone knew that it wasn't a real lie if you crossed your fingers. If it was a lie.

'Good,' said the Master.

'Good?' said the hooded figure, fingers sweaty and crampy.

'Just let me know if they leave it,' said the Master, not sharing the concern about Vlad with the minion.

'I will, Master,' said the hooded figure as fingers slipped apart. Oh dear, he thought as he tried to re-cross them without success. Too slippy. Please don't ask me another question. But at least the cramping had stopped.

'Good,' said the Master. A pause. A thoughtful pause. A long, thoughtful pause that had the hooded figure holding his breath while frantically trying to cross his toes. Because everyone knew that it wasn't a lie if your toes were crossed. Then, a click. The Master was gone.

Then, another click. The hooded figure was gone. In a heap on the ground. He had dislocated a toe.

CHAPTER 54

Vlad had, for the sake of his sanity, decided to try and not think. Go with the flow. Believe Percy was a ghost. Which was surprisingly easy, as Percy was so good at it. But whether he was a ghost or wasn't a ghost. Whether he was an avatar or wasn't an avatar. It was no matter. As far as he could see. As long as they got where they were going and did what they needed to do, then what was the point? So, no point in the questions or the ifs and buts that swam in his head. Much better to ignore them and deal with the here and now. If Percy said he was a ghost, so be it. If there were no portals out of the place, so be it. For now. So, no more questions. Or thinking of ifs or buts. But why has Percy stopped? Drat, he thought, but at least there hadn't been an if. Unless that counted?

Vlad shook his head and focused on Percy, who was a few steps ahead.

'Percy?' he called as he went to catch up with him. When he did, he saw that Percy had not only stopped he wasn't moving either. Percy, the ghost slash avatar, now appeared to be a statue.

Vlad waved a hand in front of Percy's face. He seemed to be in a trance. 'You okay?' Vlad asked. Then, remembering Percy couldn't see his hand, he picked up a stick and waved that.

Something happened. Percy's eyes, until that moment open, closed. Vlad stepped closer. Percy's eyes opened again, making Vlad start. He stepped back. Percy's eyes closed again. Now Vlad could see that Percy's eyeballs were moving rapidly under his eyelids. It looked as if he was dreaming. Vlad watched and wondered. And then Percy's eyes were open again, giving Vlad another start. Percy was back in the here and now.

'Hello there,' said Percy, as if he was surprised to see Vlad.

'Percy?' said Vlad, looking concerned. 'You okay? What just happened?' Percy looked a little out of sorts. If a ghost could be out of sorts.

'Yes, strange,' muttered Percy. 'I had another nightmare.'

'Oh,' said Vlad. 'The potato one?'

'No.' Percy staggered slightly. Vlad went to steady him, but Percy managed to stay upright. He waved Vlad away. 'I'm fine, just a bit of a shock. That's all.'

'What was?' asked Vlad, who wasn't entirely sure Percy was fine.

'The nightmare,' said Percy. 'It was someone else's.'

If they weren't invisible, Percy would have seen Vlad's eyes grow wide.

'Someone else's?' Vlad was not sure what to make of what Percy was saying.

'Yes,' said Percy. 'And I think I know whose it was.'

'Whose?'

'Danrite's.'

'Danrite's?' exclaimed Vlad.

'There was an awful lot of cheese.'

Vlad didn't ask; some things were best left well alone.

'But why Danrite's?'

'It came to warn us,' said Percy. 'It would seem Danrite and the others have been given a helping hand so they can get to where they're going a little quicker.' Percy suddenly looked tired as he explained. 'It looks like time is most definitely not on our side.'

A worried Vlad started to go back on his word and think. 'Can't they help us?' he wondered. 'The nightmares?'

'They're not sure.'

'They visited you. Can't they visit them? Warn them?'

'Sadly, no.' Percy explained. 'They can only visit as a nightmare, so whoever they visited would have to be asleep. Which is possible, I suppose, but not to be relied on. It's complicated.'

'But you weren't asleep,' Vlad pointed out. 'You were walking.'

'I asked about that. Seems ghosts are in perpetual sleep mode.'

'Oh,' said Vlad. He then had a thought. 'So how do the nightmares know about the helping hand?'

'Ah.' Percy smiled. 'A little luck there. Someone had a nightmare about it.'

'Who?'

'The nightmare wouldn't say.' Percy frowned. 'Something about nightmare confidentiality.'

'Like a doctor, patient thing?'

'Yes. I suppose.'

Vlad thought about this. 'But Danrite's nightmare visited you,' he said, slightly puzzled. 'Isn't that against the confidentiality thingy?'

'Family,' explained Percy. He being Danrite's uncle. 'But only in an emergency. And friends, but only in the most urgent of need. Like I said, it's complicated. Though I do think they make a lot of it up as they go along.'

'Grief,' said Vlad, thinking of some of his relatives, one in particular. He hoped he didn't have one of his nightmares come visit. 'I suppose some could be quite scary.'

'Thankfully, only cheese and potatoes so far.' Percy smiled. 'Not too scary. So far.'

So far, thought Vlad. He now had something else to try and not think about. Also, did that mean Percy was a ghost after all? The family link. Who knows? thought Vlad. And as he had enough to think about already, he left it. Good if he was, but not that important in the scheme of things.

'Well,' said Percy, no longer as tired as he had looked, 'we should move. Time is against us.' He took a step and then stopped. For a moment, Vlad thought he was having another nightmare. 'Oh, and something else, the nightmare told me. Whoever had the nightmare isn't working alone. They have someone on the inside.'

'Inside?'

'Here, in this Otherworld. We have to be on our toes.' Percy was now ready to take another step, Which he did. Quickly followed by others. Quick steps.

Grief, thought Vlad as Percy sped off, it never rains, but it pours. There were so many more things to try and not think about now. He hurried after Percy.

'Ah, there I am,' said the creature with the unimportant name. His head had seen his body. Now, all he had to do was guide his body over to it and pop it back on. Easier thought than done.

Wibble. Wobble. Stumble. Bump. Repeat.

As Pablo continued to lead the way, the other others, those that weren't Pablo, Wazzock, Wrinkle, or Von Vlod, finished their picnic.

Picnic packed up, the other others now realised something. Well, some of them did. Those who were not asleep or hadn't wandered off had noticed. Pablo, Wazzock, Wrinkle and Von Vlod were no longer in sight.

A hurried meeting was called. Those who were asleep were woken. Those who had wandered off were mostly rounded up. Those who weren't rounded up would turn up eventually. Mostly would. Some would just disappear. It's what happened sometimes. Blame it on a lack of imagination. The meeting started. The meeting finished.

All those in favour of staying in this Otherworld; one. All those in favour of leaving it; the rest. Though, it turned out the one who had voted not to go had had an itchy armpit. All in favour, then. Then they had better get a move on if they wanted to catch the others up.

CHAPTER 57

Talky-walky packed away, toe put back into place, the hooded figure made ready to check on the others and the other others. He felt he should do after his last chat with the Master. He didn't want to dislocate another toe. It had mightily hurt. Off he limped.

Then stopped. Perhaps he should check on the ones he was following first. The lot with the hero. The ones who lost their friend. Danrite and Co. Happy in his mind, he knew who he was checking on, he went to check on them.

He found them on the brow of a hill. They had stopped. Puzzled as to why, he inched as close as he could get without being seen. Making sure he was downwind of the chihuahua's nose. They appeared to be staring at something. He carefully sidled to the left until he was looking at Danrite and Co side on.

What is going on? he thought. He inched closer. Not too close. Was that a look of awe on their faces? At least, that's what he thought he saw. He was a fair distance from them, to be fair. They then started to move down the hill. Now what? The hooded figure decided he had better have a look see what it was they had seen and where they were going.

Easing his way through the undergrowth, he eventually emerged from it with a clear view down the hill to where Danrite and Co were heading.

And once again, his hand clamped across his mouth to save him from giving himself away. It was his turn to stare in awe. What the heck? he thought. He couldn't believe his eyes. He had better tell the Master. But as he raised the talky-walky, he remembered what he was supposed to be doing. The others and the other others. Drat, he thought. He looked at his foot. His toe was still throbbing. Not much, but enough to remind him what lying to the Master could do. He had better do what he was going to do then; he didn't want the Master asking questions he might hurt himself with. To the cave first and then back here. He just hoped nothing happened while he was away. He limped off at the double.

CHAPTER 58

'Thank goodness,' said Basil when the Font answered. 'I've only just been able to contact you.' As Basil spoke, he cast a wary glance in the direction of Danrite and the others. He had made sure he could still see them from his hiding place. They were at the bottom of the hill he was on, still staring at what they had found. It was safe to talk for the moment.

'Is all going to plan?' asked the Font, who had started to worry a little. She had expected Basil to contact her ages ago.

'So far,' said Basil. 'A few hiccups, though.'

'Hiccups?' The Font didn't like the sound of that. 'What do you mean, hiccups?'

Basil thought he had better start at the beginning. 'They have the compass.'

'How?' demanded the Font. 'You were supposed to hide it.'

Basil cringed. 'I know, but they caught me looking at it. Good news, though, is they're following it.'

'I suppose,' mumbled the Font. But the truth was, as long as they destroyed the evil, then all would be well, whoever had the compass. Then she remembered Basil had mentioned hiccups. 'You said hiccups. What else has happened?'

Basil took a deep breath. 'Vlad's disappeared.'

'What!' cried the Font, shaken by the news. 'How? When?'

'When we arrived,' said Basil, bracing himself.

'And you're only telling me now!' fumed the Font.

Basil, who had been expecting to be blamed by the Font, as he was when anything went wrong, anywhere, even if it had nothing to do with him, defended himself. 'Like I told you,' he said, 'it's the first chance I've had to contact you.'

The Font, not totally unreasonable, calmed herself. She supposed she couldn't expect miracles where Basil was concerned. 'And you haven't seen him since?' She thought she had better check. Especially where Basil was concerned.

'No,' said Basil, thinking it a stupid question. 'We looked, but there was no trace of him. We don't think he landed with us. Frida thinks he might have disappeared into another portal before he could.'

This is worrying news, thought the Font. Something was afoot. Could someone be meddling? If so, who?

Patiently waiting for the Font to reply to what he had just told her, Basil twitched for a bit, then waited some more. He began to wonder if he should mention the thing Danrite and the others were looking at or leave it for the moment. A triple whammy. No, best to leave it. Let her digest what she had just been told first. Or not? Or did he carry on waiting? Might be best to, he thought. But she had to be told. Drat. He then began to wonder if the Font remembered he was still there. He politely coughed.

The cough brought the Font from her thoughts. 'Sorry, I was miles away.'

'There's more,' said Basil, deciding it might be for the best to tell her what he knew, triple whammy or not. And before the Font could say anything else, he told her what the more was.

CHAPTER 59

'It's beautiful,' said Frida. 'In a grey kinda way.'

'It is,' agreed Twinkle.

'It's magnificent, is what it is,' said Salor.

'Suppose,' said Danrite, who wasn't at all taken with all those black roses.

As for Jose, if his tail had really been a sword, it would have done some serious damage to the legs it was pounding against. 'Sí,' he said. 'Magnifico! It is as I am already with the tasting of the biscuits.'

A multitude of frowns formed as Jose's words were digested. Frowns that grew into puzzled what-the-heck looks.

'Biscuits?' said Frida, the first to ask the question on everyone else's lips.

'Sí,' said Jose. 'Marrowbone and Tequila.' He proceeded to lick his lips.

But before anyone else could ask Jose what he was going on about, something, a vague memory that had been lurking at the back of Salor's mind, suddenly came to the fore, causing Salor to have a sudden realisation. 'Oh, good grief,' he exclaimed.

'Salor?' Twinkle was suddenly on high alert for Salor nonsense.

'It's the same,' said Salor.

'What is?' asked a bemused Frida.

'That is.' Salor was pointing at what they were all gaping at.

CHAPTER 60

The hooded figure's boss tracked back and forth across the floor. Things were moving too slowly. But a plan had been hatched. A plan that was now in place. All they had to do was fall for it. Walk in, and their journey would nearly be at an end. And then the world would be there for the taking. All the worlds. They just had to walk in. Hands were wrung. And if it weren't deemed beneath the Master to do so, a burst of cackling laughter would have followed.

But then. A thought. What if they didn't go in? And then, when the Master thought on it, why hadn't the minion made contact? He must have seen it by now and wondered. Should have been in contact by now, reporting it. The Master stopped walking and reached for the talky-walky.

CHAPTER 61

The Font waited for Basil to answer. Surely, it wasn't difficult. He had told her that Danrite and the others had seen something, and she had asked him, what?

At last, the talky-walky spoke. 'Well,' said Basil, 'it's difficult to say.'

The Font raised an eyebrow. 'Try.'

'It keeps changing.'

'What keeps changing?' asked an increasingly frustrated Font.

'The thing they're looking at.' Basil was trying his best.

Give me strength, thought the Font. She took a deep breath. 'Start at the beginning, with what you saw first.'

Basil thought for a moment. How did he explain what he had seen? And which had been the first? He couldn't remember. It was a jumble. He then remembered the black roses.

'Ah, cottage-castle-saloon-towers-concrete. But maybe not in that order.' Basil paused. 'The cottage had black roses on it.' Why he had noticed that amongst all the other things going on, he didn't know. The oddness of it, perhaps. But it had helped.

'Cottage?'

'With black roses,' said Basil helpfully.

'And a castle?' The Font was beginning to wonder if Basil had hit his head on something. She wouldn't put it past him. 'And what do you see now?' she asked. If the Font had been there with him, she would have asked him to count how many fingers she held up.

'Wait a mo.' Basil looked. He froze. 'Agh!' This last uttering was because he had just seen something he hadn't seen before. That hadn't been there before. And yet there it was, standing where the others had stood. A giant television set with a door set in it just below the on-off knobs. Unbeknown to Basil, he had just seen his heart's desire. Weird as that might be.

'Basil?' said the Font. Wondering what in the wondering wonders was going on. 'What's going on?'

Basil couldn't answer; he had clamped a hand across his mouth to stop other utterings from escaping. Surprise had caught him by surprise. So he wanted to make sure more words of fear, terror, want, and longing didn't escape after his last one. He had also moved deeper into his hiding place, afraid someone might have heard him. Thankfully, on checking, it appeared they hadn't, so immersed were Danrite and the others in their own wonderment. He doubted they would have heard thunder if it had clapped directly over them.

'Speak to me,' demanded the Font, losing some of her famous cool. 'What's happening?' She was staring at the talky-walky. 'What do you see?'

Basil slumped. He had to be going mad. And to make things worse, he was about to admit to it, to the Font. 'A television,' he replied. He felt weak.

The Font looked at the talky-walky in her hand as if it were the crazy one here. 'I don't understand,' she said. She didn't. Basil was obviously not himself.

'A television,' Basil repeated. 'I saw a giant television set with a door in it.'

So, not himself, the Font decided. 'And did this television speak to you?'

'What?' said Basil. He then realised the Font was thinking what he thought she would be thinking on hearing his babbling. 'No, it was just standing there. Like a house.'

The Font didn't know what to think, except that Basil definitely wasn't himself at the moment. 'Did you bump your head?' she asked.

'No,' wailed Basil. 'I saw it. It's real.' He snuck a tad from his hiding place and looked again. It was still there. 'It's still there.'

The Font didn't know what to think. A giant television with a door in it? Towers. Castles. Saloons? Black roses? It sounded nonsense. But she would humour him. How did that all work? She asked the question gently, trying to imagine a television with towers and black roses. She had no idea how the castle, cottage and concrete fitted in. Unless the television was made of it.

'No,' snapped Basil, 'they were separate from each other. I saw the cottage first, I think, then the towers, and so on. The television was the last thing I saw.' He chanced another look from his hiding place. 'Still see.' He wasn't sure if he'd preferred it to have vanished. It would have made his life much simpler. He could have felt for bumps then.

The Font – convinced Basil had done himself a mischief without realising it – had been about to turn the talky-walky off and make a nice cup of green tea – to drink while mulling over the more sensible news Basil had reported – when a thought popped into her head stopping her. A thought that was both confusing and a tad disturbing but just might throw some light on what Basil had told her he was seeing. He might not have bumped his head after all. She told him to go and take another look at it.

Basil did.

'Well?' asked the Font.

'It's still there,' Basil confirmed.

'And you see nothing else?' the Font asked.

'Just that and everyone staring at it,' said Basil.

'Right,' said the Font, doubting that. But, why Basil should see what the others saw was a mystery. But never mind for now. If she were right, they would be staring at something completely different. Their hearts desire. She had realised this when she remembered what Basil wanted most in all the world: a television set. His heart's desire. Though he had never mentioned, he wanted to live in one. Perhaps he didn't know himself it's what he most wanted. But that was by the way. Something was up. Wrong. It was doubtful that what they were seeing was really what they saw. Which meant it must have been put there on purpose. Someone was up to something. A trap? They mustn't go in. Go around it. 'Whatever you do, don't go in.'

It was something that hadn't entered Basil's mind until now. 'What's going on?' he asked. A puzzled mind. One suddenly worried by the urgency in the Font's voice.

'I think it might be a trap,' said the Font. 'Stop them from going in. Use force if you must. They need to go around it.' A quick pause. She needed to think. 'Call me back when you're safely away from it.'

The talky-walky went dead in Basil's hand. He stared dumbly at it. However, his mind was a whirr. Don't go in? A trap? Use force? Did the Font know what she was asking? And why would the others want to go into a giant television set in the first place? Nothing made sense. Oh, woe was he!

CHAPTER 62

Percy, who was now setting a relentless pace after the visit by Danrite's nightmare, kept glancing at the compass in his hand. Straight and true was Percy's mantra as he followed the point's direction. Straight and true.

Which was slightly different to Vlad's. No, completely different to Vlad's. Actually, Vlad didn't have a mantra. He just followed. Followed as fast as his little invisible legs could carry him. While trying not to think about anything. Which wasn't easy, as he kept wondering why his little invisible legs were getting heavy. They were tired little invisible legs. And vampires' legs didn't get tired. Invisible or not. Vampires didn't get tired. Invisible or not. So, what was going on? No, no thinking.

But Vlad was finding the no-thinking rule was getting harder to stick to. And so tired was he getting that he decided he needed to sit. He sought the nearest thing that looked like a seat. It was a medium-sized boulder. He sat. And when he did, he found he wasn't only tired, he was feeling sleepy as well. A sleepy vampire? He had never heard of such a thing.

A rest, Vlad decided he needed. Just a moment or two. He looked to where Percy was striding. He would soon disappear into the distance if he were to stay too long. But he and Percy had been following a path, and it would be easy enough to keep to it. Unless Percy veered from that path. Oh dear, thought Vlad, perhaps he should keep moving. But in a moment. He watched Percy for a moment longer. At least his eyes weren't letting him down. He blinked. At the moment. He blinked again. Perhaps he had spoken too soon. Though, it was his eyelids, not his eyes, that were on the blink. He smiled at that. His eyelids on the blink. Then they weren't. They had closed.

A second later, Vlad's eyelids suddenly shot wide open again. What was he doing? He couldn't go to sleep. He didn't sleep. Vampires didn't. Well, some did, if they had a coffin handy, but that had more to do with tradition. And it was more resting. He needed to catch Percy up. He stood up. He looked for Percy. And that's when he noticed. Noticed he wasn't alone.

'Ah-ha!' exclaimed the someone who was stopping Vlad from being alone.

'Waa!' wailed Vlad, who was taken by surprise even though he knew he was no longer alone.

'You're awake,' deduced the someone who was keeping Vlad from being on his own, even though Vlad was supposedly asleep. 'Though you're not, of course, otherwise I wouldn't be here. Then again, I would, as you're technically a ghost. Being dead. It's complicated.'

'Sorry?' said Vlad. When what he wanted to say was, who are you? 'What do you mean, a ghost?' He had another go. 'Who are you?' he asked. He didn't need complicated.

'Of course, how thoroughly rude of me,' said the someone. A someone that Vlad now noticed was dressed in early Victorian clothes. 'Let me introduce myself.' He bowed slightly. 'My name is Bert, and I am a vampire.'

Bert, thought Vlad, what kind of name is that for a vampire? It was then that Vlad noticed something else. Saw it. A stake. A wooden stake. It was sticking out of Bert's chest. 'Yikes,' cried Vlad, though it sounded more like "Vikes." He backed away.

'Oh.' Bert looked down to where Vlad was staring. 'I forget it's there sometimes.' He looked at Vlad. 'Didn't frighten you, did it?'

Vlad didn't know what to think. He glanced over his shoulder. No Percy. No path. No path? Vlad was a moment or two from panicking. No, only one needed. Vlad started to panic. And as he did, he began to move away. Slow, he thought. One step, two steps. The second was a quick step. No time to dance, though. The third, even quicker step that Vlad attempted, which would have led to a run, sadly wasn't completed. Because, for some reason, he was now back seated on the boulder.

'Sorry,' said Bert. 'Boundaries, I'm afraid.'

'Boundaries?' said Vlad in a small voice. He was staring at the bottom of the boulder between his feet and wondering how it had got there. How he had got there.

'Yes,' said Bert. 'There's precious little room in my nightmare, you see. Though not my nightmare. Whoever's nightmare this is.

You know what I mean.'

Vlad wasn't sure he did.

'Must be a relative's, of course. Otherwise, I wouldn't be able to visit you.'

Nightmare? thought Vlad, I'm in a nightmare? Vlad now eyed Bert suspiciously. His wits gathering together again. Was this what had happened to Percy? He guessed so. So why? 'What do you want?' he asked, not taking his eyes from Bert.

'I'm here to help.'

'How?'

'You are lacking powers, are you not?'

Rude, thought Vlad, but true. He had fangs. But that was about it. He couldn't glide like some could. And he couldn't change into things either: bats and the like. Or fly. But at least he was invisible. That had to count for something. Didn't it?

'I'm invisible.'

'So, it would seem,' said Bert, raising an eyebrow. 'But I mean vampiric powers.'

'I can bite,' hissed Vlad, showing Bert a clean pair of fangs. He hadn't meant to hiss. It just happened.

'No offence meant, I'm sure.' Bert raised his other eyebrow.

'Sorry,' said Vlad. 'Likewise.'

'So, as I said. You have no powers.' Vlad narrowed his eyes. Bert continued. 'And that being so is why we are here. We are here to help.'

'We?' said Vlad, giving his surroundings a quick once over.

'Royal we,' said Bert.

'Oh.'

'There,' said Bert, 'all done.'

'What is?'

'You have a power.'

'I do?'

'Two in a way,' said Bert. 'One inherited from the other.'

'Sorry?' Vlad was lost.

'One begets the other.'

'What?' Vlad was still none the wiser.

'Never mind,' smiled Bert. 'You will find out soon enough.'

Vlad was confused. 'What power?'

'Sorry,' said Bert, 'I have to go.'

'Wait.' There was something else Vlad wanted to ask.

'Like I said,' said Bert. 'You will soon find out.'

'Not that,' said Vlad because he was sure he would. Bert looked puzzled. 'How are you a nightmare? The stake isn't that scary.'

'Ah.' Bert looked down. He smiled. Bert supposed there was time to answer that question. He touched it and looked at Vlad. 'That's not the nightmare,' he said.

'Then what is?' asked Vlad.

Bert laughed. 'The name, dear boy, the name. Which vampire in his right mind would want to be called Bert? A real nightmare, right?' And he was gone. Just like that.

And just like that, Vlad opened his eyes and promptly fell off the boulder.

CHAPTER 63

The hooded figure was idly humming as he limped. For some reason, he felt happy. He didn't know why for sure, but he guessed it was because, for the moment, he was on his own. He had turned the talky-walky off. He would find an excuse for why he did that should his master try to contact him and ask precisely that. That had given him a little peace. Mix that with those he had been following now behind him and out of earshot, out of sight, out of mind, and the little peace became a touch larger. And the cherry on the peace cake would be finding, and he was sure about this, the others and the other others safely skulking in that cave of theirs.

The humming grew a little louder. A triple helping of peace. And talking of helpings, perhaps he might have the chance to sit and eat that rosy red apple he was carrying. A treat. He decided to tempt fate and take it out. He looked at it. Okay, it was a rosy grey now, but it was an apple, and he was going to enjoy it. He almost dribbled at the thought. Should he stop now? he wondered. Eat it now? he thought. Why not? he thought. The others and other others could wait. He knew where they were. He looked for a suitable place to sit, found it, sat down and prepared to eat. And as he sat, he thought back to what he had seen, back there with the ones he had been following. A traveller's caravan. All painted brightly – he imagined – and covered in brass. There had been a horse tethered beside it. A grey one. The hooded figure smiled. Well, it would be, wouldn't it? The hooded figure liked grey horses. He would like a caravan like the one he had seen. It was a dream of his. His heart's desire. He would also have a grey horse, one that was properly grey, not just looked grey.

The hum turned into a whistle. A whistle that gently subsided as the hooded figure put the apple to his lips. And that was as far as it got. Resting there. He thought he had heard something. He listened. There it was again. He got up and slipped from sight into the surrounding grey greenery. He was certain now. Someone was heading his way along the path he had been taking. From the direction he was heading. He suddenly worried that whoever it was had heard him whistling. The noise he had heard was getting louder. Was someone arguing?

The hooded figure crept further into the grey greenery and waited. He wondered who it could be. It wouldn't be long before he found out.

CHAPTER 64

It was the same but different. Different for everyone. The same as they had seen before. But different to what they had seen before. Apart from Frida, who was seeing her heart's desire for the first time. That said, it was doubtful it would have looked any different if she had seen it before. A concrete bunker being a concrete bunker. Grey like.

Salor was seeing a single white tower. At least a slightly off-white tower. This time.

Twinkle was seeing a castle, not golden this time, but magnificent all the same.

Jose, his tail wagging furiously, stared longingly at the cantina. Its lights flashing a dull welcome in grey, darker grey and off-white.

Danrite saw the same cottage as before, but its walls were no longer a brilliant white. Instead, they looked dirty. Neglected. The roses no longer a vibrant red as they climbed and rambled around the front door. Now black. As if covered by blight.

But none of them should have been there. They only appeared as your heart's desire to guide you from the world of men to the worlds beyond, the Otherworlds. Worlds of myth, magic and make-believe. A portal to them. Fronted by your heart's desire.

It was what Salor was pointing at.

'It's the same,' Salor repeated.

'As what?' asked Frida.

'As the portal,' said Salor. 'The one we passed through from the mortal's world.'

'He's right,' Twinkle realised. The novelty of seeing her heart's desire wearing off a little. 'It's grey, but it's still my heart's desire.'

Frida couldn't remember seeing a bunker before when she had passed through to the Otherworlds. Only a gate. She was puzzled. A bunker, her heart's desire? But then she had to admit, it probably was. But Twinkle's? Her secret wish was for a bunker? All their wishes were for a bunker? Even Danrite? And what about Jose? His had biscuits in it! What the heck, she thought. So she asked.

And everyone explained what they saw. That it was different for everyone. All at once.

'Hold up,' cried Frida. 'One at a time. Danrite?'

He explained.

'A cantina?' Frida gave Jose a long look.

'Sí,' said Jose happily. 'With Tequila flavoured marrowbone.'

Frida made a disgusted face at the little chihuahua. 'So I would have seen a bunker if I had entered the Otherworlds the same way as you?'

'A bunker?' said Salor.

'Each to their own,' smiled Twinkle, winking at Frida.

Frida ignored her. 'So we're all seeing something different?'

'Yes,' said Salor.

Frida looked at the bunker. The others did the same, but obviously, at what they were seeing. A full minute went by without anyone saying anything. Then, the inevitable question surfaced.

It was Frida who asked it. 'Now what?'

They all looked at each other.

'Go in?' suggested Twinkle, not sounding at all convinced by her own idea.

'Why?' asked Salor, who was most definitely convinced it wasn't a good idea. The tower didn't look inviting.

'It's what we did last time,' said Twinkle.

'But where will it take us?' Danrite wanted to know. 'Because if it's back to my world, what's the point?'

And point Danrite had. Everyone agreed on that.

'You're right. It would be pointless,' agreed Frida. 'But it must be there for a reason. So, the question is, who put it there and why?'

'The Font,' said Salor. 'It has to be.'

'Has to?' said Frida.

'Then who else?' said Twinkle, not liking the sound of where the conversation was going.

'Could someone be out to stop us?' asked Danrite, saying it so quietly it was as if he didn't want to hear the question himself.

They all looked at him. They all looked at the supposed portal. Could someone be out to stop them? Could someone have put it there as a trap? They became lost in thought.

'Maybe we should be being asking the Basil man,' suggested

Jose, making everyone start. He looked up at the faces staring back down at him. 'I go now. I am seeing a suspicious tree.' He turned and left.

Faces followed him as he wandered off. The faces then looked at each other. Why hadn't they thought of that? Occasionally, Jose could surprise you. Mostly by accident. Sometimes, it could be unnerving. But occasionally…

CHAPTER 65

'Wait up,' cried Wrinkle, raising a hand. 'Oof,' she then uttered as Wazzock walked into her. 'Oi!' she then said. They had only just been talking, rather loudly, about the need for personal space.

'Oops,' said Wazzock as he rubbed his rather large nose.

Thankfully, Von Vlod and Pablo had listened and were far enough back not to walk into anyone. The other others, who hadn't been there to hear the conversation about personal space but would have most likely ignored it anyway, had caught up but were keeping their distance, so had not been in any position to invade anyone's personal space, whether they wanted to or not.

'What is it?' asked Von Vlod, hurrying forward.

'Yeah,' groaned Wazzock, still with the rubbing.

Wrinkle was staring ahead, her eyes narrowed. 'I thought I saw something.'

'Where?' exclaimed Von Vlod, eyes darting here and there.

'Over there.' Wrinkle pointed to somewhere over there.

'Where?'

'There.'

'There?'

'No, there.'

'There?'

'Yeah.'

'Oh, there.'

'Yes, there.'

'What did you see?'

'I don't know.'

'You don't know?'

'No.'

'How do you know you saw something then?' said Wazzock.

'Because I did,' growled Wrinkle. 'And heard something.'

'Heard something?'

'Yeah.'

'What did you hear?'

'I don't know.'

'So,' said Wazzock, 'you don't know what you saw and you

don't know what you heard?'

The growl was deeper this time. 'There was something.'

'Perhaps you are seeing a goblin,' said Pablo, trying to be helpful.

Wazzock looked down at Pablo and took a step back. 'Perhaps someone should investigate,' he suggested, meaning anyone but him.

'Perhaps,' agreed Wrinkle. 'Any volunteers?' She made a point of staring at Wazzock.

'Why don't we all go?' said Von Vlod. 'Safety in numbers?'

'Sí.' It made sense to Pablo. 'We all go.'

They would all go.

They cautiously crept forward.

Until they were nearly at the place where Wrinkle thought she had seen something.

'There.' Wrinkle pointed to the exact spot the hooded figure had been in before dodging into the grey greenery.

Meanwhile, in the grey greenery, the hooded figure was having a bit of a panic.

Drat, he thought. Drat! Drat! Drat! he thought. It's the others, he thought. Now, what did he do? he thought. They mustn't find him, he knew.

He watched as one, two, no, all of them started to inch cautiously forward. Inch forward in his direction. They were going to find him as sure as sure was sure. He began to fidget. Look this way and that. He needed a way to get away. He couldn't go forward; that much was obvious. Back the way he had come then? Or across the path? No, he decided, to both. If he went back the way he had come and one of them was faster than he was, they would catch him. And what waited across the path for him? What if a deep ravine was hiding there, waiting for him to fall into it as he fled? Amongst the grey greenery. Or he got snagged on something and couldn't wriggle free? He couldn't take the chance. So deeper into the grey greenery he was already in then.

But it looked dense. How far could he get? They were bound to see him. And if he got caught up in it? But what choice did he have? Unless?

The hooded figure had had another idea. They would see him,

113

but if he was quick enough, perhaps not, a non-descript shape instead. That was it. He would be as noisy and as scary as he could make himself. He would catch them by surprise and make his getaway before they regained their senses. It was still a stupid idea and bound to fail, but the hooded figure couldn't think of any other way out of the spot he was in. Here goes nothing, then.

As the others got close, the hooded figure suddenly sprang from his hiding place and squawked, flapped and yelled, and waved as loud and as fast as he could, for all he was worth, and then ran as fast as his limp could carry him back the way he had come.

'Agh!' yelled Von Vlod as something suddenly sprang from the undergrowth. Something all shouty and whirry that then shot past and sped away down the pathway they had been heading for and into the distance.

Pablo, who would have yelled in fright as well if it wasn't for the swallowing of the stick he was still carrying, had started to choke instead.

'After it!' shouted Wazzock from behind the tree he had found as the thing had appeared.

'You go after it,' said Wrinkle, shaken but not stirred enough to give chase.

Meanwhile, Von Vlod was kneeling and worrying over Pablo, who was turning a vivid shade of grey. Blue not being an option. 'What's wrong?'

'Iz-a-stit,' choked Pablo in answer.

'Oh, good grief,' said Von Vlod, realising what had happened. 'He's swallowed his stick.'

My stick, actually, thought Wazzock.

'Grief,' said Wrinkle, the whatever it was that had suddenly appeared forgotten about for the moment. 'What do we do?'

'Hold him upside down and shake him,' suggested Wazzock.

'Oh, I know,' said Wrinkle, 'pat him on the back.'

But neither suggestion was needed. Von Vlod had noticed the end of the stick was still visible in Pablo's mouth. Von Vlod gently took hold of it and pulled. A second later, it was free.

Pablo gasped and took in a large gulp of air. He then flopped sideways onto the ground.

'Is he all right?' asked Wrinkle.

'I don't know.' A worried Von Vlod, shook him gently. 'Pablo?'

One of Pablo's eyes opened. He looked up at Von Vlod and coughed. 'Sí, I am thinking that I am,' he croaked.

'He's fine,' said Von Vlod. 'He's a little hoarse though.'

Pablo's eyes shot open as wide as saucers. 'I am being a horse?' he wailed, wondering how that had happened. 'I am not wanting to be a horse. I am a Xolo.' He quickly got to his feet and stared at them. He saw no hooves. And why was everyone laughing?

'Not a horse, Pablo,' laughed Wrinkle, rolling her eyes. 'Hoarse, as in a sore throat.'

'Oh,' said Pablo, his cheeks growing a deep shade of light grey. Red not being an option. 'I am seeing what you are meaning.' He then growled.

'Just picking it up,' said Wazzock, who had been reaching for the stick Pablo had almost swallowed.

'It is being mine.' Pablo snapped it up. It was his chew toy and no one else's.

'Are you sure?' asked Von Vlod, worried Pablo might choke on it again.

'Sí,' hissed Pablo through his teeth while showing them and the stick to anyone who wanted to question his choice.

'You know best,' said Wrinkle.

The attention now turned to whatever it was that had caused Pablo to nearly swallow his stick.

'It's gone,' said Wrinkle, looking to where whatever it was had disappeared to.

'Should we go after it?' said Von Vlod.

'Sí,' said Pablo. 'I am using my nose. We find it, and I am giving it pieces of my mind for making me to being a horse.'

'But what if it was a goblin?' argued Wazzock, not keen on catching up with one of them. 'Best leave it, I say.'

'Perhaps you're right,' agreed Wrinkle. 'We don't know what it was.'

'We'll have to be careful, though,' warned Von Vlod. 'It went the same way we're heading.'

'Oh,' muttered Wazzock, not liking the sound of that.

No one liked the sound of that.

That, though, wasn't strictly true. The other others, especially the ones lying on the floor, the ones who had laughed themselves silly when the hooded figure had jumped out from hiding, all whirry and flappy-like, scaring the others when he did, loved the sound of that. They couldn't wait to see what happened next.

CHAPTER 66

Head firmly on shoulders once again, the creature with the unimportant name decided he would chance a peek outside. He set off and promptly walked into the cave wall.

'Oof!' groaned the creature with the unimportant name, staggering backwards. He wondered what the heck. Ah, he then thought, when realising he couldn't see the wall he had walked into. He tutted and turned his head the right way around.

Wanting to shake his head at his stupidity but not wanting to lose it again, he instead tutted once more and, with great care, wibbled and wobbled to the cave entrance. But not out of it.

What did he expect to see? He didn't know, just the feeling that he should. But it was a dangerous thing to do. What if someone was out there? Within distance of seeing him? What then? An end to his miserable existence? An end to his nightmare?

Somewhere far, far away, a nightmare waiting in the wings gulped and spilt their tea.

CHAPTER 67

'Vlad!' shouted Percy.

Percy had been happily striding along, straight and true, when he had noticed Vlad was no longer with him. He had stopped. Frowned. Shouted.

He now headed back whence he had come. What now? he thought as he strode. He stopped again. 'What the?' he exclaimed when he saw Vlad sitting beside a boulder. He hurried forward.

'Are you okay?' asked Percy when he reached Vlad.

Vlad looked up. 'I think I've had a Percy moment.'

'A what?' Percy looked puzzled.

'I had a nightmare,' said Vlad.

'A nightmare?' Percy was alarmed. 'While you were awake?'

'I think I was nodding off a bit but not asleep.' He saw the puzzled look on Percy's face. 'I know. I'm not a ghost,' Vlad explained, 'but it seems I qualify.' He then added. 'It's complicated.'

'Oh,' said Percy. 'So, what did it want?' Percy guessing it hadn't been a typical nightmare, going by what Vlad had said. He offered Vlad a hand and helped him up.

'Hey!' said a surprised Vlad. 'You can touch me.'

'So, I can,' mused Percy. 'Well, I never.' He looked at his hand and shrugged, then turned back to Vlad. 'So, what did it want?'

'It said it wanted to give me a power,' explained Vlad, wondering at the lack of wonder from Percy at being able to touch things. Oh well. Percy had always been a bit of an odd fish.

'A power? What kind of power?'

'I…' Vlad stopped, suddenly realising he couldn't remember being told. 'I don't know. I don't think it told me.'

Percy looked thoughtful. 'Do you feel different?'

Vlad didn't think he did. He patted himself all over. Shook his arms. He didn't know why he shook his arms; just felt natural to do so. He thought no more of it. Perhaps he should shake a leg or two as well? But before he could, he was pulled from his thoughts by a cry from Percy.

'Flipping gravy!' gasped Percy after his cry had died away.

118

Vlad gave Percy a questioning glance. Percy was looking this way and that.

'Vlad?'

'Percy?'

A confused Percy immediately looked up. But on seeing nothing continued with his looking this way and that. 'What's going on?' he wanted to know. 'Where are you?'

'I'm here,' said Vlad, who was starting to worry there was something wrong with Percy. Why couldn't Percy see him? Vlad shook his arms again. No, flapped them about a bit.

'Where?' said Percy, increasingly worried by the lack of Vlad.

Vlad flapped his arms. Why couldn't Percy see him? Vlad was well confused. He was standing right in front of him. Except he wasn't; not any more. He hadn't been for a little while. Vlad then saw his cloak was in a heap on the ground. No wonder Percy couldn't see him. Being invisible, the cloak was the only thing that showed people he was there. But why was it on the ground? Why wasn't he wearing it? And why was he looking down on it as if from above? Because, he suddenly realised, he was no longer on the ground with it. He was above it. He was above Percy. What in the world of nonsense was going on? He flapped his arms. And then he knew.

'Agh!' Vlad, making the sound of knowing.

'What?' worried Percy, still with the looking about, but now with the looking up again. Because that was where Vlad's voice was coming from. Above. Way above. But of course, Percy couldn't see Vlad because he was invisible. Couldn't see Vlad flapping about above him. Vlad, who was now a bat. An invisible bat. An invisible vampire bat!

'I'm a bat,' yelled an excited Vlad. 'And I can fly.' Vlad had a power.

CHAPTER 68

Basil peeped through the grey greenery. He had better stop them from going in, he thought, as he watched Danrite and the others talking. Basil went to go but then had another thought. If he told them they shouldn't go in, he might have to admit to being in contact with the Font. That wouldn't do.

Grief, thought Basil, what do I do? He thought some. And as he did, he grew a little angry. Typical, he thought, no longer thinking of what he should do but rather who to blame for his predicament. Do this. Do that. No thought for what he had to go through to do this or that. The worry. The fear. The trampling. Though, that had only happened once. It was typical Font. Go there; it didn't matter how you did it; just do it. No thought for him whatsoever. Basil was working himself up. Do you know what? He told himself, I have a good mind to go down there and tell Danrite and the others the truth. That the Font was a user. A tyrant. Well, perhaps not a tyrant. But a-a... He couldn't think of anything else. But then. And a slave driver. There, now, he had covered everything. He was sure.

Basil started to calm down a little. He had told her exactly what he thought. But he hadn't. He had just told himself. In no uncertain terms. But himself. Basil's shoulders sagged. He had better go and tell them, he supposed. Not to go in. He then perked up. But he would tell them because he wanted to. Shoulders de-sagged. It would be his decision. He would tell them he thought it was dangerous to go in. He didn't know why. Had a feeling in his bones. If asked. Yes, that is what he would tell them. It was now decided under his terms. He would tell them under his terms.

After crawling quickly through the undergrowth, Basil emerged and stood up. He would stride purposely forward and tell them. He. And well, he might have if he had seen Salor – who had been sent up to get him when it was realised he wasn't with them – coming the other way. He hadn't, and the two collided, sending Basil sideways to teeter on the brow of the hill. A teeter that was no match for gravity. Basil fell on his back and rolled. Rolled to the edge of it. Rolled over it. And screamed as he careered down it.

'Oh, dear,' offered Salor, watching the little man roll away.

'Flipping 'eck!' yelled Danrite as he saw it happen from below.

'Oh, heck,' cried Frida, watching Basil bouncing from one small boulder to another.

'Ouch,' winced Twinkle as Basil arrived at a much larger and pointier boulder, 'that's gotta hurt.'

'Sí,' Jose agreed, also wincing at the sight. 'He is being rocking and rolling.'

'Oh, dear,' repeated Salor. This time, because his hand was empty. The hand that had been holding the compass. 'Oh, dearie, dear me.' This followed because he shouldn't have had the compass. Frida had accidentally dropped it when faced with her heart's desire, and he had picked it up. He had meant to hand it back to her. Really, he had. Oh dear. He now forgot about Basil and began frantically looking for it. He had no idea where it had gone.

Sadly, for Salor, looking on the ground for it wasn't going to help him one little bit. It wasn't on the ground. For, not far behind, the no longer screaming, bouncing Basil bounced something smaller. A small circular object that was catching Basil up. Basil was about to get the compass back again. But it was doubtful he would know anything about it.

CHAPTER 69

'Are you there?' demanded the hooded figure's master with a total lack of talky-walky etiquette.

On the other end of the talky-walky, the hooded figure stared at the talky-walky in his hand. He had accidentally turned it back on in his haste to escape the others. Did he answer? Did he have a reason not to? No. Drat.

'I'm here,' said the hooded figure reluctantly, 'over.'

'About time,' said the Master. 'I've been trying to contact you. Where have you been?'

Here and there, thought the hooded figure. Chased by the others. Seen my heart's desire. None of which he dare say. Although all true. He instead plumped for a lie. 'Sorry, I must have accidentally turned the talky-walky off.'

The hooded figure's master didn't believe him for a minute. A suitable punishment for lying would be dealt out later, but until then, there were more important matters at hand. 'Is it there?' asked the Master.

'What there?' asked the hooded figure back at him. 'Over.'

'The shortcut I put in place,' said the Master. 'You must have seen it by now.'

Shortcut? Oh, that, thought the hooded figure. So that was what it was. Though how it worked as a shortcut to anywhere was beyond him. He would let the question lie, though. His toe was feeling much better. Must have been all that running. He decided to keep his answer short. 'Yes,' he said. 'Over.'

The Master wasn't sure if it was the truth. 'What did it look like?' asked the Master.

Ah, thought the hooded figure. He didn't want to say. It was his heart's desire, after all. He didn't want his master to know about that, but he couldn't lie, not this time, in case the shortcut was indeed a caravan.

'Well?'

'A caravan,' said the hooded figure, deciding to keep with the short answers. No need for details. 'Over.'

Well, thought the Master. A caravan? It takes all sorts, the Master supposed. But a poor heart's desire by any standard. Then again, he was only a minion. Can't expect too much. 'And have they gone in?'

'In?'

'In.'

Drat, thought the hooded figure. He didn't know. And then, like a fool, before he could stop himself, he admitted it. 'I don't know, Master.' Drat!

'What do you mean, you don't know?' exclaimed the Master. 'Why don't you know?'

Drat-oh-drat, thought the hooded figure, what an idiot. The last thing he needed was the Master, knowing he wasn't doing his job. Now what? The truth again? He had dug himself quite a hole. He needed help. No, he thought, what he needed was something to take the Master's mind off what he had told him. He needed a distraction. The others! It wasn't going to go down well. But how much deeper could the hole he was in get? A lot, he decided. He took a deep breath anyway. 'Because the others have left the cave,' said the hooded figure, steeling for the onslaught. He wasn't to be let down.

'What!' stormed the Master. 'You told me they were still in it!'

'They were,' said the hooded figure, which was true. 'But, they must have come out after…' He looked? Which he hadn't. His toe started to throb again.

'After what?' said the Master, pouncing on the hooded figure's words like a hungry dog after a bone.

'They were in it,' said the hooded figure, grabbing at straws while hoping it hadn't sounded – as it had in his mind – like he was asking a question. He needed more. He grabbed one of the straws. 'Perhaps it's something to do with the missing Vlad. Maybe they disappeared like he did but then appeared again.' The straw must have been made of rubber because he was stretching it a bit. 'Or something like that.' What was he babbling about? He hunkered, waiting for the storm to hit. It never came.

On the other end of the line, the storm that had been brewing went out like a damp squib. The hooded figure's master was suddenly struck by doubt. Was such a thing possible? Were things taking a turn for the worse on the Otherside? Things getting beyond

123

control? Perhaps it had all gone on too long? Was going on too long? Maybe someone was meddling? The Master straightened up. Or was the idiot minion making it all up? Whatever, things needed to be hurried along. Things had been taking too long.

'Right,' said the Master, 'go and see if they've gone in and if they haven't, make sure they do.'

The hooded figure was caught on the hop. They were back to the caravan again. What had happened? Don't ask. But how did he do that? Get them to go in? He asked the question.

'An excellent question,' answered the Master coldly, who didn't care how the minion did it as long as it happened. 'Let's just say that your very existence may well depend on it if you don't. Over.'

And over it would be, thought the hooded figure, if he didn't do it. But again, how?

'NOW!' yelled the Master, who could hear the hesitation in the hooded figure's breathing.

The hooded figure jumped and started to run again. For now, that was all he could do. He would worry about everything else when he got back to the caravan.

CHAPTER 70

The Font had been thinking.

Nothing made sense. But then, these days, wasn't that the norm?

The Font had also been waiting. Waiting for the talky-walky to spring to life, to tell her all was well. That they had avoided the trap. If that was what it was. A trap. What else could it be? Thinking and waiting and...

Worrying. So now the Font was worrying. She should have heard from Basil by now. Shouldn't she? Even if they had gone in. The worst had happened. Perhaps. Either way, something should have been said. Relayed. Good or bad. Unless. Unless he was still trying to stop them. They would want to know why they shouldn't go in. Want to know why they should listen to him. And he couldn't tell them. That it was she who had said not to. It had to be that. He was between a rock and a hard place.

So she would wait. She looked at the talky-walky in her hand. She could call him. No. Wait. Give him time.

But she feared the worst.

CHAPTER 71

What it meant, neither Vlad or Percy knew. The nightmare had given Vlad a power. The question was, why?

'It's handy, I suppose,' said Percy, 'but I can't see how it helps us.' Percy looked at the compass in his hand, something he did often. It still pointed forward, so he followed. He was forgetting about Vlad's power already. There was no need for further discussion. He just couldn't see how it could help them.

Vlad was back in his cloak and trying to keep up with Percy, who had resumed his relentless striding. Like Percy, he had no idea how his newfound power could help them. Though he was more optimistic, it had to have been given to him for a reason. It didn't make sense otherwise. Time would tell, he guessed. Perhaps it was so I could keep up with you, he thought, looking at Percy striding on. And he was sorely tempted to do just that, fly, to save his aching legs. Perhaps it was this place. But for now, he needed to keep up with Percy, which he was managing. Until he wasn't.

'Hi,' announced Bert, 'I'm back.'

'Grief,' spluttered Vlad, taken by surprise.

'Well,' said Bert, looking awkward, 'this is embarrassing.'

'It is?' asked Vlad, checking to see if he was still wearing his cloak. He was. He might be invisible underneath it, but who knew what a nightmare could see? He looked up. 'What is?'

'It appears I forgot to tell you why you were given your new power.' There were no appears about it.

'I was wondering,' said Vlad, all ears.

'It's to help you stop Danrite before he and the others take the shortcut,' Bert explained. 'Otherwise, you may not be able to reach them in time.'

'What shortcut?' asked Vlad.

'The one you have to stop Danrite and the others from taking.'

'Oh,' said Vlad, who had the feeling that asking again wasn't going to get him anywhere. 'How? I don't know where they are.'

'Use your compass,' said Bert.

'If Percy lets me use it,' said Vlad, who was doubtful.

'No, not that one,' laughed Bert, 'your internal one.'

A mystified Vlad looked down. What he had expected to see, he didn't know. 'I don't think I have an internal compass.'

'Oh, but you do now,' said Bert, 'now you can change into a bat.'

'Do I?'

Bert smiled. 'It will help you navigate,' he said. 'You just have to home in on whatever you are seeking.'

'How?' Vlad was still mystified.

'You'll know.' Bert winked knowingly. 'Now, I must go. I'm wanted.' And then, without another word, Bert was gone.

Vlad blinked, opened his eyes, and then nearly jumped out of his cloak. Percy was standing directly in front of him, their noses almost touching. Percy didn't know that, though, as he had been staring at where he thought Vlad's head was.

'Another nightmare, eh?' said Percy when Vlad had got over his fright.

'Yes,' said Vlad, 'and now I know why I have my power.' He filled Percy in.

'Then you must go,' said Percy, seeing light at the end of the tunnel. 'I'll carry your cloak.'

'But I can't leave you.'

'Yes, you can,' said Percy. 'Danrite needs you.'

'Now?'

'No time like it.'

'If you're sure.'

'Go.'

'Okay.'

Vlad stepped from his cloak and changed into a bat. As he rose into the air, he watched Percy pick it up. 'And the mirror,' yelled Vlad, seeing it fall from a pocket. It was the only way anyone could see him. He being the only vampire in existence – that he knew of – who could be seen in a mirror. Vampires were notorious for not being able to be seen in mirrors; that and other things.

'You still here?' said Percy, squinting skyward.

'Going now,' said Vlad. 'I dare say I'll meet you at the end.'

'I hope so,' said Percy, cloak and mirror in hand. 'Now go, and good luck.' Percy turned and looked at the compass in his free hand. The relentless pace immediately picking up again.

'And you,' said Vlad, still rising. But it was doubtful Percy had heard him, as the distance between them had already lengthened.

Vlad waited and watched Percy go for a moment longer before setting off to find his friends. But how he was going to do that was still a mystery.

CHAPTER 72

'Quick,' shouted Frida, moving forward, as she realised what had just hit Basil on the head and was now spinning at speed past him. She had no idea how it got where it was, but that was for later; right now, her mind was on catching it before it disappeared somewhere. 'We have to get the compass!'

'I thought you had it,' said Twinkle, looking at Frida.

'So did I.'

The compass hurtled towards them. Frida positioned herself, ready to catch it. Twinkle stood beside her, arms outstretched. Danrite did the same on the other side. Jose set himself ready to pounce. It rolled towards them. Closer and closer. And then...

It hit a jutting rock, which sent it high. High and arcing above the waiting catchers. Over them. Behind them. To roll once more on the ground. Towards the anomaly. That's what they were calling the vision of their heart's desires. It was a lot shorter. Everyone turned as one to watch it head towards the anomaly's door. A door that now looked like any normal-sized door. How else would one get in?

'Good job, it's closed,' said Danrite.

'Thank goodness,' said Twinkle.

'Sí,' said Jose, who had just landed after performing an airborne pirouette. 'It is being good.'

Frida, just pleased to see it was safely on the ground, went after it.

The compass rolled on. Rolled closer to the anomaly. Frida stooped, ready to pick it up, when it came to a stop against the door. The door that had just inexplicably opened. Allowing the compass to continue rolling. To roll inside.

'Noooo!' wailed Frida as it disappeared within. She made a desperate lunge for it, but it was too late. The compass had rolled, and the door had shut. Frida had also rolled, landing in a heap to the right of it.

'Flipping heck!' cried Danrite.

Twinkle, who had been following Frida, offered her a hand. 'Looks like we have a problem?' She pulled Frida to her feet.

Jose trotted up to join them and, keeping well away from the door, sniffed the ground around it. 'It is being gone.' His tail firmly sheathed between his back legs.

But before they could even begin to think about what to do next, a thumping noise drew their attention. Basil had arrived and was rolling at them at speed. They jumped clear and then watched in horror as he, too, headed for the door. But as they started to think about stopping him, a scream drew their attention. Salor, who had begun to run down the hill after finally realising where the compass was, had tripped to start somersaulting down the rest of it.

Finding it was only Salor who had screamed, they quickly turned back to Basil. But it was too late. He was gone. The door had opened and shut, just as had happened with the compass. The anomaly had swallowed him up. Attention turned back to a groaning Salor, lying face down at the foot of the hill.

Frida walked over to him. She wasn't happy. She wanted to know why Salor had had the compass. She was joined by the rest of the gang, who were also eager to hear his excuse. And there would be one.

'Ow,' moaned Salor, joints cracking and creaking as he raised himself onto an elbow. He looked up and saw a line of accusing ankles. Uh-oh, he thought.

'Here,' said Twinkle, 'let me help you up.'

'Ouch,' wailed Salor, 'you're pinching.'

Back on his feet, Salor now saw a line of accusing faces. He immediately knew why. 'I found it,' was his feeble defence. Four faces now either frowned, rolled eyes, or gave a little growl. But they knew it was pointless to say or do anything more.

'So,' said Danrite, turning to stare at the door.

'So indeed,' said Frida.

'Well, I say we leave the little idiot in there and go around it,' said Twinkle, meaning Basil and the anomaly, in that order.

'Ditto,' agreed Salor, who got a withering glare from Twinkle.

'But we need the compass,' Danrite pointed out.

'Drat,' said Twinkle.

Drat, thought Salor.

'I am thinking it is being decided then,' said Jose. 'Sí?'

130

'Yes.' Frida looked glum. 'We have no choice. We have to go in.'

'But we don't know what's in there,' whined Salor.

'If you hadn't dropped the compass, we wouldn't have to go in and find out,' snarled Twinkle.

Salor's face took on a sullen look.

'It's decided then,' said Frida.

'Ladies, first,' said Salor, stepping aside to let Twinkle past.

'Why you—'

But before Twinkle could finish or do something worse, Frida grabbed Salor by the arm and dragged him towards the door. It opened when they drew close, and together they – Salor eyes wide and feet dragging – entered the anomaly.

Danrite and Twinkle exchanged glances and then looked at Jose. He shrugged an "in for a penny" shrug, and together they walked forward. Danrite led the way, and on his approach, the door opened. He took a deep breath and stepped over the threshold. Jose deftly skipped after him before the door could close. This just left Twinkle on the outside. She stared at the door. But it was only a moment of hesitation. The door opened. Twinkle stepped in. The door closed. And then there were none.

CHAPTER 73

The hooded figure appeared at the brow of the hill moments after Salor had landed at the bottom. He hid and then watched. The tall one with tacky make-up – he thought he might be a wizard – had got up and was now being stared at. No one looked happy. They began to talk. The hooded figure crept as close to the edge as he dared so that he might hear what was being said. But he heard nothing.

What now? he thought. But his job had been made clear; he had to get them to enter the caravan. But how? Rush them? No, not with that big fairy there. One swipe from her, and she would swat him from here to next week. Scare them? How? He wasn't exactly frightening. Wait until they just walked in? Yeah, and pigs might fly, he thought. And then, as he settled down to mull further, a whole flock of flying pigs must have flown over.

Because, to the hooded figure's surprise and utter delight, they did just that. They walked into the caravan. The one with tacky make-up didn't look much pleased about it, but the woman with him was giving him little choice. Then, the others followed. Well, I'll be, thought the hooded figure, hardly believing his luck. Job done. He stood up and did a little jig. It was time to check in with the Master and tell him of his success.

'Yes?' said the Master.

'They're in,' said an excitable hooded figure. 'Over.'

'All of them?'

'Yes.' The hooded figure was hardly able to contain himself.

'How did you do it?'

The hooded figure hadn't been expecting that. What he had been expecting was praise. A kind word, perhaps. A job well done. Even though he hadn't earned any. The Master wasn't to know that, though. But no. "How did you do it?" he sneered. In his mind. No, well done. In his mind. But what had he really expected?

'Well?' said the Master impatiently.

'I didn't,' admitted the hooded figure through gritted teeth.

'Ah,' said the Master. 'So, they walked in without your help.'

'Yes,' said the hooded figure, wondering how his master knew.

Mmm, thought the Master, I wonder why? The Master hadn't expected that. Surely they weren't that stupid? To just walk in?

'Master?' said the hooded figure, disappointed but curious. 'How did you know?'

The Master looked at the talky-walky and smiled. 'I know everything. You should know that by now.'

The hooded figure went white. That couldn't be true. It couldn't be; the others and the other others not being in the cave had been a surprise to his master. The colour, or at least a shade of grey, returned to his face. But he couldn't be sure. Not entirely. His master could be tricky. So he decided a little sucking up wouldn't go amiss. Along with acting dumb. Just in case.

'Oh, Master,' said the hooded figure, 'you are so wise to know everything.' He hated himself for it.

The Master sighed. It had been deduction, nothing more. The fact the minion was able to report back spelled out he had had no part in their going in. It would have been doubtful he would be in any condition to talk had he attempted to force them. So they had gone in of their own accord. And for the minion to say they had gone in, he would have had to see them do it. He would undoubtedly have said if something else had caused them to enter.

'Right.' The Master had had enough. 'Now, get going and follow them. Report back to me when you have them in your sights again.'

'Follow them?' queried the hooded figure.

'Yes. Follow them.'

'How?' he asked. He looked at the anomaly. Oh, he then thought. 'You mean in?' said the suddenly fearful hooded figure.

'How else are you going to follow them?'

Cripes, thought the hooded figure. He looked down the hill at the caravan and gulped.

'So?' said the Master.

'On my way, Master.' The hooded figure reluctantly started down. No choice. The caravan got closer. He gulped again.

CHAPTER 74

The others, and the other others, arrived just in time to see the hooded figure head over the brow of the hill. The others cautiously followed, edging towards it. The other others, staying put.

When the others reached the brow, they peered over and gasped. There were suddenly questions galore. But for now, whatever it was they were looking at would have to wait. It was the small hooded figure they were most interested in. For the moment.

'Do you think it's the creature that was hiding in the bushes back there?' asked Von Vlod.

'Sí,' agreed Pablo, sniffing at the ground. 'I am thinking so. I am smelling them both the same.'

They watched the hooded figure go down the hill. Foreheads furrowed; something strange was occurring. The hooded figure was having some sort of episode. He had started to wave his arms wildly about his head and shout.

'What's he doing?' said Wazzock.

'Could it be some kind of weird dance?' suggested Wrinkle.

'But he is with the shouting also,' said Pablo.

'Perhaps he's singing,' said Von Vlod.

'A song and dance routine, you think?' said Wazzock.

'Now, he's running,' said Wrinkle.

'He's heading for the door,' said Von Vlod.

'But it is being too small for him,' said Pablo, wondering how he would fit through it.

'Too small?' said Von Vlod. 'It's gigantic.'

'I wouldn't go that far,' said Wazzock. 'Big though.'

'Big?' stammered Wrinkle. 'It's tiny. He'll have a job getting his head in, let alone the rest of him.' It was here that everyone took a moment to stare at each other.

'It is being small,' said Pablo, 'but not being the teeny tiny.'

'Big,' argued Wazzock.

'Gigantic,' said Von Vlod.

'A fairy castle with a gigantic door?' frowned Wrinkle. 'Don't be so ridiculous.'

'A fairy castle?' Von Vlod looked insulted.

'A castle?' Wazzock looked puzzled.

Pablo stared up at the other three. 'Sí,' he said. 'I am supposing, but as long as it is being a luxury kennel, I am not with the worrying what you call it.'

It was now the turn of the other three to stare at Pablo. 'Kennel?' they chorused. They then looked at each other again. It slowly dawning on them that they may not be seeing the same thing. But Pablo didn't answer; his attention had returned to the hooded figure.

'Look,' exclaimed Pablo. 'The creature, it is going in.'

They looked just in time to see the hooded figure scramble within, an arm still flailing above its head.

'It's gone,' said Wrinkle.

'We should go down,' said Von Vlod.

'We should talk about what we are seeing,' said Wrinkle.

'And then we'll go down,' said Wazzock.

This perhaps would have been the wise thing to do if Pablo hadn't already started down the hill.

So down everyone went. Carefully. There were small outcrops of stone everywhere, just waiting to trip someone up. With caution. Hoping they would not fall victim to the same flapping episode that had befallen the hooded figure.

Meanwhile, the other others had now arrived at the brow of the hill. They watched the others descend.

'Looks dodgy to me,' said one of them.

'Who else is seeing a kennel?' another other other asked. Three paws and a leg went up.

'I see a castle,' said another.

'Has it got towers?' someone asked.

'Who sees a lovely squidgy marshmallow?' said another, who suddenly found themselves standing on their own.

'So, do we follow them?' asked the other other, who was standing closest to the other other who had made the dodgy observation.

'Wait,' suggested someone at the back.

'See what happens,' suggested another.

'I've got a deck of cards.'

'Ooo,' cooed Vlad, as something, he knew not what, a new sensation, kicked in. 'Ooo-oo-oo!'

And as soon as whatever it was that had kicked in finished kicking in, Vlad veered dramatically to the West.

Bats have a built-in compass. A magnetic source that helps them navigate. In Vlad's case, as he would find out, it was stronger and more precise than that of your common-or-garden variety of bat. Because right now, it was leading him straight to Danrite and Frida. Danrite and Frida and not the rest because they were the only two humans in the group. And they possessed something all vampires loved: blood!

Not that that was on Vlad's mind as he flew toward them. He actually only drank milk, a personal choice, and it had to be skimmed. But at the moment, his inner vampire bat compass was working as it should. He did wonder, though, how it worked in a world full of humans. Would he be flying in constant circles? There had to be something in place to stop that. But those thoughts would have to wait for another time. For now, he had to find his friends and warn them. Find his friends and, on the safe side, think milk-milk-milk!

Vlad didn't have that far to go as it worked out. Unbeknown to him and Percy, they had been travelling on a parallel route. The distance between them was roughly five kilometres, as the bat flies. A distance soon travelled. But not travelled quick enough to stop his friends from entering the anomaly.

What the heck? thought Vlad on seeing a daunting grey castle of the Transylvanian type. This was, in turn, followed by a good grief as he saw his friends entering it. Entering the trap he and Percy had been warned about. He shouted, but it was to no avail. No one heard him. To be fair, it had been more of a squeak than a shout. He flew toward the castle and fluttered above it.

What did he do now? Did he follow them? Go back to Percy? His mind was fluttering as fast as his little wings. Or did he go and see what that hooded figure standing on the brow of the hill was doing? He thought he would.

Vlad swooped. Then stopped. The hooded figure had started down the hill towards the castle. Vlad waited. He fluttered. He waited some more. Then, when the hooded creature was nearly down, Vlad swooped again.

'Who are you?' squeaked Vlad as he flew around the hooded figure's head. 'What have you done with my friends?' He dodged a flailing arm. 'Why are you following them?' He rose and swooped again, causing a breeze to tickle the hooded figure's face. He again dodged a flailing arm.

'Wah!' wailed the hooded figure in panic as Vlad swooped again. 'Who's there?' yelled the hooded figure, looking all around but seeing nothing. He did a full circle, his arms flailing as more squeaks and breezes came at him. 'Leave me alone!' He took another desperate swing at nothing, then, deciding he needed to get out of there, ran for the caravan's door. The door to his heart's desire.

'Come back,' squeaked Vlad, caught on the flutter.

But the hooded figure was in no mind to do so. He was in full panic mode. But at least his mind had been made up for him as to what to do next. He reached the door. It opened. The hooded figure sprinted in.

Vlad, his mind working overtime, had but a second to decide what to do next. Percy? No? Then in. But if the door closed and he was trapped inside? But if it closed and he was outside?

Mind made up, Vlad swooped for the already closing door.

137

CHAPTER 76

The creature with the unimportant name stood looking out from his cave. He sighed deeply.

This wouldn't be such a bad place, he thought, even with its lack of colour, if it sparkled a little. It reminded him of home in a way. Home to the creature with the unimportant name was cold and bleak, as was this place. But his home was full of wonder. Things sparkled. White's shone. Even the blackness was beautiful, with its countless stars sparkling so far away. Here, though, there were no stars. Nothing sparkled. The whites dull. But for all that, it still reminded the creature with the unimportant name of home. He sighed again and turned to go back in. As he did, he suddenly wobbled. He reached out to steady himself. He wobbled again.

The creature with the unimportant name turned back and waited. Nothing. But something. Something in the air. It was as he had thought. Something or someone was coming. And they were getting closer.

CHAPTER 77

The realm of the Nightmares wasn't as bad as it sounded. Oh yes, there was scary stuff around. Monsters, creatures of the dark, the usual creepy fare. But there were also towels, cheese, a lot of cheese, slime, bubbles, short trousers, split trousers, laughing and pointing, missing eyebrows, big eyebrows, mono eyebrows, toilet paper – mostly in knicker and underpants scenarios – nudity of the hilarious type, stakes, top hats, the list goes on. So, not that bad. But still a place of nightmares. Yet, to the nightmares, it was home, a wonderful place. Somewhere to kick back and relax. They were family.

As were the people who had them. The nightmares regarded them as family. Each nightmare belonged to someone. You see, it isn't the nightmares that scare or worry you and cause you to wake up sweating. No, the nightmares are just there to help. Help untangle the mess that a person's mind is trying to undo. To help. Help a member of their family.

That said, the realm of the Nightmares isn't some massive waiting room where nightmares waited until they were needed. Not at all. The realm of the Nightmares is a fun place. Parties. More parties. And even more parties. Dancing, singing, games. You could say the realm of the Nightmares was one long rave. Or was.

Was, until imagination started to disappear. Things were changing. Nightmares were becoming bland. No fun. Nightmares were beginning to fill with computers, phones and pads. With no imagination, what else was there? There was even a nightmare who just sat in a corner in a constant data stream. And the blandness was growing. Spreading to all corners of the realm. Soon, parties would be a thing of the past.

And what hope for those people who had those bland data stream nightmares? A world of mindless zombies? If one could imagine such a thing. Useless zombie nightmares.

'Oi!'

Oops, some zombie nightmares can be a bit sensitive.

Something needed to be done. And until the evil was destroyed and imagination had returned, there would be no parties. No games.

Some games. It was time for a different type of action. Thinking caps had been donned. Brains had been exercised. And after a while, the nightmares had come up with an idea. A plan. A flimsy plan. But it could just work. All it needed was some colour, some magic, and a whole lot of luck.

CHAPTER 78

Percy had been worrying about how things were going to pan out. Would everything go back to normal if they managed to save imagination? He doubted that. Not exactly. He would still be a ghost, but he worried about his friends. He wondered if they would get back to how they were. He had a feeling that not all would. And how would they feel about that? Salor would be devastated, of course, not being able to choose decent make-up ever again. Twinkle? He expected her anger issues would probably get worse; she missed her flitting here and there fairyness. As for Vlad, Percy had a sneaking feeling he loved being invisible. And now, with his new power? Vlad would be okay. And Jose, little Jose, well, Jose was Jose, he would go with the flow. As long as he could sniff and find a tree, he would be happy. Percy smiled at that.

But for now, it was all about the here and now and the compass. So far, it has been straight and true. With the tiniest nudge, now and again, towards the West. So not so straight and true. Percy's stride had also changed. His stride a little faster now he was on his own. No one to slow him. Vlad's cloak and mirror no hindrance. He had been surprised he could pick them up, him being a ghost and all. Perhaps it was thanks to this Otherworld. Who knows? Percy hoped Vlad was okay.

Without thinking about it, Percy hefted Vlad's cloak a little higher on his shoulder. He looked up. All was as it was, but something was changing. He could feel it. Really feel it. It was getting colder. How could that be? How could he feel it? Wasn't it supposed to be the other way around; ghosts made places suddenly colder? He had a quick check. No, no ghosts, apart from him. He frowned and walked just a little faster.

CHAPTER 79

'What do you think?' asked Wrinkle, suspiciously eyeing the door to the anomaly. They, too, were now using the word.

'I think we should talk about it,' said Wazzock.

'That's what we're doing,' said Wrinkle.

'We should be the going in,' said Pablo.

'But what if that thing we saw is waiting to ambush us?' said Von Vlod.

They all looked at the door suspiciously.

'What about the new arrivals,' said Wazzock. 'What if they went in there?'

'Sí,' agreed Pablo. 'What if they are being there?'

'But what if they aren't?' said Von Vlod. 'They might have gone around it.'

'True,' said Wrinkle, not liking the look of the door one little bit. She was sure it had moved when they had first arrived. 'Perhaps we should go around it.'

'But what if that hooded thing was following them?' said Wazzock, who then wondered whose side he was on. The last thing he wanted was to go in.

'But it was spying on us,' said Von Vlod.

'Sí,' said Pablo. 'It is spying.'

'But what if he wasn't,' said Wrinkle, thinking Wazzock, for once, might be onto something. 'What if it *was* them it was following, and we just happened on it.'

They had themselves a dilemma.

Above them, on the brow of the hill, some of the other others were watching.

'What are they waiting for?' said one.

'Beats me,' said another.

'Oi,' said another other other, 'how many flipping aces you got in this pack?'

'Well, I'd go in,' said another, ignoring the card players.

'Why?' asked another other other, not the other other who had asked about the aces.

'Why else would it be there if it wasn't to go into?' reasoned the other other who had ignored the card players.

'That makes sense,' said another.

'Could be a trap,' suggested another other other.

'Course it's a trap,' said another other other, behind the other other who had just spoken.

"Ere,' yelled a voice from behind those on the brow, 'how many of us are there?'

Heads turned. Was it important?

'Why?' asked someone, who was ignored.

They started to count.

'I count ten,' said someone. Not the one that had been ignored.

'You counting yourself?'

'Eleven.'

'I count twenty-four,' said someone else. 'And yes, I counted myself.'

'How many times?' shouted some other other, which brought a number of chuckles. No one counted how many.

'Twenty,' chipped in another other other.

'One hundred and eighty!' shouted another, who then remembered he hadn't counted himself. 'One hundred and eighty-one!' Which, of course, wasn't possible. Especially not if you wanted the jokey comment to work. 'Bother.'

'There are forty of us,' said some other other, who sounded as if they knew.

'What about those two in the bushes?'

'I counted them.'

"Ere, what are they doing?'

'Counting cards,' said someone.

'Ten aces,' said someone else. 'Ten flipping aces.'

Counting now done and forty being the final figure everyone agreed on, they turned their collective attention back to the foot of the hill and the anomaly. Why they had decided to count, no one knew, and no one could be bothered to ask.

'It's what we would have done when we arrived,' said Wazzock, who still didn't know why he was on the side of going in.

143

'And where has that got us?' said Wrinkle.

'But we know better now,' said Von Vlod.

'Which means we should definitely not go in,' said Wrinkle.

'Which means that if we didn't know better, it's what we would do,' said Von Vlod. Which, if thought about sanely, made a lot of sense. Even though it's the point Wazzock was making.

But sanity in the Otherworld they now existed in wasn't always to be relied upon. You only had to talk to those watching from the brow of the hill to figure that out.

Pablo, who had been quietly watching on and quietly listening, had had enough. He looked at the door. Then, back to the others. And as it didn't look like any decision was about to happen, he decided to make one himself. What could happen? Get stuck in there? Like they were stuck in this Otherworld. What was the difference? None that he could see. And if it was a trap? At least it would be something different. He gave a little shrug of the shoulders and headed for the door. There might even be some tequila-flavoured dog biscuits in there.

'Look,' said an other other. 'The dog's going in.'

'Pablo?' said Wrinkle when she saw where he was heading.

'What's he doing?' cried Von Vlod.

'Wait!' yelled Wazzock.

But it was too late. The dog had entered the building.

'He's gone in,' said Wazzock, stating the obvious.

'We should follow,' said Von Vlod.

'Drat,' said Wrinkle.

So they followed. Some a tad more reluctant than others.

'They're all going in,' said someone other than the other other who had seen Pablo going in.

'Time to move then,' said someone else.

'Surely we've got time for another hand or two of cards first,' suggested another.

'Not with you, we haven't.'

The other others started to move.

'Wait for me.'

'And me.'

''Ere,' said some other other, as he watched the two who had been in the bushes emerge from them, 'they haven't got any cards.'

'I said they were counting them, not that they had any.'

'Oh.'

Now, they were all heading down the hill to the anomaly.

CHAPTER 80

The compass took a bounce as it landed inside the anomaly. There was a whooshing noise. The compass was no longer in the anomaly.

Basil had rolled to a stop just inside the anomaly. There was a whooshing noise. Basil was no longer in the anomaly.

CHAPTER 81

'I can't see anything,' wailed Salor.

'That's because it's dark,' sighed Twinkle, rolling her eyes.

And then there was a whoosh, and Salor was no longer in the anomaly.

More whoosh's followed.

Frida was no longer in the anomaly.

Neither was Danrite.

Nor was Twinkle.

Jose, on the other hand, had not whooshed anywhere. Yet. 'Hello?' he ventured. Then, 'Ay caramba!' as an invisible force enveloped him. A whoosh.

Jose was no longer in the anomaly.

CHAPTER 82

It's dark in here, thought the hooded figure as he stood in the anomaly, but at least he had escaped whatever had been attacking him. He thought too soon.

'Ow,' wailed the hooded figure as something whacked him on the forehead. He waved his arms about. Not again! he thought. Then there was a whoosh, and he was gone.

There followed another whoosh.

But Vlad was still there. He had felt whatever the whoosh was grabbing at him and had dodged it. Another whoosh. Another dodge. Vlad didn't like it. It felt wrong. Unnatural.

Whoosh.

Dodge.

Whoosh.

Dodge.

Vlad looked for the way out. The way he had come in. But he could neither see nor sense it, even with his bat senses.

Another whoosh.

Another dodge.

Vlad didn't know how long he could keep this up. He felt it would only be a matter of time before the whooshing got him. Until then, he would keep on dodging, looking, and sensing. And then, just as Vlad feared the next whoosh could be his last, he saw it. The door had opened again. Just a crack. But he took his chance and headed for it.

CHAPTER 83

Poor Pablo never got a chance to see if there were any dog biscuits of the tequila-flavoured variety behind the door of the anomaly. As he stepped in. As Vlad flew past him. There was a whoosh. A whoosh that was intended for Vlad. Instead, it grabbed Pablo. And so, Pablo, who you could argue was never wholly or actually in the anomaly, was no longer in it.

Wrinkle, who had been the first to follow Pablo, saw what had happened to him and, as she was only on the threshold of the anomaly, went to turn and make haste out of there. Something was wrong. She didn't like it. Sadly, someone who was eager to get things over with, thinking that if they were going to go in, then let's get it done with, a quick pull on the plaster if you like, bumped into her, knocking Wrinkle off balance and into the dark. There was a whoosh, and Wrinkle had gone the way of those before.

'Oof,' had said Wazzock on bumping into Wrinkle. 'Sorry, didn't see you.' He now opened his eyes and peered into more darkness. Darkness that had enveloped him when the door to the anomaly had closed behind Von Vlod. 'Hello?'

But there was no answer, just a whooshing noise. Quickly followed by another.

CHAPTER 84

Only one mishap had occurred as the other others navigated the slope down the hill. The one with the cards had to stop to pick them up from the ground after someone had asked him if he wanted to play fifty-two card pick up, or fifty-eight, if you included the six extra aces. He wouldn't fall for that again. Perhaps. Meanwhile, most of the other other others had reached the bottom of the hill and were now milling about outside the door to the anomaly.

'Oi! Stop pushing,' shouted someone.

'It's not me. It's someone else,' said the someone who was being blamed. 'Someone else is pushing me.'

'It's not me,' said Someone Else, who hated his name. He was always being blamed for something.

It wasn't; it was the hill. There had formed a melee of thirty-nine other others that pressed between it and the anomaly, and those still on the bottom of the hill couldn't help but press forward and downward as the slope, urged on by gravity, forced them into the rest.

'For goodness sake, will someone move!' suggested an other other who could no longer feel the ground beneath her.

'That was awfully polite of you,' observed Someone Else.

'Why thank you,' replied the hovering other other.

'To heck with that!' yelled an other other, who could no longer feel his toes. 'Will some of you move your bottoms!'

'Language,' said someone, before the numb-toed other other could utter another word.

Things were now getting desperate. No one would give an inch. They had become wedged. There was only one thing for it.

'Open the door!' yelled someone else other than Someone Else.

'I'm trying,' said the sensible other other who had counted forty. But it was no good; the door wouldn't budge.

'It opened for the others,' said someone, meaning Wazzock, Von Vlod, Pablo and Wrinkle.

'Perhaps you have to say a rhyme,' suggested another other other. It was something one did when opening a portal in the human world to get to an Otherworld. And sometimes the other way around.

150

'Yes,' said the sensible other other. 'Anyone know one?'

'The others hadn't,' said an other other whose eyeballs were starting to bulge from his head because of the pressure of the other other others squidging him.

'No, they didn't,' gasped an equally observant other other.

And then the sensible other other had an idea. Perhaps they were too close? They had ascended almost all at once. What if, because of that, the door hadn't sensed there was anyone there? Too many at once? As reasons went, it was one. 'Back!' she now shouted. 'Get back!'

The other others now pushed back. Why? Not many knew, but if it stopped eyes from popping from heads and toes from growing numb, then they were all for it.

They grunted. They groaned. They swore. They were told to watch their language. They pushed. And then some more. The ones on the slope inched higher. And then, finally, there was space between them and the door. A space where the sensible one stood. The door started to open.

A cheer went up. The sensible one stepped forward and in. Then, not wanting to be crushed again, the other others steadily but quickly followed until all were in. And when that happened, the door closed behind them. They were all in.

'Oi!'

No, they weren't.

The other other with the playing cards, who had just finished picking them up, had discovered he was all alone. He looked up. Looked down. Looked left and right. Scratched his head. Then looked at the door. He put his cards in a pocket and headed for it. It was the only place everyone could be.

Inside the anomaly, the other others huddled together, not sure what to do next. And then there was a whoosh. This was followed almost instantly by another. And then another. And each time, the whoosh was louder.

Outside the anomaly, the other other with the cards stopped in

151

his tracks. The latest whoosh had been so loud it could be heard outside. He took a wary step forward. Another whoosh. This one even louder. So loud that the ground trembled. Eyes widening, he now took a step back.

'What's happening?' wailed an other other as the anomaly appeared to shake.

No one knew. What they did know, though, was that every time there was a whoosh, an invisible force tugged at them, and each time it did, the noise it made got louder.

The problem was there were too many of them in the anomaly, and the whoosh was trying to grab them all at once. And it wasn't able to.

'We should go back!' yelled someone.

'I can't see the door,' yelled Someone Else.

Another whoosh. Much bigger and louder than the rest, but again, no one moved. No one could. No one could see the exit. And then something began to give.

'I don't like it!' wailed someone.

There was a scream.

Another whoosh. A gigantic one. One so huge it was bigger than all the others put together. One big enough to do its job. The other others had finally gone. Popping like a cork from a bottle.

The other other with the cards looked on in horror as the anomaly started to shake. Began to drift in and out of focus. A sudden bang, like a sonic boom, threw him to the ground, the final whoosh. Then nothing. No noise. No shaking. No anomaly. Just a frightened other other looking on in dismay. Only one thought on his mind. Who was he going to play cards with now?

CHAPTER 85

It was getting colder. Percy wasn't imagining it. A cold breeze had picked up and was tickling his ghostly visage.

Should I be feeling wind? thought Percy, head down, pulling Vlad's cloak tighter around his shoulders. Should I be feeling the cold? He decided as it was his first time as a ghost, that he didn't know. But, then again, as he was feeling them, perhaps it was normal for a ghost to feel things. He frowned. Did that mean he could feel everything? As when he had been alive? He suddenly hoped not. Paper cuts were nasty. Thankfully, the thought disappeared as a sudden, stronger, colder wind tugged at his hair, causing him to look up for the first time in a while.

So that's where the cold is coming from, thought Percy, on seeing, in the distance, the outline of mountains. But it wasn't the mountains themselves bringing the cold. It was what was covering them. There was a whiteness there. Snow.

CHAPTER 86

Out of the anomaly flew Vlad. Higher and higher in the air. Up until he felt it safe to stop.

Vlad hovered where he had stopped and looked down. That was a lucky escape, he thought. But no time to think, time to make with the skedaddle. Percy needed to know what had happened. But as Vlad prepared to do so, he saw something out of the corner of his eye. Something that made him frown.

Climbing down the hill were… Something. Something strangely familiar. Four, something strangely familiar. Vlad, curiosity taking over, decided to hang around for a moment.

As Vlad watched, the four strangely familiar creatures reached the anomaly. There, they started to bicker amongst themselves. Or three of them did. The fourth was heading towards the door. What sort of dog is that? thought Vlad while wondering if he should shout a warning. But that would give him away, and he didn't have time for explanations. He had to go. But yet he still hovered. He couldn't shake the idea that he knew them somehow. The dog thing entered the anomaly. The others had now realised they were missing someone. They began to head to the door. Some, Vlad thought, somewhat reluctantly.

When the door closed behind the other three, Vlad, instead of immediately flying to Percy, tried to figure out why the four looked so familiar. He felt, he knew not why, that it might be important to do so. The shadow creature? Something about it. But what?

But then, stopping him from mulling further, something else caught his eye. A whole lot of somethings. Weirder than the somethings before. A whole lot of weird somethings staring down from the top of the hill.

'Yikey-yikes!' exclaimed Vlad. How long they had been standing there, he didn't know, but he counted at least forty of them, give or take. They now started down the hill. Vlad watched them with wonder as they, too, appeared to be heading for the anomaly. There were one or two similar to those that had just entered it, but the others…

What? thought Vlad as a sudden spray of what looked like playing cards flew into the air. Oh, he then thought, smiling, the old fifty-two card pick-up. He had fallen for that before. But why do it there? Weird. While he watched whatever it was that was picking up the cards, the others reached the anomaly all at once. Shouts drew Vlad to see what was going on. He grimaced. They had wedged themselves against the anomaly. Vlad gasped. That poor fellow's eyeballs! More shouts, this time telling everyone to back up. They did. Thank goodness for that, thought Vlad, as the fellow's bulging eyeballs gradually returned to normal.

A space now appeared between the crowd and the anomaly, leaving one of the somethings standing alone at the door. Must be the one in charge, thought Vlad. The door now opened. The one in the space stepped into the anomaly. Quite soon, they were all in there. Except for the one picking up the cards.

'Oi!' shouted the card picker-upper.

Which was a signal to Vlad that he had seen enough. Time to go, he thought. And so he would have if it hadn't been for the noise. At first, Vlad thought he had imagined it. A whooshing noise. Like the one he had heard in the anomaly. But there came a second one, a much louder one. And then another. And another. All louder than the last. Was the ground shaking? He stared at the anomaly; it appeared to be shimmering. And then another whoosh. Like a sonic boom. The card picker-upper was knocked to the ground. Vlad was blown higher.

Managing to take control of his unexpected ascent, Vlad turned and watched in horror as the anomaly shook, shimmered, and then disappeared. Oh, woe, he thought. But there was nothing he could do, so he shrugged sadly, swooped and headed to find Percy.

The card-picker upper, oblivious to the invisible onlooker, brushed himself down and looked at the deck of cards in his hand. He suddenly smiled. Patience, he thought, I could always play patience.

CHAPTER 87

The Font sat on her chair, which looked remarkably like a throne, and fretted.

There had been no word from Basil. The Font worried. What had happened? Did they fall for the trap? They wouldn't be so stupid. Would they? They had to know not to enter.

Rising from her chair, the Font sighed. She looked at the talky-walky in her hand. In her heart of hearts, she knew they had gone in. Especially Frida. Not that she was stupid, far from it, quite the opposite. Frida was an adventurer and an explorer, brave but not reckless. She would have wanted to go in because it was who she was and what she did. Frida would have needed to know what lay inside. But she wouldn't have endangered the others. Would she? Unless she had no choice.

The Font's eyes narrowed. Basil, on the other hand, was an idiot. An explorer of the television pages of a magazine. Not an adventurer. Most certainly not brave. And because of that, he wouldn't have gone in. He would have avoided danger. It was his job to talk them out of going in. But he was Basil. The Font sighed again. She felt one of her headaches coming on.

CHAPTER 88

The hooded figure's master, mind awhirl, was waiting for a call from him. Had he entered the trap yet? Was he out the other side yet? Had it even worked? But as much as the Master worried, however much of a pain it was, there was nothing the Master could do but wait.

But waiting wasn't easy. The Master's head hurt. The Master rubbed at aching temples. The projection into the Otherworld, the anomaly, was taking a toll. It wasn't supposed to be open this long. Why wouldn't it close? Surely they're through? The Master wanted to blink it from existence. But couldn't. Too much depended on it. Concentration was needed. The Master decided there was a need to know what was happening.

Mind probing, the Master sought the reason for the delay. Across the void between the Master's world and the dark Otherworld went the Master's mind. And the closer it got, the worse the pain became.

'By the stars!' thought the Master as his mind finally made contact. 'What is going on?' The anomaly was shaking. Going in and out of focus. The Master's mind was inside it now. And inside, it was chaos.

At first, the Master couldn't understand what was happening. But then, slowly, realization came. There were too many inside for it to work. Who were they? Why were they there? Something was going to give. And that something might well be the Master's mind if the Master didn't deal with it quickly. There was a blockage, and the blockage needed to be cleared.

The hooded figure's master, seated on a chair, gripped its arms and concentrated. The pain was almost unbearable, but the Master had no choice. The whooshes needed a boost. There was a whoosh. Not quite. Another whoosh. Still not enough. The Master's fingernails dug into the arms of the chair. The pain. A gigantic whoosh like a sonic boom. Then there was no pain. No blockage. No anomaly. But the effort had taken a toll. The Master slipped from the chair to land in an unconscious heap on the floor.

CHAPTER 89

The evil compass rolled to a quick stop. As did Basil. Except he
had skidded to a stop. He lay there, on his own, for a moment. Until
everyone else started to arrive.

'Yikes!' yelled Danrite as he slid, arms waggling for balance.
'Look out!'

Frida, who had arrived a moment earlier with Salor, dodged as
Danrite slid past, but Salor was a little slower and was knocked
sideways. He landed on his face. His mouth, open from yelling
his surprise, filled with something cold and wet. A moment later,
Twinkle and Jose arrived.

'What the heck,' shouted Twinkle.

'Ay caramba!' wailed Jose. 'It is being slippy.'

Thankfully, no one else had landed on their face. Even Danrite
had managed to stay upright after his collision with Salor. They now
stood there, Salor on his feet again, gawping at their surroundings.
All about them was white. All about them was snow.

CHAPTER 90

Thankfully for the hooded figure, when he arrived, he didn't land slap-bang in the middle of those who had come before. Instead, he had somehow squirted sideways from the anomaly – due, perhaps, to his arms still waving at an invisible foe – to land in a heap far enough away from anyone to notice him. Land in a heap but in cover. Land in a heap inside a deep snowdrift.

CHAPTER 91

Pablo appeared, skidding on the snow. He stopped, stood up, then slipped and landed on his bottom. He stayed there as it seemed safer. He then watched as the others arrived.

Wazzock was immediately on his bottom. Wrinkle managed to stay upright, relying on a lot of arm waving. Von Vlod had no such problems on arrival and glided gracefully to a stop to stare at the surroundings in awe.

Then, there was a boom, a sonic one.

CHAPTER 92

Arriving with a bang, a sonic boom of a bang, the thirty-nine other others landed in a gigantic bundle of arms, legs, tails and other things that, thanks to the lack of imagination, couldn't be explained, then skidded as one along the snowy ground. And then, when they looked to be stopping, skidded some more. And some more. Until they came to a rest amongst the massive snowdrift they had caused. At least no one was hurt. Well, not no one.

Out of the massive snowdrift popped a groaning head. And then another. And then a tail, which was pulled upon to eventually reveal another groaning head. Then something else appeared. It might have been a head. It, too, was groaning.

Thankfully, the sudden bang had acted as a warning to those who had already arrived, giving them time to dodge to safety as the other others bulldozed past. It had also interrupted a lot of staring and frowning that had been going on. Staring and frowning, that now concentrated on the newcomers.

The first to realise who the newcomers were, quickly ducked behind his own snowdrift. The next to realise, four of them, now scowled. It was the last thing they needed. The last group to realise, didn't. They had no clue as to who it was in the snowdrift. They also had no clue as to who the ones who had been frowning at them moments before were. And as for the hooded one, who had now ducked behind a snowdrift, who that was was anyone's guess. Basil was still out for the count, so missed out on the frowning and wasn't wondering anything.

CHAPTER 93

Vlad didn't know what had happened to his friends or where they had gone, but he knew they had gone somewhere; he could sense them. Danrite and Frida. Hopefully, the others would be with them.

Good news, but the problem was they were now, somehow, further away. A long way away. And because of that, he doubted Percy would be able to get to them in time to stop them from destroying the evil. Perhaps he could find them and tell what he knew, but would they believe him? Maybe. He didn't know. No, he had to find Percy. Tell him what had happened. Something was telling him he needed Percy.

Percy was closely following the compass, his stride unwavering, but he didn't feel he was getting any closer. He was. But it didn't feel like it. The mountains looked no closer, even though he had been walking for a while since first seeing them. They were. But they didn't look it. Because of that, he was beginning to doubt he would be able to stop Danrite from destroying the evil. But he would keep going. Keep looking at the compass. Keep an eye on the mountains. And so he did. With the occasional glance skyward. He knew he wouldn't be able to see his friend, but something told him Vlad was needed if he was going to succeed.

Vlad was flying as fast as he could. Determined to get to Percy and tell him what had happened. Hoping his friend would know what to do next.

Percy looked at the compass. Looked at the mountains. Glanced up. Hurried with his walking. He looked at the compass. Glanced at the mountains. He looked up. He walked. He stopped. He looked up again. Caught something out of the corner of his eye. Percy turned slightly and squinted at the sky. What was that? Something looked out of place. There was a blur. No, a haze. He stared harder. But was none the wiser.

He walked on. He stopped. Could it be Vlad? For a moment, he brightened at the thought. But then he remembered he couldn't see him. He started to walk again. So, if it wasn't Vlad? He took another glance toward the haze. Percy's stride suddenly lengthened. He broke into a trot. Whatever it was in the sky, it appeared to be heading straight for him. Then again, it could be nothing. Eyestrain from staring at the compass. The cold that had got colder, affecting his eyesight. But, just in case it was something, perhaps he should make with the hasty moving. Percy started to run.

Strange, thought Vlad, who had made better time than he had expected; why's Percy running? Vlad, without realising it, was causing a minor disturbance to the air around him, so fast were his wings flapping. A shimmer. A haze. Something so small no one would notice it unless you were a ghost, it seemed. The haze Percy had seen.

'Hey!' shouted Vlad as he closed in. 'Percy!'

Percy continued to run.

Vlad now flew past Percy and hovered a couple of metres above him. 'Percy? It's me, Vlad. What's going on?'

Percy looked up but still didn't stop. All he saw was this thing hovering above him, all shimmery-like. But he did slow a little. Did he just hear Vlad? He slowed a little more. 'Vlad?'

'I'm here, in front of you,' said Vlad, who, now that his wings had slowed, was no longer creating a haze.

'Where?' Percy looked nervously behind him at the sky. The shimmery thing, it appeared, had disappeared for now.

'Here.' Vlad was no longer in bat form.

'Where?'

'In front of you.' Vlad was wondering what was going on with Percy. 'You'll see if you pass me my cloak.'

Percy held it out.

'Thank you.' Vlad took it and put it on.

'Ah,' said Percy when Vlad was cloaked. 'Am I glad to see you. I was being chased by this weird thing in the sky.' He glanced again skyward. 'But it appears to have gone now.'

'What weird thing?' said Vlad, scanning the sky.

Percy pointed to where he had seen it. 'It was there and was heading straight for me just before you arrived. It then hovered just in front of me for a second before disappearing into thin air.'

Vlad looked; there was nothing there now. But it was where he had been moments ago. It then dawned on Vlad what it might have been that Percy had seen. 'I think that might have been me,' he confessed.

'You?'

'That's the direction I came from,' said Vlad. 'And I did hover in front of you just now.'

'Blimey,' said Percy, feeling slightly better now that the weirdness in the sky had been explained. 'How?'

'I don't know,' said Vlad, 'but I had been flying quite fast. Perhaps it was that?'

'Perhaps.' Percy was not sure what to think. 'But you're here now.' He patted Vlad on the shoulder and returned to being Percy. 'So, what news of Danrite and the others? Did you find them?'

Vlad told his tale.

CHAPTER 94

'Wuz-up?' muttered a bewildered Basil, who had not long come round. The cold of the snow helping him regain some of his senses.

'You're up,' said Twinkle, pulling him to his feet. 'It's here.' She stooped to pick up the compass and handed it to Frida.

Frida took it and helped Twinkle drag Basil to where Danrite and Salor were standing. Jose was stood a little apart from them, baring his teeth and snarling at all and sundry.

It was time for Frida to put her business head on. 'Okay, keep close until we know what's going on,' she advised as she eyed the creatures that had arrived after them. 'We don't know if they're friend or foe.' She joined Jose. The others did the same. She took something from her pocket.

'What's that?' asked Twinkle, now in sole possession of Basil.

'It's a gun,' said Danrite, his sword now in hand.

'A gun?' said Salor.

'It's not a gun,' said Frida, frowning at her brother. 'It's a tazer.'

'Oh,' said Salor, none the wiser.

Free of the snowdrift, the hooded figure chanced a look to see what there was to see. He was also curious to find out what had caused the noise. Sadly, he hadn't used the stealth he had hoped for. He was seen, grabbed, and now stood miserable in the grips of Wazzock. Unknown to him, the dodging of the other others had placed Wazzock and the rest of the others within a metre or two of him and his snowy hidey-hole. He and they now watched as the other others continued in the process of discovering which way was up.

They watched and kept close. Not too close, but close enough to call on them if they needed help. What help they could offer was another thing, but there was strength in numbers, and there were a lot of them. They watched and kept close but also had one eye on those who were staring at them. With most of that eye trained on the little one with the massive teeth.

'Who do you think they are?' asked Von Vlod.

'No idea,' said Wrinkle who glanced at the hooded figure. 'Perhaps he knows.'

165

'Never seen them before in my life,' lied the hooded figure.

'Perhaps it's them,' said Wazzock, giving them the once over.

'You mean the ones that came through?' said Von Vlod.

'Could be,' said Wrinkle, studying them. 'Weird looking lot.' Especially the big one with the little wings, she thought. But familiar. Perhaps they've met before? No, she would surely remember.

'So what do we do now?' asked Wazzock. 'They've seen us.'

'Nothing, for now, is my feeling,' suggested Wrinkle.

'But what if they want us to join them?' asked Von Vlod.

'We'll worry about that when we have to.' Wrinkle again. Everyone agreed.

Pablo, who had been strangely quiet since they had arrived, now spoke. 'He is smelling,' he said.

'Smelly?' Von Vlod wondered how he could tell from this distance. But he was a dog, so.

'No being smelly,' said Pablo. 'No, I am saying he is being smelling. He is being smelling at us.'

'Sniffing us, do you mean?' said Wrinkle.

'I don't like the look of his teeth,' whispered Wazzock, steering the hooded figure so he was standing in front of him.

'Sí,' said Pablo, 'he is the sniffing at us. The smelling.' He now gave the one with the big teeth an intimidating stare. He was sure he could take him one to one. But then again, those teeth were very big teeth. Perhaps not, then. Bravado slipping away, Pablo returned to just normal staring instead.

'Should we do something?' asked Von Vlod.

'Wait and see what they do,' said Wrinkle.

'Wise,' said Wazzock. 'Perhaps a step or two back until then would be just as wise?' He was still staring at the huge teeth.

'Wouldn't be a bad thing,' agreed Wrinkle.

'Good idea,' said Von Vlod.

'Sí,' said Pablo.

''Ere, get off me hoof,' moaned one among the pile of other others.

'That's a paw,' another other other pointed out.

'I know what I have on the end of my leg,' argued the other other with the hoof, who then stared at it. 'Wait a minute, it is a paw.' He now compared it with the other three. 'Well, I'll be!'

And so they continued until all the other others were on their feet-hooves-paws and other things. They then checked their surroundings. They stared with curious eyes at an equally curious Danrite and his friends. Much eyebrow-raising and frowning ensued. Finished with them, they turned their attention to the others, mainly at Wazzock and the strange hooded figure in his grip. They knew him. They didn't know the little one. They studied him. They now looked at each other. Eye to eye. Which led to some having to crouch. Some having to be held aloft. A meeting of tall, small and the in-between. They talked. They cogitated. Some didn't know what that meant, so they had a good think instead. They decided. They turned, and one walked forward. All that was looking on now waited to see what came next. She spoke.

'We, the other others, as some of you call us, have come to a decision,' she announced to everyone. 'If you need us, we'll be somewhere over there building a fire.' She pointed to somewhere over there. 'It's flipping cold.' With that, she and the other others went to look for firewood.

'That was strange,' declared Danrite as the other others wandered off. As understatements went, it was up there with the best.

'You think,' said Frida, unsure what to make or think of the creatures that had emerged from the giant snowdrift.

'What are they?' asked Twinkle, not expecting an answer. She was particularly unsure about the one that hadn't realised it had paws.

'Who knows?' said Salor.

'Grr,' growled Jose, bringing everyone's attention back to the other group. 'I am being smelling the fear,' spouted Jose suddenly. 'It is being from the one in the hood.'

'That tall weird one does appear to have him by the neck,' observed Salor.

'Perhaps he's a prisoner,' suggested Danrite. His grip on his sword tightened.

'But is he good or bad?' wondered Twinkle.

'Are any of them good?' said Salor, offering up a fair point.

'Do you think they're the evil?' said Danrite.

167

Frida glanced at the compass even though she doubted they were. But better to be careful. It wasn't pointing at them. 'No. But that doesn't mean they're friendly.'

'And what about those?' asked Danrite, absentmindedly pointing his sword at the other others. 'Baddies or goodies?'

'Uh-oh,' cried Wrinkle. 'That one's raised his sword.'

'What do we do?' wailed Von Vlod.

'Form a circle,' suggested Wazzock.

'I am with the snarling at them,' snarled Pablo, snarling.

'Maybe they want him,' said Wrinkle, looking at the hooded figure.

'I knew he was with them,' growled Wazzock, tightening his grip on the hooded figure's hood.

'I've never seen them before,' lied the hooded figure again.

'No, it's okay.' Von Vlod sounded a little calmer. Relieved. 'He's pointing at them.'

Heads quickly turned to see what the other others made of that.

Nothing much as it turned out. Some had found a small copse and were eagerly gathering firewood. Others were engaged in a rather frenetic snowball fight. Two of them were sitting on a blanket having a picnic. And as for the other others, they couldn't be bothered to even notice the sword that Danrite pointed at them. Nothing at all, as it turned out.

'The strange bald dog with the haircut has started to snarl at us,' warned Salor.

'Really?' Twinkle looked. 'Why?'

'The sword.' Basil, who had finally regained his wits, pointed at it. 'I think they think we want to tumble.'

'Tumble?' said Danrite, lowering it.

'I think he means rumble,' explained Frida, who then suddenly realised why the snarling dog and its friends seemed so familiar. Good grief, she thought.

'He's lowering the sword,' said Von Vlod.

'Perhaps they're surrendering,' said Wazzock.

'Surrendering to who?' asked Wrinkle, frowning at Wazzock.

'I am thinking the girl, she is being staring at us most strangely,' said Pablo.

'Pablo's right, she is,' said Von Vlod. 'Most strangely. Should we say something?'

'Like what?'

'Hello?'

It wasn't the worst suggestion. The sword looked sharp, and the little dog's teeth were way too big and pointy. But should they?

'Might be worth a go,' said Wrinkle.

'But she's holding something. Two things.'

'Weapons?'

'What about running?' suggested the hooded figure, who got a tap on the head for his trouble.

'Who asked you?'

'Just saying.'

'Well, don't.' He got another tap.

'What about running?' suggested Wazzock.

'For goodness sake,' groaned Wrinkle. She peered at Frida and then the others with her. Something so familiar.

'Perhaps he should say it,' said Wazzock, pushing the hooded figure forward.

'But what if he's one of them?' said Von Vlod.

'Don't worry.' Wrinkle cupped a hand to her mouth. 'I'll do it.' She gave a loud hello.

'She just said hello,' said Twinkle, even though they had all heard.

'It might be a trap,' warned Salor.

'Or they're being friendly,' said Danrite.

'Enemies are friendly until they're not,' said Salor, all doom and gloom. 'I expect that's what they said to the one in the hood before they grabbed him.' Everyone looked at the hooded figure.

'Perhaps he didn't say hello back,' said Danrite.

'Oh,' said Salor.

'Hello,' said Twinkle.

CHAPTER 95

Percy's face was a picture of dismay when Vlad finished telling him what had happened. It appeared they would not be able to stop the evil being destroyed. They had failed. Imagination would be no more.

'We've lost,' groaned Percy glumly, head in hands. 'There's no way we can stop them now.'

'It would seem not,' agreed Vlad, shaking his invisible head.

Percy looked up. 'At the mountains, you say?'

'Somewhere at the foot of them,' said Vlad. 'If my senses are to be believed.' He meant his new bat senses.

'Miles away then,' said Percy, glancing at the mountains before returning his head to his hands. His shoulders slumped. All of Percy slumped. He looked at the compass. Fat lot of good that was now, he thought.

'That's true,' said Vlad, who, though as glum as Percy, still harboured hope. 'But they have to find it first. The evil, I mean.' That was also true. There might still be hope, then. A chance. And if Vlad had known how many had looked and failed in their search for the evil before, that hope would have grown even more.

It was Vlad's turn to look at the mountains. They were vast. So much space for something to hide in. He perked up a little. 'Perhaps they won't be able to.' He smiled. 'And we have something they don't have, an evil compass to help us.' If only he knew.

But hope was hope. Percy brightened a little. He looked at the compass. It was pointing at the mountains. And while it pointed, there had to be hope. He unslumped. 'Then what are we waiting for?' He had regained some of his mojo. 'Let's go.' He started to walk.

Vlad, happy to see his friend cheer up, fell in beside him.

CHAPTER 96

The hellos were just background noise to Frida as her sudden realisation took hold. 'Good grief,' said Frida under her breath. She grabbed Danrite's arm and pulled him closer to her. 'They're them.'

'What?' said Danrite, not in a whisper.

'Keep your voice down,' hissed Frida. 'Look at them.'

'Who?' said Danrite, this time keeping his voice low.

'Them.' Frida nodded at the ones holding the hooded figure. 'Who do they remind you of?'

Danrite looked. He thought about it. And then. 'Flipping heck,' he exclaimed quietly, 'they're them.'

And they were. The ones holding the hooded figure were dead ringers for their friends. Well, nearly dead ringers. Sort of. Nearly. There were differences. Quite large ones, in truth. But there was no denying the fact that who Danrite and Frida were looking at were of the same ilk as their friends. A wizard. A vampire. A fairy. And a dog. Which may or may not be a were-something-or-other.

CHAPTER 97

The ground beneath the creature with the unimportant name trembled, causing him to wobble even more so than before.

That was big, thought the creature with the unimportant name. Never before had he wobbled so violently in his cave. And that wobble had nearly been the wobble to end all wobbles. The creature with the unimportant name shivered at the thought.

Mind aquiver, the creature with the unimportant name, retreated into the depths of the cave to think. What did it mean? he wondered on arriving there. He didn't know. But one thing he did know for sure was he wasn't as brave as he thought. He no longer wanted to face what was coming. Hunters?

He had done. Before. On a number of occasions. They hadn't seen him. But he had seen them. And each time, he had managed to scare them away in some way or another. Always four of them. Always with one amongst them that wasn't as brave as the others. And the fear that that one had easily passed on to others. They had run eventually. But so had he. To find a new, safe place to hide. To wait for the next ones to stumble across it. And so on. But it had been a while since the last time. This one had even begun to feel like home; he had been there so long. But this time, it was different. Something was different. He had felt it when they had arrived. And he felt he would once again be stumbled upon. And this time, he wasn't so sure he would be able to scare them away.

The creature with the unimportant name was scared. More so than ever before. He just hoped that when they found him, the end if there was to be an end, would be quick.

CHAPTER 98

'Basil?' The Font almost pleaded into the talky-walky. There was no reply. There hadn't been for ages. What *had* he done? thought the Font for the umpteenth time.

'BASIL!' she now shouted, knowing it wouldn't help. The umpteenth before hadn't.

The Font sighed. She was tired. And then, going for a hat-trick of umpteenths, she let the hand holding the talky-walky drop to her side and bump, for the umpteenth time, against her leg. She would have a bruise. Had a bruise. It had hurt. And now, to cap it all, she was getting another headache. She hoped it wouldn't get as bad as the last one. It was her own fault. She shouldn't get so stressed. Time for another lie-down. She would try again later.

CHAPTER 99

The Master carefully got up from the floor. How long have I been out? he wondered. A clock was sought.

As it happened, it had been no time at all. But a lot can happen in no time at all.

The Master picked the talky-walky up from where it had fallen. The unblocking had been a success. The Master could feel it. A button was clicked. But what has happened since? A lot can happen in a few minutes. He needed to know.

'Hello?' said the Master into it. 'Are you there?'

No reply.

'Hello?'

Still no reply.

'Hello?'

'HELLO?'

Why won't he answer? It was worrying. Where was the fool?

'HELLO!'

But to no avail.

'HELLO-HELLO-HELLO!'

'Now what?' asked Wazzock, now the ice had been broken with a couple of hellos. No one knew. But someone had a suggestion.

'You could put me down,' wailed the hooded figure, who was not strictly off the ground as the toes of his boots were touching it.

'Who said you could talk?' snarled Wrinkle, who, with everything that had happened, had all but forgotten the creature was there.

'Yes,' said Wazzock, giving the hooded figure a shake.

'Those two are whispering,' said Von Vlod, taking the attention away from the hooded figure for the moment.

'Sí,' said Pablo, 'and they stare.'

They all decided to stare back, apart from the hooded figure whose hood had fallen across his eyes.

'What do you think they're whispering about?' said Wrinkle as she watched the girl saying something in the boy's ear. 'Looks suspicious.'

'Plotting to get their little friend back, no doubt,' said Wazzock, his eyes narrowing until they were nothing but slits. He gave the hooded figure another shake.

'Oh, for goodness sake,' groaned the hooded figure. 'I told you, they're not my friends.'

'But you would say that, wouldn't you?' Wrinkle wasn't believing him for a moment.

Pablo, whose nose had taken a break from proceedings, mainly due to the crisp coldness it had endured since leaving the anomaly, suddenly did a quick double sniff. 'It is being they,' he said. 'The whisperingers. I am now smelling it.'

'Who is they?' quizzed Von Vlod.

'They are being the humans that are not being the humans,' Pablo replied helpfully. Thankfully, they all knew what he was going on about.

'They could be dangerous.' Wrinkle turned to Pablo. 'Are they?'

'I am smelling no,' said Pablo.

'That's good,' sighed Von Vlod, who had been somewhat worked up over the idea of humans. Humans were dangerous.

'Unless you are with the poking with of the stick at the girl one,' said Pablo, who then remembered what he had in his mouth. He quickly dropped it. The stick landed softly in the snow.

'Perhaps it's their friends who are the dangerous ones,' suggested Wazzock.

'Dangerous is as dangerous be,' uttered Wrinkle wisely.

'What?' said the hooded figure, frowning through the side of his hood at her. He got another shake for his trouble.

'Sniff them,' urged Wrinkle.

'Sniff?' Pablo gave Wrinkle a look.

'Oh, okay,' said Wrinkle. 'Smell them.'

Pablo did as he was asked. He frowned. He did it a second time. That is not being right, he thought. He did it a third time.

'Well?' asked Wazzock.

When there was no immediate answer, Wrinkle glanced down at Pablo. She frowned. Pablo's nose was so wrinkled it looked like a prune. 'Pablo?'

Wazzock, now also smelling something, as in was up, voiced concern. 'Wrinkle?' She nodded at Pablo. Wazzock saw his wrinkled prune nose. 'Pablo? What is it?'

'I am thinking I am smelling wrong,' said Pablo, looking concerned.

'How?' asked Von Vlod, wondering how one could smell wrong. Unless wrong was a something. And weren't wrong things bad?

Wrinkle had had the same thought. 'What's wrong with them?' she asked, fearing something terrible was amiss.

'It is being us that I am smelling,' said Pablo.

'What?' stammered Wrinkle. 'What's wrong with us?'

'No,' said Pablo. 'I am being smelling them, and they are smelling us.'

'Are they?' said Wazzock, glancing across the way at the little dog with the big teeth.

'I'm lost,' said Von Vlod. It was doubtful Von Vlod was the only one.

'He doesn't look as if he's smelling anything,' said Wazzock. 'I mean, sniffing.'

'No,' snapped Pablo sharply, wondering how dogkind wasn't the dominant species. He then remembered the thumb thing. Not having one. He sighed. 'They are being smelling the smelling like as we are.' How much simpler could he put it?

'Uh-oh,' murmured the hooded figure, suddenly thinking he knew what the weird-looking dog thing was going on about. The problem was he had spoken aloud.

'What's that supposed to mean?' demanded Wrinkle on hearing him. She grabbed him by the scruff of the neck and took over dangling duty from Wazzock.

'You know something, don't you?' snarled Wazzock, who took to giving him a vigorous shake. And who then quickly hid his hand when he remembered he wasn't holding him anymore.

'Well?' growled Wrinkle menacingly as her grip tightened on the hooded figure's scruff.

The hooded figure now found himself in a caught between a rock and a hard place situation. Time to spill the beans. But not all of them.

'They're you,' said the hooded figure, preparing for a shake. It didn't come, so he took a chance and continued. 'Or at least the next yous to be sent through.'

'It *is* them?' said Wrinkle, forgetting the hooded figure and dropping him as realisation hit home that they had found who they were looking for.

'Well, flip me sideways!' exclaimed Wazzock as he stopped the hooded figure from making a run for it. He stared hard at the supposed latest them. 'But they're nothing like us.'

'Oh, they are,' said Von Vlod, eyeing them up. Or at least three of them were. The resemblance was there to be seen. But what of me? thought Von Vlod. Where is the other me? Surely it's not that little strange one? Von Vlod was looking at Basil.

CHAPTER 101

'What do we do?' whispered Danrite. 'Shall we say something?'

'Not for the moment. Best to find out who they are first,' warned Frida, meaning their friends, almost, lookalikes.

'Do you think they are the evil?' asked Danrite.

'No,' said Frida, 'I checked. None of them are. At least not the evil we're looking for.'

'Oh,' said Danrite, not sure if that made him feel any better.

'Let's see what the others think.'

'What are Danrite and Frida up to?' said Salor. 'They've been whispering for ages about something. It's quite rude, you know.' He was feeling a bit miffed as he felt he should always be in the loop – whether it was his business or not.

'Perhaps it is being a twin thing,' suggested Jose.

'Perhaps they don't want you to hear what they're saying,' said Twinkle, aiming her remark at Salor. She also thought it was a bit rude but didn't say anything as she didn't want Salor thinking she was agreeing with him.

'Oh-oh,' said Jose, 'Frida, she is being coming this way.'

As she reached them, Frida noticed there was a touch of frostiness coming from Twinkle and Salor. 'Everything okay?' she asked.

'All okay here,' replied Salor haughtily. 'You okay?'

'All fine,' said Twinkle hesitantly.

'They are being of the thinking that you and Danrite are being of the rude,' said Jose, drawing dirty looks from the other two. 'What?'

'Well, I…' stuttered Twinkle.

'Ha,' muttered Salor nervously, 'Jose and his little jokes.'

It then dawned on Frida that they must have seen the whispering. Better not say why they were whispering, she decided. For now.

Danrite, who had lingered a moment or two to stare at the paw thing, now caught up. As he did, he also noticed there seemed to be an atmosphere. 'What's going on?' he asked.

Jose went to open his mouth, but Frida stepped in. 'They saw our twin thing.'

'Twin thing?'

'See,' said Jose, mouth now free of Frida, 'I am being right.'

'Whispering,' nudged Frida, winking at Danrite. 'You know, when we're nervous.'

'What? Oh, yeah.' Danrite had caught on at last. 'Nervous.'

'Though it's not technically whispering,' explained Frida, 'it's more your talking quietly sort of thing.'

'Ah,' said Salor, who knew all about nervous and its friends, fear, run, etcetera. He knew there was a good reason.

'Why didn't you tell us you did that?' said Twinkle, feeling a little more included and a tad foolish.

'We only just found out ourselves, really,' said Frida. 'Didn't we?'

'Yeah,' agreed Danrite brightly. 'Just now.'

'And now we have sorted that out,' said Frida, 'I was thinking that perhaps someone should go talk to the ones that said hello, see who they are and what they're doing here. What do you think?' Tables turned.

'Well,' said Salor, expecting to be chosen but ready to graciously turn down the privilege if he was. 'What do you think, Twinkle?'

'A good idea,' said Twinkle. 'But who's going?'

'I shall be doing it,' said Jose, with a swish of his tail. 'I am being as a black knight. I am being afraid of no one.'

'Perhaps a big black knight heading their way might be a bit frightening,' said Frida gently, thinking a swishing black tail and overly large teeth might not be seen as the extending of an olive branch. No, someone else would need to go, and she had just that person in mind.

'What about Danrite?' Salor was getting in quickly as the choice to go had just become smaller, even though he felt he was the obvious candidate.

As it happened, Danrite was also Frida's choice. 'Just what I was thinking,' she said, to Salor's disappointment and relief.

'Me?' said Danrite.

'Put your sword away, though,' said Frida.

'But he is being like a knight with it,' said Jose. 'Oh, yes, he is being the scary. I am now seeing.'

'Why me?'

179

'Because you're the leader,' said Salor, who got stares and frowns from everyone.

'Yes, he is,' agreed Twinkle, who meant it.

'Okay,' said Danrite, 'I'll do it.' Even though he wasn't feeling much like a knight or a leader. But he was a hero. So, it had been written. He took heart from that.

'Good lad,' extolled Salor. He was ignored.

'And while you're at it,' said Frida, who had just noticed a fire coming to life amidst the other others, 'ask them who that lot are.'

'And who that is they have by the scruff of the neck,' wondered Twinkle.

'He looks a bit weird,' Basil chipped in. He had been keeping himself to himself. He now took a step back from the limelight again.

'Sí,' said Jose, 'as weird is as weird being.' He looked Basil up and down suspiciously.

'Be careful,' said Frida.

'I will.' Danrite. He took a step forward.

'Look,' said Pablo, 'one of the human not human, he is coming.' He was.

'What do we do?' worried Wazzock.

'We greet him,' said Von Vlod.

'But he isn't one of the four.' Wazzock didn't like it.

'Then let's find out what he wants,' said Wrinkle. 'It might be this thing.' She gave the hooded figure a shake.

The hooded figure doubted it.

'I…come…in…peace,' said Danrite, for want of a better greeting, but thinking it might be the right thing to say in moments like this.

'Who are you?' asked Wazzock, pushing himself forward, now free of the hooded figure.

'My…name…is…Danrite,' said Danrite, though why he was talking so deliberately or loudly, he didn't know.

'We…can…hear…you,' said Wrinkle.

'Oh-sorry,' apologised Danrite, 'it's just that I'm a little nervous.' Should a hero admit to that? Hey-ho.

'What's a little Nervous?' demanded Wazzock while wondering

what a big one would look like. 'Never heard of one before.'

'He's nervous,' said Von Vlod, 'not a Nervous.'

'Ah,' said Wazzock. 'Just checking.'

'My name is Von Vlod,' said Von Vlod, extending a shadowy hand to Danrite. 'I'm a vampire.'

Danrite took it and shook it without the slightest hint of surprise. And while it had looked as if the offered hand would blow away in the wind, it felt solid enough. And although tension now eased a little on both sides, wariness remained.

The tall woman dressed in white with large white wings introduced herself. 'My name's Wrinkle.' If it wasn't for the black eyes set deep into her white face, you might easily not have noticed her in the snowy surroundings.

'Are you a fairy?' said Danrite, hoping he wouldn't upset her by asking.

'I am,' Wrinkle replied, amazed that anyone could still tell after all the changes the lack of imagination had caused. She smiled. She didn't do that very often anymore. Not with warmth, at least.

'And I am a wizard,' announced Wazzock grandly, keen to get in the act. 'A great caster of spells and a great master of magic.' He bowed. Wrinkle rolled her black eyes.

With the long robe, the pointy hat, the grey beard and the air of self-importance, the introduction had not been needed as far as Danrite was concerned. He smiled and shook the offered hand. It was warm and clammy. A lot like Salor's. Although, unlike Salor, this wizard wasn't wearing make-up or a tie.

'I—' started the hooded figure before being stopped abruptly by Wrinkle. If Danrite noticed, he didn't show it.

'And I am being Pablo,' came a voice from below. He dropped the stick, which he had just picked up again, to introduce himself. 'I was being a Xoloitzcuintle. But I was also being a god. A dog-god.' He suddenly looked sad. 'But now I am being a mere were-Xoloitzcuintle.' He raised a paw.

Danrite leaned down and shook it and then attempted to say Xoloitzcuintle. He failed.

Von Vlod came to his rescue. 'It's Show...low...itz...queent...ly. Show-low-itz-queent-ly. Or Xolo for short. We just call him Pablo.'

181

'Sí,' said Pablo, 'I am being a were-Xolo.' He then gave a smile of sorts and wagged his tail, which was as hairless as the rest of his body. Apart from the spot between his large ears where a tuft of hair grew. A sort of tufty Mohican haircut.

'But you're a god?' said Danrite. He had never met a god before. Did he bow?

'Was,' said Wrinkle. 'Before he was bitten by a werewolf. And before you ask, no, no one knows how that happened. Not even Pablo.'

'Oh,' said Danrite, just a tad disappointed not to be meeting a god. But then again, an ex-god. Wow.

'He's shaking their hands,' said Salor.

'So I see,' said Twinkle. 'I'm taking it that's a good sign?'

'I am being ready for the rescue,' offered Jose, just in case it was needed. His tail rigid.

'I don't think that will be needed,' said Frida as she saw the tall one smile at Danrite. It looked genuine enough.

'Do you think we should go over?' said Salor, eager to impose himself upon the others, now it appeared safe to do so.

'Not yet,' said Frida. 'Let's wait for Danrite to call us over.'

'And what are you?' Wrinkle asked, knowing full well he was human. At least, if believing Pablo, some of him was.

'What am I?' Danrite was puzzled by the question.

'What manner of creature?'

'Oh,' said Danrite, realising what he was being asked. 'I'm a human. Well, most of me is, I think.'

'You think?' worried Wazzock.

Danrite looked uncomfortable, mainly because he was. 'I think I'm a little bit magical as well.' He really didn't like talking about it, especially amongst strangers.

'Magical?' said Wrinkle, growing warier.

'At least that's what I've been told.'

'By whom?' asked Wrinkle.

'My friends.' Danrite turned and pointed towards Twinkle and Salor.

'What sort of magic?' asked Wazzock, feeling under threat.

182

What if he was a wizard in disguise? Or something. A good one.

Danrite was starting to feel the same way. Not the wizard bit. 'I don't know,' he admitted. 'But I think it's something to do with me being the hero.' He then remembered his sister. 'Or one of them.'

'What hero?' asked an intrigued Von Vlod.

Danrite pulled himself together. 'The one that saves imagination.'

'Really,' snapped Wazzock. 'But you're not a wizard.' It was obvious, he had now decided: no pointy hat.

'So that's why you're in this Otherworld, to save imagination?' said Wrinkle, ignoring Wazzock.

'Yes,' said Danrite. 'Well, me and my sister. Who I think might be the real hero.'

At this point, some of the others were getting a little lost.

'Your sister?' said Von Vlod.

'Yes,' said Danrite, again turning. He pointed at Frida. 'The tough-looking one in the shorts.' He gave her a wave, which she returned.

'So, you're both heroes?' said Von Vlod, trying to get it clear in the mind. 'And both of you are here to save imagination?'

'So it is written,' said Danrite. 'Or at least it was about me, I believe.'

The others looked at each other. Blank looks. It was as clear as mud what the human, partly human, was talking about. And then, just as it looked as if they were all going to be swallowed by that mud, a small length of string, as in Wazzock's weary memory, was offered forward to help pull them clear.

'Ye-gads!' yelled Wazzock suddenly, loud enough for some of the other others to look up. 'You're the one that it's written about.'

'Yes,' said Danrite, sure he had just said that. Not too bright this wizard.

Three pairs of eyes turned to Wazzock, who quickly explained how it had been written many years ago that a hero would come and save everyone. A hero that was half giant and half dwarve, as in the mythical sense.

Three pairs of eyes then turned to Danrite.

'Half giant, half dwarve, you say,' said Wrinkle, looking Danrite up and down.

'It's what was written,' said Danrite, on the defensive.

'Oh, I get it,' said Von Vlod.

'Do tell,' said Wrinkle.

Von Vlod told her.

'Ah,' said an enlightened Wrinkle, 'so imagination has been in trouble for a very long time.'

'Would seem so,' smiled Von Vlod. 'Perhaps they were trying to make it sound a little grander.'

'Um,' pondered Wrinkle. 'So you're a half giant, half dwarve hero, are you?'

'Yes.' Danrite thought they had already covered that.

'Which makes you, when putting the two together, an about average-size hero?'

'I'm five feet, eleven and three-quarters inches tall,' said Danrite. 'Six feet in my shoes.' He didn't know why he felt he always had to add that last bit.

'But a hero?'

Der, thought Danrite, but didn't say it. 'That about sums it up,' he said.

'So that's why there are six of you,' said Wazzock, who was eager to believe as it was said to have been a Master Wizard that had written it. Said amongst the wizards. So it must be true. 'Four like the rest of us, but with the two heroes tagging along.'

'There were actually seven of us,' Danrite decided to say, thus adding a tad more mud, 'but Vlad disappeared when we arrived.'

'Vlad?' Von Vlod's shadowy ears pricking up.

'He's a vampire, like you,' said Danrite, 'but he's invisible.'

'Then how you know he is being disappeared?' asked Pablo.

'He wears a robe,' Danrite explained. 'That disappeared too.'

'Invisible?' said Von Vlod.

'But he can be seen in mirrors.'

'Ah,' said Von Vlod, understanding. The gradual lack of imagination could be a cruel thing.

'And the others?' asked Wrinkle.

Danrite told her.

'And what is Basil?'

'I don't know,' Danrite admitted. 'The Font sent him.'

'She sent us here too,' said Wazzock. 'But we haven't heard from her since.'

'She sent those lot too, as far as we can make out,' said Von Vlod, gesturing towards the other others. 'Not all of them are, well, easy to talk to. If you get my drift.'

Danrite looked over at the other others. One saw him looking and stuck out a tongue. It was forked. It also didn't belong to him. Danrite quickly looked away. He most definitely didn't want to talk to him. If it was a him.

'So, it looks like we're on the same side,' said Von Vlod. 'All looking for the evil?'

'Looks like,' said Danrite.

And, as the mention of the evil hadn't phased Danrite, Von Vlod and the others decided they were.

'Trouble is,' said Wrinkle, 'we have no idea where it is. We've looked and looked but never found it. So, I fear it's doubtful, even with you and your sister's help, we ever will.'

'And I doubt we have time to anyway,' said Wazzock.

'Sí,' agreed Pablo. 'Time, it is being running out, we are thinking. We are feeling it.'

'They're right,' said Von Vlod.

'But we have a compass.'

'Danrite's waving at you,' said Twinkle.

'Should we go over?' said Salor, feeling Danrite had been there too long. He would say something in a minute.

'Might be a trap,' said Basil, wondering why he was still drawing attention to himself.

Frida waved back. 'It's just a wave,' she said, but pleased as it meant things were going well.

'I don't like it,' said Salor, after a minute. 'He's been over there too long.'

'Sí,' said Jose, 'I should perhaps be being rescuing him.'

'Not yet,' said Frida, confident her brother was coping.

'He has been over there a long time, though,' said Twinkle, looking at her wrist where a watch would be had she had one.

'All in good time,' said Frida. She was sure she would know if

185

Danrite was in trouble. Until then, they would wait.

'Compass?'

'Yeah, a compass,' said the hooded figure, the words coming out before he could stop them. Oops, he thought.

All of a sudden, the air became quite frosty, and it wasn't the weather doing it. Well, it was doing some of it, but not the air around Danrite. Well, it was doing some of that as well.

'I knew it,' yelled Wazzock, 'he's one of them.'

'Have you been lying to us,' snapped Wrinkle, staring hard at Danrite, her friendly demeanour melting away like a snowman on a hot day. 'You said you didn't know him.' She gave the hooded figure a shake.

'I didn't,' said Danrite, wondering what was happening and how that hooded figure hanging by the scruff of its neck could possibly know about the compass.

'You did,' said Wazzock, though not entirely sure he had. But mustn't let the fairy take the lead.

'He didn't,' said Von Vlod.

'What?'

'He didn't say he didn't know him.'

'He didn't?'

'No, because we never asked him,' said Von Vlod. It had been on the list of questions, but no one had thought to ask.

'Sí,' said Pablo. 'We are not being of the asking yet.'

'Then we should ask him now,' said Wazzock, not wanting to back down.

'Yes, perhaps we should,' said Wrinkle, her voice less sharp now.

Von Vlod did the asking. 'Do you know this creature, Danrite?' Pointing at the hooded figure. No one as yet having thought to remove his hood. But where's the sense in that?

'I've never seen him before in my life,' said Danrite. True.

'I believe him,' said Von Vlod.

'Then how did he know about the compass?' asked Wrinkle, who was also tending to believe Danrite and already regretting her outburst.

'Sí,' said Pablo, 'I am believing too, but how is it the hooded

186

one is being knowing about the compass thing?' Even though Pablo had no idea what a compass thing was?

'Perhaps we should ask him,' suggested Danrite. 'Because I'd like to know as well.'

'A good idea,' said Von Vlod. 'And I suggest your sister and friends also hear what he has to say.'

'Yes,' agreed Wrinkle. 'Please call them over.'

'Sí,' said Pablo, who would also like to know what a compass thing is being.

'Right.' If we must, thought, Wazzock. 'Sound idea.'

Danrite called them over.

CHAPTER 102

Up ahead, Percy had come to a stop. Just like that. No warning.

A second later, just after Vlad had thought, now what? He did the same.

Percy was having a nightmare. The potato one.

'You're taking too long,' said the nightmare.

'Tell me something I don't know,' said Percy.

'Okay,' said the nightmare. 'That's why I'm here. You're as light as a feather. In fact, you weigh nothing.'

A frowning, Percy went to ask what the heck the nightmare was going on about, but he was too late; his chance had gone, along with the nightmare.

'Hi,' greeted Bert.

'Grief!' exclaimed Vlad, 'you startled me. Again.'

'Sorry,' said Bert, 'but I have something to tell you.'

'Okay?'

'You're taking too long.'

'I know,' said Vlad, screwing his face up for none to see. 'But there's nothing we can do about it.'

'But there is,' said Bert.

'Is there?'

'You can fly.'

'I know that,' said Vlad, 'but I can't very well go on my own. Percy needs to be there.'

'Does he?'

'Doesn't he?'

'Yeah, he does, actually,' said Bert, making no sense. 'I suppose.'

'What does that mean?' asked Vlad. But the question fell on deaf ears. No ears. Bert was gone.

Vlad woke with a start and discovered he was sitting on the ground again. Which was strange. Or was it?

'Hey,' called Percy as he approached the still-sitting Vlad. 'You see one as well?'

'If you mean a nightmare, then yes.' Vlad started to get to his feet.

'Here.' Percy offered a hand to thin air. Vlad took it, and when on his feet, Percy asked him what the nightmare had said.

'Nonsense.'

'Yeah, same here,' said Percy. 'Made no sense. Told me I was as light as a feather.'

'Told me I could fly.'

'We already knew that,' said Percy, brow creasing.

'Makes no sense.'

'A head-scratcher, and no doubt,' said Percy, doing just that. He looked at the compass. Whatever the nightmares had meant, it had changed nothing. They still had a job to do. 'We should go. Enough time's been wasted.'

Vlad agreed, and side by side, they continued on. Pondering as they went on what the nightmares had told them.

CHAPTER 103

A large bonfire was now blazing happily, and many of the other others were sat around it. Had been sat around it.

Those that now weren't were the ones that had sat too close to the fire to begin with. They had been mostly put out now. Their clothes. Through snow rolling. Being stamped on. And watered. We won't go into that. Other other others that were no longer sat around the fire were the dousers, rollers, and stampers. Then there was the unconscious one. Victim of the old accidental rock in a snowball trick. An accident. It happened. So, the guilty party claimed. Also, not beside the fire were the couple having a picnic. But then, they hadn't sat around it anyway.

So now, all in all, only two other others were sat around the fire. Something tall and not green and the one with paws. The one with paws liked his paws now that he knew what they were and had names for nearly all of them. There was Paw, Another Paw, Also A Paw, and his favourite, because he thought it was rather cute, was named Paw Paw. He hadn't named his fifth paw – which he had only recently discovered having – because he was angry with it, as it was constantly tripping him up. He was telling it off when a shout went up.

'Oi,' went up a shout. 'They're meeting up.'

Heads turned. Except one. No, even his head had turned. Thanks to a kind bystander who felt that just because he was unconscious, it didn't mean he should miss out.

The other others watched as the others and the new ones met.

'Hang on,' said an other other, 'shouldn't we be there as well?'

'You got a point,' said another other other.

'Perhaps we should wait a minute,' said some other other.

'Why?' said someone.

'They might be going to have a punch-up,' said another.

'Stay back then,' said the unconscious one. Helped by the kind bystander.

'Don't get involved,' shouted an other other with wet clothes.

'But we are involved,' exclaimed the tall and not green creature out of the blue, causing the one with paws to trip over them.

'Good idea, like a good fight I do,' barked a rough-looking other other wearing a tiara and muscle t-shirt, who pushed herself to the front. 'Let's get at it!'

'Fight-fight-fight!' encouraged the unconscious one. The kind bystander, who was sitting on the fence on this one, was appalled.

The tall and not green creature got up and marched to the front of the other others. There, it grabbed the rough-looking one by her braces and rolled her out of the way. 'That's not what I meant,' it growled.

'Ooo,' whispered an other other to another, 'it's the sage.'

'Is he lucid?' whispered another.

'What colour's that?' asked another.

'I think so,' said another other other.

'Makes a change,' uttered someone.

The tall and not green creature was a sage. Even though he looked remarkably like a long stem of broccoli. That's a lack of imagination for you. A sage of the wisest kind. One that, before he ended up in this Otherworld, was sought after for his wise words by the kings and knights of fairy stories and tales of lore. Admired and respected by all who knew him or knew of him.

But that was then, and this is now. The sage was now something resembling a stem of broccoli. A stem of broccoli that frequently swayed from side to side. That frequently fell over because it was top-heavy.

But now and again, he would stop his swaying and become thoughtful. Return a little to his former self. And one of those times, it appeared, was now.

'I think we should wait,' advised the sage.

'I said that,' said the other other that had said it.

'Blimey,' whispered an other other, 'he is lucid.'

'Is that a sort of grey?'

'We had better wait and watch then,' suggested an other other with ash on his shoes.

'Thank goodness for that,' said another other other, who was still dousing – or so he said. 'I can't just stop mid-stream, you know.'

And so they decided to wait and see what happened next.

191

CHAPTER 104

The parties met.

'Nice tie,' said Wazzock, on seeing Salor's neckwear. All stars and moons.

'Why, thank you,' said Salor, puffing out his chest.

'What colour is it?' asked Wazzock.

'Silver moons and gold stars on a royal purple background.' Salor was set to explode. 'It's the finest silk, you know.'

'Noice,' said Wazzock.

'I'm Wrinkle,' said Wrinkle, holding out a hand.

'Twinkle,' said Twinkle, shaking it.

'You're a fairy,' said Wrinkle as their hands touched.

'Ditto, back at you,' smiled Twinkle.

'Please take no notice of them,' said Frida and Von Vlod as one. They laughed.

'Von Vlod,' said Von Vlod, with a bow that could have been a curtsey. 'At your service.'

'Frida,' said Frida. 'Are you the one in charge?'

'No, thank goodness,' laughed Von Vlod. 'One of those are.' Von Vlod nodded at Wrinkle and Wazzock. 'At least that's what they tell each other.'

Frida smiled. 'We've just got the one of those.'

Jose and Pablo were also exchanging pleasantries. If you can call it that. Danrite, whose nose was wrinkled at the sight, nudged Jose with a foot.

'But it's being how we are greeting,' said an indignant Jose.

'Sí,' said Pablo.

'Sí,' said Jose.

This just left Basil and the hooded figure.

They eyed each other suspiciously. Basil eyeing the hooded figure's boots. The hooded figure, who had been raised, eyeing the top of Basil's head from the depths of his hood. And that is how it would stay until Wrinkle put the hooded figure down. Something that would happen as soon as everyone had met everyone else and finished discussing the where-they-went-from-here's, the well-I-never-goodness-graciousness's, the what-was-all-that-anomaly-malarky-about's, the what-the-heck-are-the-other-others and the compass.

'So, we want the same thing,' said Wrinkle. It *was* them. The new arrivals. Perhaps they did have a way out.

'So, it would seem,' said Frida.

'Look.' Danrite, who now held the compass, showed it to everyone. 'The pointer's got bigger.'

They looked. It was also flickering from side to side quite quickly.

'The evil. It's on the move,' declared Wazzock with confidence.

'It's getting bigger,' said Salor, with equal self-assurance.

They exchanged a glance and nodded. Weren't wizards the best?

'Or it's because we've got closer to it,' said Frida.

The anomaly-malarkey had been the last thing to be agreed on. It had somehow moved everyone to somewhere else. Why? Where? For good or bad? No one knew. But maybe now they did.

'Oh,' said Wazzock, he hadn't thought of that.

Oh-oh, thought Salor, closer. He didn't like the sound of that.

'But whatever,' rallied Frida, 'I think it's time we made a move.' She looked at the others. 'Together?'

Wrinkle, Wazzock, Von Vlod and Pablo exchanged glances. Pablo shrugged. Wazzock looked nervous. Von Vlod gave a tentative nod. It was decided.

'Together,' said Von Vlod, who was still slightly disappointed at not meeting Vlad the Vampire.

'Together,' agreed Twinkle and Wrinkle.

'Danrite?' said Frida, remembering her brother was their leader. She should have said something. 'Sorry,' she whispered.

'That's what we're here for,' said Danrite. 'No prob,' he whispered back with a wink. He knew who was really in charge. He was just the letterhead. Was that right? Never mind.

'It's decided then,' said Frida.

'But what if it is moving?' worried Wazzock.

'Then we need to keep our eyes open,' said Wrinkle.

'Or getting bigger?' worried Salor equally.

'We're bigger,' said Twinkle. 'There are more of us now.' She

193

cast a glance at the other others. Was that one's clothes smoking? She looked away. 'What about them? Can we count on them?' she asked.

'They want to get out of here as much as we do,' said Von Vlod. 'But that's not a guarantee.'

'Then onwards and upwards,' said Danrite brightly. He held the compass out.

'Onwards,' said Wazzock, holding back any doubts.

I suppose, thought, Salor. 'Onwards,' he said, keeping his.

'Upwards,' cried Twinkle and Wrinkle as one. They looked at each other. There followed the slightest of fist-bumps.

'Sí,' said Jose. 'It is being upwards and the onwards.'

'Sí,' said Pablo. 'It is the onwards and upwards.'

'Onward,' said Von Vlod.

Well, said the glances between Frida and Danrite, that was easier than had been expected. But then...

'Wait a minute!' It was Twinkle. 'Where's Basil?'

In all the excitement and chit-chat and introductions, Basil and the hooded figure had been all but forgotten.

'And who is that hooded figure?' said Frida, remembering they hadn't asked.

'Well, I never,' said Wrinkle, looking down. 'I'd completely forgotten about him.' Even though she was still holding him by the scruff of his neck.

'Here,' said Basil. He had thought of finding somewhere away from everybody to call the Font, but everybody was now everywhere. So, instead, he had decided to keep out of sight out of mind as best he could until a chance appeared. He had been keeping an eye on the hooded figure, though. Something about the creature was familiar, but he couldn't quite put his finger on what that was.

Wrinkle placed the hooded figure on the ground but kept a firm grip on him. 'We thought he was with you, but Danrite said he wasn't.'

'I never saw him before we arrived here,' said Frida.

'Ditto,' said Twinkle.

'Then it's about time we found out just who he is,' said Wrinkle, grasping the front of the hooded figure's hood.

Basil, who had now ventured closer, waited. There was something about this hooded figure. Something that wasn't sitting right. Who was he? And why did he remind him of someone?

Wrinkle pulled back the hood.

CHAPTER 105

Percy and Vlad were still walking. The pointer on the compass was still the same size and was not moving from side to side. The mountains still didn't look any closer. And they were still pondering on what the nightmares had told them.

'I wish I knew what they meant,' said Vlad.

'Talking in too many riddles for my liking,' said Percy. 'Why can't they just say what they mean?'

'Light as a feather,' pondered Vlad.

'Weighs nothing,' said Percy.

'And that,' said Vlad.

'And you can fly,' said Percy, rolling his eyes.

'I know,' said Vlad. 'What's that all about?'

They shrugged. They pondered. They walked. The compass stayed the same. The mountains didn't look any closer.

CHAPTER 106

And while Percy and Vlad pondered and walked somewhere, far, far away, a group of nightmares were playing Ludo.

'Back you go,' laughed one of them as his counter landed on someone else's.

'You'd think they'd have worked it out by now,' said another as he took his turn to throw the dice.

'Why don't we just tell them?' said the nightmare, returning his counter to the start.

'Because another attempt at imagination would be lost,' replied the fourth nightmare, 'and there's not a lot of it left.'

'True,' said the nightmare, counting the dots on the dice he had just thrown, 'but it's not exactly rocket science. Eight-nine-home.'

CHAPTER 107

'They seem quite pally, don't they?' observed an other other.

'Didn't see that coming,' said another other other. 'Didn't happen when they arrived and saw us.'

'Yeah, do you remember what the fool of a wizard wanted us to do when he first saw us?'

'Ha-ha, yeah, wanted us all to bow down to him.'

'Soon knocked some sense into him, though, didn't we.'

'The bigfoot did.'

'Shouldn't have been standing so close, should he.'

'Head like a sledgehammer, that bigfoot.'

'Out for two days if I remember right.'

'Never came near us after that.'

'Wonder where he is now?'

'Over there with that other wizard.'

'What? No, not him, the bigfoot.'

'Just a small one now. One of the first he was, you know. Imagination, eh?'

'A small bigfoot?'

'No, just a foot. That's him over there stamping on the one with the smouldering clothes.'

'Oh yeah, I remember now.'

'Strange that they're getting along, though.'

'The foot and the smouldering guy?'

'No, the fool of a wizard and those new ones.'

'Ah, yeah, strange.'

'Look!'

'What?'

'Look.'

'Where?'

'There.'

Both looked. Then some other others did. Then they all were. Even the still unconscious one. Thanks to the kind bystander.

'The big fairy's taking the little weird ones hood off.'

'Blimey.'

There followed a few oohs and ahs.

'Never expected that.'

'Nor did they by the look on their faces.'

'Ha, especially that little new one, looks like his eyes are gonna pop out of his head.'

'First dibs,' said a voice behind them. It was the one with the paws.

CHAPTER 108

'Ay, caramba!' cried Jose.

'Sí,' agreed Pablo.

'Flipping heck!' gulped Danrite, thinking perhaps he *had* seen him before.

'What the!' said Twinkle.

'By the stars!' exclaimed Salor.

'Well, I never,' said Von Vlod.

'Good grief,' said Wrinkle.

'Basil!' yelled Frida. 'Get over here!'

Basil, for his part, was as dumbfounded as everyone else was by what he saw. So dumbfounded was he that he couldn't talk, let alone walk. Frida helped him with that by grabbing him by the arm and pulling him to the front.

'Well?' said Frida sternly. 'Care to explain?'

But Basil just stood there. Stunned. Just staring.

'What's wrong with him?' asked Wrinkle.

'Looks like he's in shock,' said Twinkle.

'I think I would be too, I suppose,' said Wrinkle. 'He wasn't expecting it.'

'Not together then?' guessed Von Vlod.

'I doubt it. Not by his reaction,' said Frida. 'Basil?' Her voice was softer now. But Basil still said nothing.

'Pretending not to know him more like,' muttered Wazzock, who hadn't yet noticed what everyone else had. 'Now look here.' He stared in Basil's face. 'Do you know this hooded creature or not?' He turned as he pointed and stared straight into the face of the unhooded hooded figure. He then stared some more. He looked at Basil again. He looked back at the unhooded hooded figure. The penny then, at last, dropped. 'Ye gads!' he exclaimed. 'Doppelgangers!'

Doubles. Basil and the hooded figure could both be looking in a mirror they were so alike.

'Twins?' ventured Von Vlod.

'Has to be,' said Salor.

'But why is Basil acting like he doesn't know him?' said Twinkle.

'I didn't know Danrite,' said Frida, who had only met her own twin brother, Danrite, at the beginning of their quest. 'But I suppose that doesn't mean *they* don't know each other.'

'How so?' asked Danrite.

'Basil is shocked to see him, but that doesn't mean he doesn't know him,' said Frida. 'He might just be shocked to see him here.'

'Or they are being the sneaky ones,' said Jose.

'Sí,' said Pablo, 'I am with the thinking of the same. They sneaky together.'

'You think they're working together?' said Danrite.

'Sí,' said Jose. 'They are being from one pod, I am thinking.'

'But looking alike doesn't mean they're working together,' said Frida. 'And the only way to find out is to ask them.' And as Basil was still far from making a sentence, Frida turned her attention to the hooded figure.

'Who are you?' Frida demanded.

The hooded figure looked at her and thought about it. He could give her his name, rank and serial number as prisoners did, which he was sure he was, but as he didn't have two of those, it would be a waste of time. So, did he run? He needed the big fairy to let go of him first. But if she did, what then? If he did run, he doubted he would get far. And he didn't like the look of the other others. Some of them looked decidedly hungry. No choice, then. He would have to make his excuses to the Master later. If there was a later. And why were that little dog's teeth so big? He wanted to be free of the fairy first, though. Okay, he thought, here goes.

'Okay,' said the hooded figure, 'I'll tell you, but she needs to put me down first.'

Wrinkle looked at Frida, who nodded and gripped the tazer. Danrite's hand went to his sword. Wrinkle let go of the hooded figure.

The hooded figure straightened his robe and looked up at Frida. 'Thyme. My name is Thyme. As in the herb.'

'Thyme?' murmured Basil. His face contorted. He stared at the hooded figure. 'No!' he suddenly wailed. His shock had turned to horror. For a moment, everyone thought he was going to attack the hooded figure, but the fury on his face, which had looked like erupting into violence, instead erupted into tears. Basil started sobbing like none had sobbed before. Great shoulder heaving sobs.

201

'Grief,' said Danrite. 'What's going on?'

But no one had the slightest clue. Feeling sorry for the little man, Frida put a hand on Basil's shoulder and steered him away. Taking him somewhere where he couldn't see the hooded figure.

'What's his problem?' the hooded figure asked as numerous faces stared at him. 'What?'

'At a guess,' said Wrinkle, 'I'd say it's you.' She grasped the hooded figure by the scruff of his neck again. 'But not only his, I'm thinking.'

'But I told you my name,' protested the hooded figure.

'Yes,' said Wrinkle, 'but not why you're here.'

'Or why you were following them,' said Von Vlod.

'He was what?' snapped Twinkle.

'Sí, and being the spying on us too,' said Pablo.

'Tell us,' demanded Wrinkle, giving the hooded figure a shake.

'Yes,' said Danrite, getting all serious.

Drat, thought the hooded figure. He just knew they would ask that. Why couldn't they keep to the questions he could answer? At least the questions it was safe to answer. The Master wasn't going to like it. And, he doubted, neither would he. From the corner of his eye, he desperately looked for somewhere to run. Perhaps they wouldn't be able to catch him? But the other others were there and were listening and staring. Did he take the chance? Then he caught sight of the foot jumping up and down on its own. It looked angry. Could feet be angry? He decided he didn't want to know. 'Okay-okay,' he said at last.

'Go on,' said Wrinkle.

The hooded figure glared at everybody. 'I was sent to make sure you finished what you came here to do.'

'And what's that?' said Von Vlod.

'Stop the evil, of course. It doesn't matter who, as long as someone does. You four. The new ones.' The hooded figure glanced at the other others. 'Even them.' But he had his doubts about them. 'I had to watch and report back on your progress.' Drat, he hadn't meant to say that last bit.

'To whom?' Wazzock demanded.

'The Font,' said Danrite, suddenly putting two and two together.

It had to be. Basil would find it, and Thyme would be there when they did to make sure they did what they were supposed to do. Even the names, he thought, herbs. They had to be working together. Sadly, the answer he had come up with wasn't four.

'The Font?' frowned the hooded figure. 'Who's the Font?' He knew, had heard of her, but he didn't have to tell them everything. But it wasn't the Font who had sent him.

'The person who sent us here,' said Salor.

'We ask the questions,' said Twinkle, stepping in. She gave Salor a dirty look. She then turned to the hooded figure. 'Who sent you?'

'Fight-fight-fight,' now rang out again from amongst the other others. This time louder, causing heads to turn. To look at the kind bystander, who looked suitably embarrassed. The kind bystander pointed to the unconscious other other. 'It was him again.'

'Sounds like they want to join in,' said Twinkle. And then, there it was: how they would get the hooded one to talk. 'But that's enough,' she said, suddenly straightening up. 'I don't think we'll get any more out of him.'

'No?' Wrinkle was surprised at her fellow fairy giving up so quickly. 'You sure?'

The hooded figure frowned.

'Let me have a word with him,' said Salor.

'No,' said Twinkle, looking at Wrinkle. 'Just have to make sure someone keeps an eye on him for the moment.' Her eyes moved in the direction of the other others.

Wrinkle glanced sideways. The other others? I don't understand, she thought. Then... 'Ah,' she said, finally catching on. 'I suppose you're right. Time is running.'

'But he hasn't said anything yet,' moaned Salor, wondering what was happening.

'He's right, he hasn't,' Wazzock agreed, wondering the same.

'The problem is,' continued Twinkle, ignoring the wizards, 'who's going to do it? He can't stay here. Basil's been upset enough.'

The hooded figure's frown deepened. Something was up.

'I know,' said Wrinkle brightly. 'We could ask the others.'

'The others?' asked Twinkle, all innocent.

'Them over there,' said Wrinkle. She took a step towards the other others. The hooded figure clenched tightly by the scruff of his neck.

'What?' said the hooded figure, going rigid.

'They won't eat him, though, will they?' frowned Twinkle, enjoying her little plan.

'Oh, no,' said Wrinkle. 'Not in one go.' She took another step. The hooded figure attempted to dig his heels in, but they weren't touching the ground.

'Wait!' yelled the hooded figure, all animated. 'I'll tell you what I know.'

'Well,' said Wrinkle, smiling at Twinkle, 'in that case.' She promptly let go of the hooded figure, who dropped and landed in a heap on the ground.

'Ah,' said Salor.

'Ah, indeed,' agreed Wazzock.

'Well done,' whispered Von Vlod.

'All Twinkle,' said Wrinkle.

'Nice one,' whispered Danrite.

Twinkle smiled at him.

'It is being they that are being the sneaky ones,' said Pablo.

'Sí,' said Jose, 'the sneaky ones.'

Twinkle turned her attention back to the hooded figure. 'So,' she said, 'who sent you?'

The hooded figure looked up. 'My master sent me.' He knew when he was beaten. 'The Master.'

Elsewhere, away from the hooded figure, Basil had managed to calm down enough to tell Frida what had upset him so. When he had finished, Frida swore him to secrecy. It would be their little secret until it wasn't. A pleased Basil had agreed. He didn't want anyone else to know why he had been so upset unless they had to.

They returned to the others.

When they returned, Frida was brought up to speed on what the hooded figure had told them. It wasn't a lot. The significant part was the part about him following everyone. That's how he knew about the compass. Otherwise, there was little else. He was in this Otherworld for the same reason they were, and that was about it.

Except he had a master somewhere that was pulling his strings. And it turned out the hooded figure knew little about him either.

It was true. The hooded figure knew little. He hadn't told them everything, though. He wasn't that stupid. But even what he had held back was precious little. The hooded figure really didn't know a lot, and when he thought about it, it worried him.

In return, Frida told everyone what had upset Basil so much. He had been shocked by the sight of the hooded figure and more so when he had heard he was called Thyme. True. You see, she explained, the hooded figure held an uncanny likeness to Basil's long-lost brother. And to make things worse, he had the same name. An awful coincidence. Not true.

And so, after all had been discussed, chewed over and digested, thoughts turned back to the reason they were all there in the first place: to destroy the evil that was destroying imagination.

'Destroy it?' exclaimed Frida on hearing there was some other significant part they should have been told about. 'I thought we were here to stop it. No one mentioned anything about destroying it!'

'Basil said we only had to stop it,' moaned Salor.

'Basil?' Twinkle glared at him.

Basil could only shrug. It was clear that was all they were going to get from him.

'Okay,' said Frida, gathering herself. 'Stop it, destroy it. It doesn't change anything. We still need to do what we have to do to save imagination.'

'She's right,' said Danrite.

'Sí,' said Jose.

'We do what we came here to do,' agreed Wrinkle.

Even Salor agreed although he would prefer not to think about it.

So, now that everyone was on the same page, it was time to do something about it. Continue on. Do what they were there to do.

Frida started the ball rolling. 'I think we should get moving, then.' She glanced at Danrite. 'Okay?'

'If everyone agrees,' said Danrite, pleased he had been asked. The wizards did.

"The dogs" did.

The fairies did.

Everyone did.

Even the hooded figure. Although he hadn't actually been asked. More lifted onto the toe of his boots in readiness.

"Ere,' said an other other, 'they're moving.'

'So they are,' said another other other.

'Hey, everyone, they're moving!' yelled someone.

Heads looked up. Turned. Even the one on the ground who was finally regaining his wits after the snowball incident.

'What do you think happened?' asked one of the more curious of the other others.

'Got fed up with talking, would be my guess,' said some other other other.

'Do you think we should follow them?' said another as it rubbed its paws.

There was a flourish of foot-tapping Morse code.

'Foot says, we always do,' someone decoded.

'Perhaps we should ask the sage now he's lucid.'

'Yellow?'

'Good idea.'

Heads turned again. Most looked up. Only one looked down. That belonged to the sage. He was swaying and mumbling to himself in a language perhaps only vegetables could understand.

'Nope,' said some other other, 'he's gone again.'

'Typical,' said another other other.

'Shall we go then?' said the one with paws.

'Might as well,' said one of the picnickers who had packed it up but a moment ago.

So they did. The other others did what they had been doing for as long as some of them could remember. They followed.

CHAPTER 109

Percy stopped dead in his tracks. But this time, he wasn't being visited by a nightmare.

'Percy?' said Vlad, thinking that was just what Percy was having.

'I just had a thought,' said Percy.

'About what?'

'What the nightmares told us.'

'Go on,' said Vlad, eager to know.

'What if we're thinking about it all wrong? What they said to us, I mean,' said Percy. 'What if we put the nightmares together?'

Vlad gave this some thought. A vampire with a stake and someone peeling potatoes. No. He couldn't see the link. 'How do you mean?'

'Think about it,' said Percy.

Vlad was. He couldn't see a link. He thought harder. Percy's had potatoes in it, and mine had a vampire. Still no link. And then, just like that, it came to him. The vampire had a stake in him. The stake. Of course. Food. Change the stake to steak and the potatoes to chips and… 'They want us to eat something?'

'What?' Percy gave Vlad a puzzled look.

'Steak and chips.'

Okay, thought Percy, not what he was thinking. 'Good thinking,' he said, 'but I was thinking of something else.'

Vlad wasn't all that sure Percy meant it. And the more he thought about it, he could see why. 'Okay. What were you thinking?'

'Well,' said Percy, suddenly afraid his thoughts would sound as ridiculous as Vlad's. Then, going on the idea that nothing could be as absurd as Vlad's idea, he continued. 'What if we put what they told us together? What if we put feather and flying together?'

'We've got to find a bird?'

'What? No.' Percy frowned. 'What I mean is…' He stopped. What he should do, as it was Vlad, was come straight to the point. It would be quicker. 'Look, you can fly, and I'm as light as a feather.'

'And?'

'I think they want you to carry me.'

'Ah,' said Vlad, not really any the wiser. He didn't know how that would help, either. Percy walked faster than he did. He pointed that out.

'Not walk, fly. You carry me as you fly.'

'Good grief,' said Vlad, 'I think you're onto something. Why didn't the nightmares just tell us that?'

'I have no idea,' said Percy. 'Would have been a lot easier. And we could have been on our way by now.'

'So how do we do it?'

'Grab me by my clothes, I suppose.'

'Okay,' said Vlad, thinking it could work. 'Let's give it a go.'

Vlad took off his cloak and handed it and his mirror to Percy. The next second, Vlad was in the air.

'Vlad?'

'Right behind you.'

Vlad hovered for a moment, then swooped and grabbed Percy by his collar as he passed. Percy instantly rose into the air as if he weighed nothing. The cloak and mirror, on the other hand. But it wasn't too bad. Vlad was sure he could handle it.

'Yahoo!' yelled Percy as he soared into the air. 'I'm flying!' He looked down at the quickly receding ground beneath him. 'You know, I think this just might work.'

'Danrite, here we come,' whooped Vlad. He just hoped they weren't already too late.

Below him, Percy already had an eye on the compass. 'Straight as you go, old chap, and full steam ahead.'

'I win!' the nightmare with the blue counters yelled gleefully. He was the Ludo champion, and as he celebrated, news was filtering through from the Otherworld about Vlad and Percy.

'They've only gone and done it!' shouted a nightmare poking his head through the doorway to the games room.

'World peace?' ventured one of the Ludo-playing nightmares without turning round.

'Someone on Mars?' suggested another.

'Don't tell me, someone managed to run trains on tracks with leaves on them?' spouted another. Everyone turned and stared at him. Then laughter.

'Get real,' joked the Ludo champion. He turned to look at the nightmare of news. 'So,' he asked, 'who's done what?'

'Percy and Vlad,' said the nightmare in the doorway. He looked pretty excited. 'They finally worked out what they're supposed to do.'

'Flipping cheese-filled undergarments,' said the nightmare whose only reason for being was just that. 'We had better make ready.'

Chairs were suddenly scattered. Counters and dice knocked to the floor. A mad rush towards the door. A nightmare of a wedge in the doorway. Four nightmares struggling to free themselves.

'In your own time,' said the nightmare of news, leaving them to it.

CHAPTER 111

'Whoops,' wailed Danrite as he slipped again. The path to the evil was getting more and more treacherous. And colder.

'Careful,' said Frida, grabbing Danrite by the arm to steady him.

'It's getting colder,' said Salor, who had wrapped his arms around his chest.

'How much further, I wonder?' wondered Twinkle.

Danrite glanced at the compass. The pointer had nearly doubled in size, and the speed of the flicker had increased. It was getting harder to determine if there was just one or many, so fast was it moving. It was also growing warmer by the minute. Which wasn't such a terrible thing; at least one of his hands was warm. 'We've got to be close,' he said. 'The compass is going crazy. It's getting warm as well.' He passed the compass to his other hand.

Frida looked at it. It looked as if it was going to explode at any moment. 'Careful, Danrite,' she urged. 'Throw it if it starts getting too hot.' She thought it best not to mention the exploding bit. Not yet. 'I think we should prepare ourselves,' she said, taking the tazer from its pouch.

'I am having the big teeth,' said Jose, snarling.

'Sí,' said Pablo, 'I am also being ready with the teeth.' And though they weren't as big as Jose's, his jaw was powerful. His stick looked in danger.

'I have my magic staff,' said Salor, pushing it forward.

'Magic doesn't work here, remember,' Wazzock reminded him. 'It's nothing more than a big stick now.' He wished he still had his big stick.

Salor now wondered if he would be better at the back as the rear guard.

Twinkle made her hands into fists.

Wrinkle did likewise but then opened them again to reveal her fingernails had been replace by talons.

'Cool,' said Twinkle on seeing them.

'I doubt they will do as much as your fists,' said Wrinkle, enviously looking at Twinkle's meaty mitts.

Von Vlod shimmered. The shadowy figure that was Von Vlod

was ready to distract and bewilder the enemy.

Behind them came Basil and the hooded figure. They had daggers, but only to stare at each other with.

And then came the other others. Some ready for anything. Some ready for nothing. One still not talking to a paw. Others wondering what was a foot. Others explaining that it used to be the bigfoot. But all were vigilant. All wary. Ready to fight. Ready to run. It depended.

Danrite pulled his sword from its scabbard. The compass was getting hotter.

None knowing how close they might be to the evil.

They went on. Warily. Watchful. Waiting for the unexpected.

They passed the place where the creature with the unimportant name had lost an eye. They walked up and on. Getting closer. Passed the spot where the creature with the unimportant name had wibbled. Wobbled. Had slithered.

They walked on. They were getting close. Everyone could feel it. Especially Danrite, who could hardly hold onto the compass now, so hot it was becoming. And then.

'I don't like it,' said Salor.

The way ahead had suddenly become more daunting. The ice looked icier. The shadows more sinister. The trees that looked on as if sentries guarding the sides of the path they now trod stood barer. And in the distance. Just visible. Was a cave. Its entrance as black as jet. As black as a pirate's heart. And just as welcoming. Do not come closer, it warned. A scene to dishearten the stoutest of hearts. And some not so.

'Perhaps we should go back,' suggested Wazzock.

But it was too late for that. They had reached the home of the evil. And it was time to deal with it. With or without slightly moistening wizards.

CHAPTER 112

It was close now. The end. But there was one last thing to try.

The creature with the unimportant name slithered, wobbled, and wibbled to the cave entrance.

It had worked before. But would it this time? Wouldn't know until tried. But if it worked again, what then? More time bought? Until the next time. The creature with the unimportant name stopped for a moment. Stopped moving. Perhaps it would be better to get it all over with?

No, he should try. Let fate deal with it. Whatever it was. You see, the creature with the unimportant name didn't know why he was being hunted. Just that he was. He had always run. Had always been chased. Here. But had never asked why.

The creature with the unimportant name looked out. He thought he could see something, someone, in the distance. He had decided. He would try again. He did.

CHAPTER 113

The mountains were now looming large.

'Lower,' yelled Percy as he dangled by his collar.

Vlad flew lower.

'There, to the left, I think I see someone.'

'Yes,' Vlad shouted back. 'Me too.'

'Is it them?'

'I'm not sure.'

'Faster Vlad,' yelled Percy. 'Faster!'

Vlad wasn't sure he could. He was tiring. But, somehow, from somewhere, he managed to.

'Flipping heck!' cried Percy as the other others came into sight first. 'There's loads of them!'

'I told you.'

'And there,' yelled Percy, 'leading them. Is that Danrite?'

'I think you're right.'

Of course, they couldn't really tell who was who. What they were seeing was slightly bigger than ants. Hope did that to you. But they did have them in their sights. But would they be in time?

And then it happened. A thunderous roar that stopped Vlad and Percy in their tracks.

Thor had sounded his defiance. At least that's what people called him. Or something like that. When his name was not unimportant.

CHAPTER 114

The cave loomed larger. More menacing. And if that wasn't enough to make wizards even damper, the thunderous roar that now erupted from it was. Pant-wettingly so!

Behind Danrite, as he and the others covered their ears and took a step back, the other others suddenly realised they had been here before. The situation, that is, not the cave. But not all the other others; just the ones quick on the uptake. And it was they who were lying on the floor with their hands over their ears while spouting garbled nonsense.

"Ere,' said a still standing other other, 'what's wrong with them?'

'No idea,' said another other other.

'They're muttering something,' said some other other.

'Sounds nonsense to me,' said another.

'Agh,' suggested someone. 'But more, aaaaagh!'

'No,' said another, 'sounds like...'

'How many words?'

'Give us a syllable.'

'Not again,' finished another, ignoring the numpties.

'Why are they saying that?'

But before anyone could think of an answer, they had it answered for them. And in no uncertain terms.

The roar gradually faded away, and in its place, a voice now bellowed forth.

'WHO IS IT THAT DARES SET FOOT IN THE LAND OF THOR?' it demanded.

It was deep and booming and came from within the cave.

'Flipping gods of thunder,' exclaimed Twinkle, the roar still ringing in her ears. 'Did I just hear that right?'

'Thor?' said Danrite, proving that she had. 'No one said anything about Thor.' A moment later, he hurriedly dropped the compass. It landed in the snow at his feet, instantly turning it to water. It had become too hot to handle.

Frida grabbed Danrite's hand. 'Are you okay?' She turned it palm up. It was fine.

'Yeah.' Danrite looked down at the compass. 'Look.'

The compass was now melting.

'Looks like we're here,' guessed Frida.

'But it's Thor,' wailed a stricken Salor. 'How are we going to destroy a god?'

'I think we should go,' cried Wazzock, siding with Salor's assessment of the situation. 'We can't destroy Thor.'

Everyone had heard of Thor, it seemed.

'We need to go,' said Salor. The union of wizards was in total agreement.

'We can't,' said Twinkle. 'We have to destroy the evil no matter the cost. We have to save imagination.'

'We have to try,' said Danrite, not feeling as brave as he sounded.

'Sí,' said Jose. 'It is just being a noise.'

'But no,' said Pablo, 'it is being a noise made by a god.' And he knew how powerful they could be. 'We should go.'

'Pablo's right,' said Wrinkle. 'We should go. We can't win.'

'We have to at least try,' said Frida, bewildered by the other's sudden change of heart.

'They're right,' said Von Vlod quietly.

'But why?' said Frida, shaken by Von Vlod agreeing. She had thought, out of all of them, Von Vlod would stay by their side.

Wrinkle looked at the others one by one, and each looked away. 'Because we've been here before,' she said.

'Here, at the cave?' asked Danrite.

'Not the cave,' Wrinkle explained. 'But here, the situation.' Puzzled looks. 'We've faced Thor before.'

'What?' said Twinkle.

'You've already fought him?' said Danrite.

It was Von Vlod who spoke next. Voice as quiet as before. 'No. Already found him.'

And then Frida understood what the others were trying to say. 'You ran away?'

'You heard what he said,' said Wazzock defensively. 'He's Thor. You can't mess with Thor.'

215

'What chance would we have had?' said Von Vlod.

'We are being going to fight another day,' said Pablo, his tail between his legs.

'Pablo's right,' said Wrinkle.

'So, why are you here now?' snapped Frida. 'And why didn't you tell us what you knew?'

Wrinkle had the courtesy to look embarrassed when she answered. 'We never planned to join you. We just wanted to be there if you succeeded in destroying the evil,' she said. 'To see if you were our way out of here.'

Von Vlod chipped in. 'If it weren't for the anomaly, we would have still been following at a distance. We kind of got carried away. Caught up in the moment. Sorry.'

'Sí,' said Pablo. 'We were being in the distance.'

'So, you had no intention of helping us?' snapped an angry Frida. 'You would have let us go on our merry way just to see what would happen to us?'

'It isn't like that,' protested Von Vlod. 'We want to help, but…'

'Then what is it like?' growled Twinkle.

'You heard him,' said Wrinkle. 'The roar.'

'And it's Thor,' said Wazzock.

'Sí,' said Pablo. 'We were being frightened.'

'It was frightening,' admitted Salor. He, out of all of them, could understand their reluctance.

Frida sighed. It had been the most frightening sound she had ever heard. But they had a job to do. God of thunder or no god of thunder, they had to try to save imagination. Otherwise, what was the point? And this time, they had something else – they had two heroes amongst them.

'Okay,' said Frida, coming to a decision. 'You can stay here and watch what happens. But we're going on.'

'Too right,' said Danrite.

'What he said,' said Wrinkle, glaring at the others.

Salor looked at the others and then at his friends. They were his friends. He gripped his staff. 'What she said.' Oh dear, he thought.

'And me,' said Basil, surprising everyone. He didn't care anymore.

'And me,' said the hooded figure. 'I want to be there to make

216

sure things get done this time.' He gave Wrinkle and the others a long, disdainful look.

'If you must,' said Frida, who then looked down to see where Jose was. She had expected a tail-swishing comment by now. He was usually the first. But he wasn't there. Between everyone's feet like he always was. That was strange. 'Jose?'

But Jose had heard enough and was already halfway to the cave. The Font had said that he, too, would be a hero. His time would come. This was it, he had decided. He didn't want his friends hurt. He swished his tail. The Black Knight would destroy the evil and save his friends and imagination.

All of the other others were on the ground now. The uptake had been well and truly taken up. And while they had been lying there, a meeting of sorts had convened and votes taken. The sorts and results were as follows:

Those who wanted to run for it. The one with the paws was the ringleader. After he had spoken to the fifth one, and it had promised not to trip him up. The other four who had voted to run wore pointy hats of the wizard variety. *Five.*

Those that were quite happy to stay where they were and pretend that they weren't. *Four.*

Those who didn't have the faintest idea what was going on, let alone why they were lying on the ground. *Two.*

Those who were kind bystanders and liked sitting on the fence. As long as it wasn't electric. *One.*

Those who liked sitting on electric fences. *One.*

Those that were concussed. *One.*

Those who wanted to have another picnic. *Two.*

Those that were Someone Else. *One.*

Those who would do anything for a laugh. The foot was one. *Eight.*

Those who were the sage. Who should have been in the haven't the faintest idea what was going on sort, but was disallowed as he was sometimes lucid. *One.*

And finally, those that still had a modicum of derring-do. *Thirteen.* Unlucky for some.

The result of the meeting would be announced as soon as

someone remembered what the meeting had been about.

'Jose!' yelled Twinkle. 'Come back!'

'Oh, good grief,' said Frida, realising what the little chihuahua was up to. 'Come on.' Frida ran.

Danrite and Twinkle were hot on her heels. Salor was also there, but he was more warm on them. Basil followed, and the hooded figure was not far behind.

'Look!' shouted the other other who had been unconscious from his vantage point on the ground, which was also, then, at that moment, everyone else's. 'The little dog's heading for the cave!'

Everyone looked. Saw the new ones following. Saw the others just standing there, like all of them before them had done. Another vote, a quick one, was taken. This time, it was unanimous. This time, they weren't going to just stand there and watch.

Still smarting from the look the hooded figure had given them, the others watched with disbelief as the other others started to advance towards them.

'Good grief,' said Wrinkle. 'Where are they going?'

'I-I think they're going to help,' stammered Von Vlod, glancing at the others. 'As I think should we.' Von Vlod started to move.

'Sí,' said Pablo, 'I am being thinking the same. I am no longer wanting to be being a scaredy-xolo. I go.' Pablo started to trot after Von Vlod. A trot that soon picked up pace.

'Yes,' said Wrinkle. 'Yes, we should. Wazzock?'

'By your side,' said Wazzock, hitching up his robe to knee high as he readied to run. Jog. He hoped he wouldn't get a cramp.

And now a horde was heading for the cave.

A cave that Jose had abruptly stopped a couple of metres short of. He now slowly crept forward. He had been expecting another roar. Thor. Thunder. A noise. But not this noise. A low noise. A sad noise. A sobbing noise. He stopped again.

Someone inside the cave was crying.

Something inside the cave was moving.

CHAPTER 115

The creature with the unimportant name had tried his best, but it looked like it wasn't enough this time.

He waited. He watched the little creature, the creatures behind it, moving closer and closer to his home. This was the end then. But at least it would all be over at last. A tear trickled down his cheek. And perhaps he would at last find out why. Why he had been hounded so for so long. It wasn't as if he had done anything wrong. At least, he didn't think he had. Couldn't remember doing so. He let out a little sob. He should go out. Meet them. Hold his head up high. But that wasn't easy when you were crying. But it was time.

Taking a deep breath that made a funny sound as it mingled with a sob, the creature with the unimportant name straightened up as best he could and headed outside to meet his fate.

CHAPTER 116

'Whoa!' cried Frida, holding up a hand as she caught up with the stationary Jose. Something was moving in the cave.

'I am being hearing the crying,' said Jose as Frida appeared by his side.

'Crying?' said Frida. 'I can't hear anything.'

'No, it is being stopping now. But I am also smelling smell,' said Jose.

Pablo sidled up beside them. 'Sí, I am also smelling it. It is being smelly.' He snorted.

No one else could, but no one else in the advance group, which now included the others, had the noses of Jose and Pablo. Some of the other others had, but they weren't close enough yet.

'What smell?' said Danrite, sniffing the air.

'It is being yellow,' said Jose.

'Sí,' said Pablo, 'it is most definitely being yellow.'

'How is yellow a smell?' said Frida.

'Yellow like straw,' said Jose.

'Sí,' said Pablo, 'straw.'

No one was the wiser, but judging by Jose and Pablo's twitching noses, the smell they could smell didn't appear to be a pleasant one.

Whatever had been moving in the cave now lingered in its mouth. The shadows hiding it.

'Steady,' warned Frida as those behind moved closer. 'We don't know what we're up against.'

'Der,' said Twinkle, 'I'm sure I heard Thor mentioned.'

'Could just be a ploy,' said Frida. 'Someone or something trying to scare us away.'

And doing a darn fine job of doing it, thought Salor.

'What's that?' said Von Vlod.

'Sounds like someone crying,' said Danrite.

'Sí,' said Jose, 'it is what I am hearing before.'

'Someone doesn't sound happy,' said Wrinkle.

'Could be a trap,' said Wazzock. 'False sense of security and the like. And then pounce.' He made with a pouncing movement that made Salor jump. 'Sorry.'

'Sounds genuine to me,' decided Frida. 'That's real sobbing going on in there.'

'Real as ever I heard,' said Von Vlod.

'Perhaps it's a prisoner?' said Salor, wits recovered.

'Maybe,' said Frida.

'Look,' cried Danrite. 'Somethings coming out.'

Everyone tensed.

The something moved from the shadows into full view.

'Flipping snowballs,' gasped Twinkle.

'What the...?' said Wrinkle.

'Yellow,' said Frida. She didn't know what else to say.

'Sí,' said Jose, 'it is the smelling yellow.'

'It's yellow,' said Von Vlod.

'It's a snowman,' said Danrite, hardly believing his eyes.

'Made of yellow snow,' said Basil.

'Sí,' said Pablo. 'It is being the yellow smelly snow.'

'Ye gads!' said Wazzock.

'Grief,' sniffed Salor, wrinkling his nose.

'It's a yellow snowman,' said Twinkle.

'But is it a prisoner or Thor in disguise?' said Salor. A strange disguise, perhaps, but one never knew.

'I told you, it's trying to lull us,' said Wazzock.

'We don't know that there is a prisoner.' said Wrinkle.

'But if it is, where's Thor,' said Danrite. His sword drawn.

'Easy now,' warned Frida. 'Prisoner or Thor, there's evil here, and we have to destroy it.'

'She's right,' said the hooded figure, seeing his chance to finish things. 'Whatever it is, we have to destroy it.'

'He's right,' agreed Basil through gritted teeth, still with the staring daggers. He didn't want to agree with anything the Thyme creature said, but it was true. 'We have to destroy it.'

But no one moved. It was a snowman, for goodness sake. Yellow snow, yes. Not nice. You wouldn't want a snowball made of it to hit you. But evil?

'We should talk to it,' suggested Von Vlod.

'It's a trap, I'm telling you,' said Wazzock.

'But it's yellow,' said Twinkle. 'It's yellow.'

'I see that,' said Frida, watching the sobbing, yellow creature carefully. She needed to think.

'What do we do?' asked Danrite, sword wavering.

Frida looked at the quivering mass of yellow snow. What did they do? The compass came to mind. They had followed it this far. Her throat was dry. It was their mission. It was why they were there. She came to a half-hearted decision. 'We destroy it... I suppose,' she whispered back. What else could they do? But she wasn't sure. The yellow. Why was it the only thing in this Otherworld in colour?

Basil, who had slipped beside Frida, heard her say destroy it. 'Yes,' he said. 'Destroy it.'

'Yes!' shrieked the hooded figure, pushing his way to the front. 'Destroy it!'

Frida looked at Danrite. At Twinkle. The others. Basil. The hooded figure. The hooded figure? 'Wait!' she suddenly shouted. Who was he? Who was his master? Why was he so keen to destroy the evil? Why did its master want the same as the Font? Something suddenly didn't feel right. An old saying then came to mind: if in doubt...

'We wait,' said Frida. 'We wait and see what the snowman has to say.' She hoped she was right. She turned to Danrite and whispered for his ears only this time. 'Have your sword ready.' He nodded.

'NO!'

Heads turned at the sudden shout that had come from amongst the other others.

It was the sage. He was lucid. He was angry. He no longer wanted to be a stem of broccoli. He wanted to be wise again. He wanted to go home.

'We must destroy it! NOW!' The sage started to charge towards the yellow snowman.

CHAPTER 117

Having recovered from the surprise of Thor's roar, Vlad and Percy were making their descent.

'Good grief! Look at that,' yelled Percy as they closed in. 'The thing coming out of the cave.'

Vlad turned his attention from seeking a landing spot to look. He did a double-take. 'Is that what I think it is?' he yelled back.

'I believe it is!' yelled Percy. 'And if I'm not mistaken, I believe it's the evil we have to save.'

They got lower, so they got closer.

'Doesn't look evil,' shouted Vlad.

'That's because it isn't,' yelled Percy. 'It's evil's, evil!'

Down they went.

They were now coming in to land. Vlad still looking for a place to put down. Somewhere between the snowman and the advancing would be destroyers if he could. He would have to be quick, though. The space was disappearing fast.

'They've stopped!' yelled Percy. 'Look, there's Danrite.'

'What?' said Vlad. Percy was right. The advance on the snowman had stopped. Vlad headed for the space he had had his eye on. 'Hold tight!' warned Vlad. 'I'm going in!'

'We're going to do it!' yelled Percy. 'Wait, what's that?' Percy had caught movement. Something was leaving the ranks of the larger group.

Vlad slowed. He looked. 'Flipping vegetables!' he cried. 'I think it's a stem of broccoli.'

They had seen the sage setting off on his rampage.

'It's heading for the snowman!' yelled Percy. 'We need to do something!'

Sage, the lucid, was moving fast. Fast for a vegetable. But fast enough to reach Frida, Danrite, and the others and scatter them before they could do anything to stop him in his quest to destroy the snowman. The evil.

'We've got to stop him!' shouted Vlad.

'Drop me on it!' yelled Percy.

'What?' shouted Vlad, thinking he had misheard.
'Drop me! It's the only way!' yelled Percy.
'Okay!' Vlad headed for it. 'Hang on.'
Vlad swooped.
Percy dropped.

CHAPTER 118

'Watch out!' warned Twinkle as the sage surged towards them.

But he was upon them before anyone could move. He barged through; the only thing on his mind was destroying the evil.

It was Frida who reacted quickest. Rising quickly, she went for the tazer, aiming to stop the crazy other other in his tracks. But it wasn't needed. As she had taken aim, something had fallen from the sky.

Percy made contact.

Sage the broccoli, and his plan suddenly went sideways.

'What the heck?' cried Twinkle.

'Giddy gads,' cried Salor, who was on his knees.

'Percy?' said Danrite, first to realise who it was that had suddenly appeared out of the blue and knocked the other other over. 'Percy!' He couldn't believe his eyes. More so when Danrite then remembered his uncle was dead. 'Percy?' he whispered.

'Percy?' said Von Vlod. 'Who's Percy?'

'A good question,' said Frida, recognising the man who had fallen from out of nowhere as hers and Danrite's late uncle. Danrite had shown her a photo. Or, as the Font had said, just an avatar she had created. She started towards him. She wanted a word with this ghost, or non-existent man, or whatever. She wanted to know what the heck was going on.

The other others had stopped and were looking on, stunned, with ever-increasing puzzlement. Never had they been so quiet. What had just happened? Someone had fallen out of the sky and knocked over the sage, that's what. They now watched as the girl in the shorts walked over to where the sky-faller had landed. The one with the paws tripped over its fifth one.

The others were gathering together in a group. Like the other others, they were at a total loss as to what had just happened. In their midst was the hooded figure, the toes of his boots barely touching the ground. Wrinkle had thought it for the best. Like the other others, they stood and watched as Frida marched over to whoever had fallen from the sky.

The creature with the unimportant name, the snowman, Thor, the evil, the destroyer of imagination, all of the above, perhaps, left to his own devices for the moment, stopped crying and began to smooth over the small furrows in his face they had caused. As he did, he wondered what had just happened. More so, he was wondering how he was still in one piece. Even more so, he was wondering about his next move.

Frida arrived to confront the so-called Percy a moment or two before Danrite did, so she bumped into him as she stepped back. The cloak Percy was wearing was detaching itself. Rising. Then floating. Eventually, stopping to hover a few inches from the ground.

'Vlad?' uttered Twinkle on recognising the cloak. By her side were Jose and Salor.

'Sí,' said Jose. 'It is being Vlad. I am smelling him.'

'I don't believe it,' said Salor.

But believe it, he had to. It was Vlad, and he had a story to tell.

'What's going on?' asked Wazzock, staring at the floating cloak.

'No idea,' said Wrinkle. 'Do you?' She shook the hooded figure. He said nothing. He knew nothing. He kept his eyes focused on the ground. Wrinkle tutted.

'I think they know it,' said Von Vlod.

'The cloak?' said Wazzock.

'They seemed to be talking to it,' said Von Vlod.

'Danrite's going over to the chap that fell out of the sky,' noted Wazzock.

'You're quiet, Pablo,' said Wrinkle.

'Sí,' he said.

'Sí?' said Wrinkle. 'Is that all you're going to say?'

'Sí,' said Pablo. 'No. I am being watching the smelly snowman. It is stopping with the crying.'

They glanced over at it. It looked as if it was thinking.

The other others didn't know what to think. So, instead, they built another fire. A picnic basket was reopened. A paw had a tongue lashing. And some other others began to smoulder. And, when all this was done, they watched and waited.

Vlad told his tale but not before gently ushering all away from Danrite and Percy. His news that the snowman wasn't evil was a welcome relief, even though there were now more questions than answers. But before anything could be acted on, a different topic needed to be discussed: The Percy situation.

It was a part of Vlad's story that needed Danrite not to be there. It was delicate. So, they had left him talking to his late uncle. No harm in that as things stood. Danrite didn't know that the Font had told everyone else that Percy was not real, just an avatar. To Danrite, Percy had always been a living, breathing person.

'So, he thinks he's a ghost?' said Twinkle, meaning Percy.

'He does,' said Vlad.

'Nothing about being an avatar?' said Frida.

'Not a murmur,' said Vlad.

'And everyone's sure Danrite doesn't know about Percy supposedly being an avatar?' asked Frida.

'As far as I know,' said Twinkle.

'Salor?'

'I've never said anything,' said Salor defensively.

'Si,' said Jose. 'I am saying nothing also.'

'Nor me,' said Vlad.

'Good, let's keep it that way,' said Frida. 'At least for now.' Everyone agreed.

'Wait a minute?' said Twinkle. 'What about Basil?'

Frida had forgotten about him.

Basil, who had been hanging around betwixt and between the others and the scene unfolding around the stem of broccoli, not knowing what to think or do, was called over.

The question was asked. Basil said he had hardly spoken to

Danrite, so no, he hadn't told him what the Font had said.

'Right,' said Frida, 'until we know what is really going on with Percy, Percy will remain a ghost. All agreed?'

All agreed.

'Okay,' said Twinkle, 'I'm thinking it's time we talked to that snowman.'

'Sorry,' said Frida, 'but there's something else I need to say while Basil's here.' She turned to the little man. He looked worried. 'I think it's time you told everyone else what you told me earlier. About that hooded creature Thyme.'

A worried Basil looked like he was caught between crying again or running. But he did neither and told all he had told Frida. Frida told them all not to say anything.

'They're coming over,' said Wazzock.

Frida thought it best to share what Vlad had told them about the evil with the others.

'Not evil?' exclaimed Von Vlod.

'A ghost?' puzzled Wazzock.

'A friendly one,' said Vlad.

'You're a vampire?' said Von Vlod to the floating cloak.

'I am,' said Vlad. Von Vlod reddened a little. No one could tell.

'Now what do we do?' asked Wrinkle, raising a familiar question.

'We talk to the snowman, I guess,' said Frida. 'See if it knows why we were sent to destroy it.'

'What about them?' Twinkle nodded at the other others.

'They'll come and have a look if they want to,' said Wrinkle.

'You know best,' said Salor, not sure he wanted them anywhere near if that crazy stem of broccoli was anything to go by.

'Ready then?' asked Frida.

'Ready,' said Wrinkle.

Frida led, collecting Danrite and an excited Percy – eager to greet his old friends again – on the way. They came to a halt at what they thought was a safe hailing distance from the snowman. Frida spoke to him.

The creature with the unimportant name had watched nervously

228

since the big, tall thing had tried to attack him. Thank goodness that man had fallen from the sky when he had. He now watched with even more trepidation as the man from the sky headed toward him, led by a girl in shorts. Her legs must be really cold, he thought. He grimaced. Why was he thinking about things like that at a time like this?

This is it, he now thought as the group got closer. He tried to close his eyes, but of course, he couldn't. But they stopped a good two metres or so away from him. He was confused. What now?

'Phewie,' grumbled Salor.

'Sorry,' said the creature with the unimportant name.

'It's not your fault,' said Frida, glaring at Salor. It wasn't the first word she had hoped would be spoken.

'Sorry,' said Salor, looking suitably embarrassed.

'I should think so,' whispered Twinkle. 'What if he is Thor?'

Salor took on a paler complexion. He hadn't thought of that. He tried to shuffle backwards but couldn't because Wazzock was close behind him.

'He is being smelly though,' whispered Jose to Pablo.

'Si,' said Pablo, whispering back. 'He is being double smelly.'

'I'm sorry about that,' said Frida. 'My name's Frida. Are you Thor?'

'I am,' said the creature with the unimportant name, thinking how nice it was to hear his name spoken again after all this time stuck in this Otherworld.

Poor thing, thought Frida, who just couldn't help feeling sorry for him. From a god to a smelly yellow snowman. It must be awful. She thought it was the worst case of a lack of imagination she had seen. Apart from perhaps the broccoli creature. She gave him a sad smile. 'And you were once the God of thunder,' she sighed. 'So sad.' Behind her, several gasps were heard.

'Used to be? What?' said the creature with the unimportant name, wondering what the girl in the shorts was talking about. God of thunder? He looked puzzled, which wasn't easy, considering his face was made of snow.

'Oh my gosh, sorry,' muttered a horrified Frida, suddenly aware

229

she had spoken out loud. 'I didn't mean... My bad.' Why had she done that? And, snowman or not, she realised, he would still be thinking of himself as the God of thunder. 'I mean, of course, you are, still are, the God of thunder,' she quickly corrected. 'I didn't mean... Sorry.' Upsetting the God of thunder might not be the best idea. Behind her, breath was being held.

The creature with the unimportant name still looked puzzled. 'No,' he said.

'No?' said Frida, wondering what he meant. 'Sorry, I-er, I don't understand.'

No one behind did either. Lots of puzzled looks were going on.

'No, I'm not,' the creature with the unimportant name attempted to explain.

'Not?' said Frida, now wondering if she had missed something.

'Not what you said,' said the creature with the unimportant name, wary but trying to be helpful.

What did I say? thought Frida. Oh, she then thought. Good grief. 'You're not Thor?' she said. Perhaps the snowman was a prisoner, after all.

'Yes... I am,' said the creature with the unimportant name.

'Then...?' Frida was struggling.

At that moment, Percy sidled up to help. 'I think he means he's not the God of thunder.'

'Not the God of thunder?' stammered Twinkle. 'Then why bellow Thor if it isn't your name?'

'It is my name,' said the creature with the unimportant name. He was trying hard not to get upset.

'Then, if you're not the God of thunder, as you say,' said Salor, 'who are you?'

The creature with the unimportant name told him.

'So,' said Danrite, trying to understand, 'you're Thor the snowman? You just have the same name as the God of thunder?'

'No,' groaned the creature with the unimportant name, now slightly exasperated. As was everyone to a certain degree. 'It's Thaw,' he said. Blank looks. 'T...H...A...W. Thaw.'

'Oh!' went a chorus of voices.

'We thought you meant Thor,' said Danrite. 'T...H...O...R.'

'No, just Thaw... the snowman,' said Thaw, relieved they were there at last. Thor, he thought. He had an internal titter. Me, the God of thunder, he thought. Titter. Even he knew who Thor was. Oh, he then thought. Another thought had struck. He had suddenly caught onto why everyone may have run away when he had shouted his name all those other times. Cool, he thought.

And, with the creature with the unimportant name now named, it turned out that his name wasn't important. Except to Thaw. Though, why anyone would call a creature made from snow Thaw was just beyond to some. Cruel even. But a name it was. An old English name. Saxon and the like. A boy's name. Oddly enough, it did mean, mostly, melt. So, Salor said.

With the Thaw or Thor saga over, the conversation turned to the idea the nightmares had had to save imagination. Did Thaw know anything about that?

The answer, in short, was no. Thaw didn't even know why everyone was looking for him.

'Well, at least he's not dangerous,' remarked Wrinkle to the huddle that had now formed away from the snowman.

'But it doesn't help us solve the problem of saving imagination,' said Frida.

'If only the nightmares were here,' said Danrite.

'At last,' said a nightmare, his remark totally unconnected to Danrite's.

'We had better get going,' said another nightmare.

'No time like the present,' said another.

And so they went.

A whole gaggle of them.

One for each.

Even though they were all awake.

It was an emergency.

CHAPTER 119

The nightmares arrived.

Danrite, Frida, Twinkle, Salor, Vlad, Jose, and Basil suddenly stood stock still, their eyes closing. Eyes closed.

The same happened to the others and then the other others. Even the hooded figure known as Thyme.

All were standing as if waiting for something to happen.

Oh, and the other other with the playing cards. He, too, was the same. Where he was, though, gawd only knew guv'nor.

'What's happening?' said Thaw to the only other person who wasn't in some sort of trance.

'It's the nightmares,' said Percy, wondering if they had somehow heard what Danrite had said and why he wasn't being visited. 'Those who had the idea.'

'Those?' said Thaw, a tad uneasy. Those with the idea. Then it struck him that he didn't actually know what a nightmare was. He thought he had better ask. 'What's a nightmare?'

Percy told him.

'Oh,' said Thaw, 'I don't think I've ever had one of those.'

'Never?' said Percy. There was no answer. He looked at Thaw and smiled. It appeared that had just changed. Thaw's frozen face had taken on a glazed look. More cake than snowman now. Then it was Percy's turn.

'Hi,' said the potato-peeling nightmare that was Percy's, 'sorry for the wait.' It then explained why Percy was the last. 'Had to make sure we were all synced before I joined.'

'What does that mean?' asked Percy.

'We wanted to make sure everyone has their nightmare at the same time so we could make a link between us.'

'You can do that?' Percy was astounded.

'Only in an emergency,' said Percy's nightmare. 'And before you ask, don't.'

'Okay,' said Percy, wondering what that meant. But he didn't ask.

'Right,' said Percy's nightmare, 'it looks like it's a go. Time to reveal our plan to save imagination.'

Instantly, as if someone had flicked a switch, nightmares appeared to all.

'Oh, hello,' said Thaw to his nightmare.

'I'm supposed to speak first,' said the nightmare.

'Oh, sorry.'

'No harm done.' The nightmare frowned. 'This your first nightmare, isn't it?' he asked.

'Yes,' said Thaw, who appeared to be enjoying the moment. Nightmares, it seemed, weren't as bad as Percy had made them out to be.

'Ah,' said the nightmare, who had been wondering why he wasn't the snowman.

'It's lovely,' said Thaw.

'Shouldn't be,' said the nightmare.

'But it is,' said Thaw.

In Thaw's nightmare, the sky was blue. The sun was shining. It was warm. A lovely day. Even if the sun was talking to him.

'Wow,' enthused Thaw, 'It's so real. Look, I'm sweating.'

'No, you're not,' said the nightmare.

'But I am,' said Thaw. 'Look.' A large drip fell from his nose. Any moment now, thought the nightmare.

'Oh,' said Thaw as now his nose fell off. 'What's happening?'

'You're melting,' said the nightmare.

'No!' squealed Thaw.

'Now you're getting it,' said the nightmare.

'But I don't want to melt,' wailed Thaw.

'And there you have it,' smiled the nightmare. 'You're having a nightmare.'

'I want it to stop,' wailed Thaw. 'I want to wake up!'

'And so you will in a moment,' promised the nightmare. 'But first, I need to tell you what is about to happen.' Later, he would explain to Thaw that he, the nightmare, would be the snowman in further nightmares. It helped.

The nightmare filled him in. As did all the other nightmares with their hosts.

233

So, the nightmares told what they knew. They had discovered the existence of Thaw quite by chance, through a dream they knew. Until then, they had all but given up hope of imagination being saved. But the knowledge of Thaw's existence had changed all that.

The dream had belonged to a worrier. A worrier of plans failing. A worrier of one particular plan failing. The plan to destroy imagination forever.

In the dream was an Otherworld where raw, untapped imagination existed, waiting to grow into a thought or an idea that would then leak into Otherworlds to become the source of stories, adventures, and even inventions. An Otherworld of colour. Rainbows. All things bright and cheerful. It was the seeding bed of all imagination.

A secret Otherworld, until its discovery. Discovered by a creature who despised all that the world of imagination stood for. An Otherworld it dreamed of destroying.

But one small piece of colour still survived. Had dodged and eluded the creature. Found somewhere to hide. This colour. This yellow. This yellow snowman. This Thaw. And until it was found and destroyed, there was still a chance. A chance, imagination could be saved.

And then the nightmares were gone.

Sadly, because of dream and nightmare rules, no one was allowed to know whose dream it was. The name of the dreamer could not be named. No, not even if everyone had their fingers crossed behind their backs and stood on one foot. It was a secret never to be told.

'What the!' cried Danrite as he woke up. His nightmare had been the one where he was wearing a dress and looked like his sister. Which he would, them being twins. He quickly glanced across at Frida, half expecting her to be looking at him. She wasn't. She had her business face on. Relief. Why he had thought she would know what his nightmare was about, he didn't know. But relief all the same.

Everyone else now awake, Frida took control of the situation.

'Right people!' called Frida, loosely covering everyone. 'Are we all on the same page?'

It appeared they were, including the other other with the playing cards. Not that he could do anything about anything, wherever it was he was. He frowned, then continued with his game of patience.

'Good,' said Frida in a loud voice.

They now knew, even though it had been there right in front of their faces, where and what the colour was that the nightmares had earlier mentioned.

'But where are we going to get the magic from?' asked Wazzock, knowing magic didn't exist in this Otherworld.

It was the question on everyone's lips.

And it was the weak link in the nightmares plan.

So, the plan.

Save the colour. This had been done. It should be noted that it wasn't Thaw that was being hunted but the colour. No one knew this except the ones that did. Thaw had always thought it was he everyone was after. And as time went by, Thaw gradually grew to believe he had always been that colour. But everyone knows snow is white until it's not. You have to turn snow yellow. Ugh. And the yellow, knowing this, used it to protect itself. Who wanted to go near yellow snow? And, after a while, had added the smell to complete the disguise.

The next step, when step one was achieved, which it had, is to spread the colour and imagination back into the Otherworld it existed in. And once that was done, the nightmares would spread the colour and imagination back into other Otherworlds. How?

Through magic, that's how.

To begin with.

And then it would be spread throughout the Otherworlds by pleasant dreams and happy nightmares. Something the Nightmare Union wasn't so sure about. But.

And that was the plan. A plan that came up short. Because magic was needed. To mix with the colour to give it a boost. To help it grow again. To create rainbows. An explosion of magical rainbows that would fill this Otherworld with colour and imagination again. To pass, as it had before, the colour and imagination to Otherworlds. BUT. Magic doesn't exist in this world.

Or does it?

CHAPTER 120

The hooded figure's master was sat brooding, staring at the talky-walky.

There was still no contact from the minion. Why not? It was worrying. Where was the little fool? What was he up to? What had he done? Should have gone myself. No point thinking that now. Too late. Or was it? Perhaps. Maybe. But surely something should have happened by now?

Outside, the night was giving nothing away.

CHAPTER 121

The Font was restless and shifted uneasily in her chair.

Why had she still not heard from Basil? Had something gone wrong? Was imagination saved? Should have gone herself. Perhaps. Maybe. No point worrying about that now. She would have to wait. Sit and wait.

No, she couldn't do that. Not without popcorn, at least. The Font rose from her chair and went to get some.

Outside, the day got on with its own business.

CHAPTER 122

'You sure your staff doesn't work?' asked Frida hopefully. A little desperately.

'Dead as a doornail,' said Salor. 'As empty as schoolboy's bottle of pop. As useless as—'

'Okay,' said Twinkle, cutting Salor off. 'We get the idea.'

'Er-hmm.' A polite cough.

'What about you?' said Frida to the others. 'Got any magic tucked away?'

'If only,' said Wrinkle. 'Sadly, Wazzock's staff is no more. And it was useless anyway.'

'Rude,' said Wazzock.

'Er-hmm,' coughed someone a second time and just as politely.

'What about you, Danrite?' said Von Vlod. 'You're the hero. Is there anything hero-ish brewing?'

Danrite shrugged. 'I don't think so,' he said.

'Frida?' said Twinkle. 'Any magical-hero vibe?' It was thought that Frida had the edge over Danrite when it came to being magical.

Frida had never felt the urge to see if she did. Perhaps now would be a good time to try. Nope, not at the moment. 'Nope,' she said.

'OI!' shouted someone impatiently. They had tried to be polite.

The shout had the desired effect. Everyone turned to see who was making all the noise.

Standing, not a metre away, was an other other. And beside that other other, another other other. And beside that other other was another.

'Hello?' said Frida, a little taken aback by the sudden closeness of the weirdness that was the other others.

'We might know something,' said the other other, who had tried to be polite and who happened to be the one with the paws. It had overcome its dispute with its fifth paw, and so all was now hunky-dory on the paw front.

'I doubt it,' whispered Wazzock over his shoulder to Salor. 'That one looks like a sheep.'

"Ere, I heard that. I'm not a sheep,' replied the other other with paws. 'I have paws.'

'He does,' said one of his fellow other others.

'And sheep don't have paws,' chipped in the other other.

'Yes,' said Wazzock. 'But you know what I mean?' He was looking for support. None came.

'Ignore him,' said Wrinkle. 'Now, what is it you might know?' He is pretty woolly, though, thought Wrinkle, as she asked. If it is a he. But sheep don't have paws. Or a beak, for that matter.

'Go on,' urged the other other that most definitely could not be mistaken for a sheep. 'Tell them.' There were curious stares sent its way.

The one with paws noticed. 'She used to be a mermaid.' He glanced sideways at his friend, who nodded stiffly. 'But now she's more fishfinger.'

The mermaid smiled a smile that was fishfingerish. Everyone smiled back.

'And he's a changeling,' Paws explained as he introduced his friend, the milkmaid.

'But I can't control it anymore. Oops,' said the small horse.

'Poor things,' said Von Vlod, who hadn't realised how hard it was for the other others. At least Von Vlod was just a shadow. A shadow of Von Vlod's former self. A shadow that Von Vlod might cast when standing in sunlight. Which, of course, Von Vlod was not able to, not if Von Vlad didn't want to burst into flames while doing so. But at least a shadow that didn't keep changing. Small mercies.

'Sí,' said Jose, 'they are being poor things. That one is being a smelly poor thing.'

'Jose,' snapped Twinkle. 'Don't be so rude.'

'It's okay,' said the fishfinger thing. 'He's right. I'm fishy. It goes with the territory.'

'Sí,' said Jose, 'it is what I am saying. I am not being a mean one.'

'All very nice,' said Percy, suddenly butting in. 'But what is it you think you know?' He was all for the charming chitty-chat in the right place but felt this might not be it. Not at the moment.

Two of the other others looked at the third and nodded.

'We think we know where some magic is.'

'You do?' said Wrinkle, finding it hard to contain the sudden flicker of hope she had felt.

'Yes,' said paws.

'Where?' asked Percy.

'There.' The small horse pointed a hoof at Pablo.

'Pablo?' said Wazzock.

Pablo, who had been doing his best to ignore what was going on until that moment, looked up from the stick he had been happily chewing on when he heard his name. '¿Qué,' he said with a wary look. Pablo would often slip into his native Spanish when he didn't want to be disturbed.

'Not him,' said paws. 'His stick.'

Pablo looked from Percy to all the others that were staring at him. He instinctively pulled his stick closer to him with a paw. Was that a sheep?

'But that's just part of my old staff,' smiled Wazzock. 'No magic there.' He gave a little guffaw. He knew about magic.

'It sparked,' said the fishfinger thing.

'Blue ones,' said paws.

'Yes,' said the one who had been a milkmaid and then a small horse but was now a picture of better days. Oil on canvas. 'And his hair had stood on end.'

Everyone now stared at the stick.

'It is being mine,' growled Pablo. He wondered if perhaps he should bury it somewhere. He glanced at the cave.

'Blue, you say,' said Percy. 'If that's true, then this stick could be our salvation. That, or very dangerous. Very dangerous indeed.'

Pablo was now thinking of burying it for different reasons.

'That's true,' said Salor. He could be a buffoon at times, but he knew one or two things about magic. 'Can anyone tell me just how it was broken?'

'He was in a temper,' said Wrinkle.

'Smashed it on the ground,' said Von Vlod.

Pablo said nothing. He was still thinking what to do with his stick.

'So, it was broken violently?' said Salor.

'And a bit,' said Wrinkle. She looked at Wazzock. 'Toy wouldn't work, so boy throws a hissy-fit.'

'Then,' said Salor, puffing out his chest. 'There could be magic in that stick.'

241

'How?' asked Danrite, beating everyone to the punch.

Now the centre of attention, Salor played to his audience. 'If a staff is broken.' Pause for dramatic effect. 'And quickly.' Pause. 'Violently.' A rub of his beard. 'Sometimes,' he waved a finger. Pause. 'And I do mean sometimes.' Another pause. A look down and up again, hand back on beard. 'Then.'

'Oh, for goodness sake, get on with it,' snapped Twinkle.

'Yeah,' begged Frida. 'Please.'

Salor pouted but continued. 'Sometimes, a fragment of magic may remain. Trapped.'

The looks went from Salor to Wazzock.

'But there was no magic in it,' argued Wazzock. 'That's why I broke it.'

And back again.

'Maybe not enough for the staff to work,' said Salor. 'But some. It's possible.'

'Is that true?' asked Frida. 'Might there be magic in that stick?'

'A small amount perhaps,' said Salor. He went on to explain that a wizard's staff was all magic. From its tip to its bottom. But there had to be enough magic to make it work. Not enough, and the power of the staff will weaken. And if that happens and it was to break, and violently so, then whatever magic was left may well concentrate into one place. One piece. 'Or not,' he said when he had finished explaining.

The feeling of hope that everyone had started to feel now started to evaporate.

'But they said they saw a spark,' said Danrite, trying to keep his hope afloat.

'We did,' said paws.

'Then we should at least try it,' suggested Frida.

'Yes,' agreed Percy. 'And there's no time like the present.'

'I'll get it,' said Salor.

'No,' said Frida, 'let Danrite do it. It's written, remember.'

'Me?' said Danrite, not keen on touching something that sparks or taking it from a dog-god were-xolo.

'Go on,' urged Frida, 'nothing has happened to Pablo.'

That was true, thought Danrite, but what about Pablo?

Nothing, thought Pablo, how dare she. I was once dog-god, I am not calling that nothing. He looked at the stick. But now I am stick chewing. Suddenly, all the fun went from having the stick. But it was a stick. His stick. They would not have it without a fight. But there were many other sticks. Less dangerous ones if that buffoon in the pointy hat was right. And it doesn't squeak. Pah, I am finished with it, it is being boring. Let them have it. Pablo then pushed the stick, although reluctantly, towards Danrite.

Danrite cautiously walked towards Pablo, and then, when it looked like Pablo was a happy dog-god, he gingerly picked it up. Phew, he thought, no shocks. But he didn't want to hold it any longer than he had to. He quickly turned and headed for Thaw. All he had to do was push it in the yellow – not a pleasant thought – and hope for the best. The best being imagination back to how it was. But halfway to Thaw, a voice spoke out. It was Thaw.

'Hold on a minute,' protested Thaw, nervously eyeing the stick in Danrite's hand. 'Shouldn't I have a say in all this?'

'It's to save imagination,' said Danrite.

'I know that,' said Thaw. 'But what will happen to me?'

'I…' said Danrite, faltering. 'I don't know,' he admitted. He turned, looking for help and was faced with a multitude of the usual blank expressions.

Percy stepped up. 'Didn't your nightmare say?' he asked.

Thaw went to say no but was asleep before he could.

'Hello,' said Thaw's nightmare, who was now a melting snowman. The sun was now high in the sky behind him. It was wearing a smile. Fairly beaming down at Thaw it was.

'Oh!' said Thaw.

'Sorry,' said Thaw's nightmare.

'Why are you here?' asked Thaw once over the shock.

'I forgot to tell you something.'

'You did?'

'Yeah,' said the nightmare, who was now in danger of forming a puddle. 'You'll be going home after all is done.'

'Will I? Wait, were you listening?'

'Not as such,' said the nightmare. 'More hanging around, really, because I'd forgotten to tell you you were going home. I was waiting for the right moment. And hey, it's great you've found some magic. The guy's back home will be pleased.'

'Yeah, great,' said Thaw, wondering if it was. But his nightmare had said he was going home. So perhaps it was. Wouldn't hurt to check one more time.

'You will,' assured Thaw's nightmare. 'And what's more, you'll be snow colour again.'

Snow colour? And then it clicked. Snow colour! 'Wahoo!' yelled Thaw. He had been yellow for so long. But just as Thaw thought to ask if the smell would go away as well, he was awake again.

'Wahoo?' said Danrite.

'A nightmare?' asked Percy.

'Yes,' said Thaw, all excited, 'and I'm ready for whatever happens next.' If he was still smelly afterwards, then so be it. At least he would be smelly at home. He would deal with it then. 'Do it.'

Danrite, urged on by all and sundry before Thaw changed his mind, stepped within reach of the yellow.

'Wait,' shouted Thaw suddenly. All and sundry took a deep breath in. 'Watch where you poke that stick.' And out again.

Danrite blushed and raised the stick before sticking it in Thaw's shoulder.

It was in.

A moment later, it was out again.

Well, thought Thaw, that was a waste of time. Still with the snow. Still with the ice. Still with the dark. Still with the… Oh goodness!

If Thaw had owned a jaw, it would have just dropped all the way to the floor. There were sparkles. On the ice. On the snow. He looked up. More sparkles way up in the dark. Stars. Now, his eyes began to sparkle. He suddenly knew where he was. It had worked. He was home.

CHAPTER 123

How they had got there, no one knew. It had happened in a flash. But got there, they had.

Danrite, Frida, Twinkle, Salor, Vlad and Jose were back where their adventure had started, in the Font's castle. The one in colour.

And they weren't alone. The others had travelled with them. As had the other others, including the one with the playing cards. And Basil and Thyme. And Percy.

'Did it work?' said Danrite, his arm still straight out as it had been when he had stuck the stick into Thaw. But now, there was no Thaw. No stick.

'I don't know,' said Frida. But what she did know, what was slowly rolling over her, was that she was no longer standing in a world of greyness.

'Ay caramba,' cried Jose, 'I am not being believing it.'

'Look,' said Twinkle, staring in wonderment. 'It's the others.' Some of them, at least. Wazzock and Pablo they recognised immediately. And was that Von Vlod?

'Good grief,' exclaimed Salor. 'And look there.' He had just noticed the other others were there as well.

They did, and none of them could believe what they were seeing. The other others were no longer creatures formed by a lack of imagination. They were back to how they should be, how imagination had created them.

A mermaid had thrown off her breadcrumbs and was now flashing her silvery tail in delight. Beside her stood a tall, handsome man, able again to change into whatever he wanted to, whenever he wanted to. He stooped and swooped the mermaid into his arms. She whooped as she put her arms around his neck and hugged him.

The sage, who was no longer a tall stem of broccoli, wisely looked on and smiled, adding his smile to the numerous others forming on the faces of the other others as they began to realise what had happened.

'I don't believe it,' said Twinkle. She had just noticed Wrinkle. Wrinkle was no longer tall and white but as small as a child's thumb. She saw Twinkle and fluttered over to land on her shoulder.

Twinkle could hardly believe it. Not because Wrinkle had changed so, but because of what she had changed into. She was the rarest of fairy kind. A Night fairy. Her body as black as ebony, wings as white as snow. Her eyes a dazzling ultraviolet.

Wazzock, his robe back to its best, his staff back in one piece, strolled across to Salor. He held out a hand, which Salor shook. 'Nice tie,' he said.

Salor looked down. The colour was back. The silver. The gold. It was a beautiful tie. 'Thank you,' he said. It was all he could think to say.

'Oi,' said Danrite.

But Jose and Pablo ignored him. It was how dogs greeted each other. Pablo, unlike the others, had not changed. He was still a were-xolo, but now he was a dog-god again. And gods could do whatever they wanted to. Pablo chose to be Pablo the were-xolo.

'It is being what we do,' said Jose.

'Sí,' said Pablo, 'it is being what we are doing.'

Von Vlod, and it was Von Vlod who Twinkle had seen, wasn't a vampire count. She was a vampire countess. And in a male vampire world where being a count was supreme, a countess was rarely treated as an equal. But right now, she didn't care. She was back. And she was staring hard at Vlad via his mirror. She had never seen such a handsome vampire.

'Hello,' said Von Vlod, holding out a hand. They had met, of course, but had not yet been formally introduced. 'I am Countess Von Vlod. And I am no longer a shadow of my former self.'

'Countess,' said Vlad, bowing. He took her hand in his and gently brushed his lips against it. 'It is a pleasure to meet you. I am Vlad.' I am also a tad bewitched, he thought.

And so, all might think that all's well had ended well. It hadn't. Not for Twinkle, Salor, Vlad or Jose. For some reason, they had not returned to their properly imagined selves. Apart from the colour. That was back. But before they could even question the why's and unfairness of it, a voice rang out, drawing everyone's attention. A voice nearly all recognised as belonging to the Font.

246

'Basil?' she exclaimed, nearly dropping the popcorn she had just been to get. She stared at the now packed room. 'What's going on?'

But it wasn't Basil she had seen. It was Thyme, formally known as the hooded figure. And that meant it was time to confront the Font with what Basil had told them.

'That's Thyme,' said Frida. The room's attention now turning to her.

'Thyme?' said the Font, looking puzzled. She lowered the box of popcorn.

'Don't pretend you don't know,' said Frida accusingly.

'I don't know what you mean,' said the Font. 'And how dare you speak to me like that?' The box of popcorn was dropped on the floor, spilling its contents across it.

'Oh-oh,' said Twinkle, who wanted answers the same as everyone else, but this was the Font. The legend that was.

'And why did you tell them I was an avatar?' said Percy, who had overheard Salor slyly telling Wazzock. Wizards, what can you do? Percy had stepped forward to add his weight to the conversation.

The Font looked visibly shocked.

'Well?' demanded Frida, wondering how Percy knew. She was sure she would find out later. She wouldn't. Percy was a ghost of honour and would pretend he had overheard them all talking about it.

'I-I thought it for the best,' said the Font.

'The best for who?' asked Percy.

'And Thyme?' said Frida.

'Who?'

The Font looked from Percy to Frida and then back again.

The Font's face hardened for a moment, causing the whole room to draw a breath, before softening again. She even smiled. 'For Danrite,' she said. 'I thought it might soften the blow of losing you.'

'But he didn't know,' said Frida. 'He was out for the count when you had Percy the avatar appear.'

'Was he?' said the Font. She looked at the spilt popcorn at her feet. And when she looked up again, her smile had gone. 'Then why didn't you tell him?'

All the while this was happening, a puzzled Danrite was looking

247

on as if a spectator at a tennis match.

'Because we thought he had been through enough,' said Frida. She turned and smiled at Danrite as Twinkle put an arm around his shoulders. 'We'll talk later, okay.' Danrite nodded.

'Then all appears to have worked out for the best,' said the Font. She looked past Frida and Percy at the menagerie of beings behind them.

Perhaps the Font was telling the truth about Danrite, but Frida wasn't finished with the Font. 'For Danrite perhaps,' she said, 'but what about Thyme?'

The stare Frida received from the Font would have wilted a lesser person, but Frida stood her ground. 'I have already told you,' said the Font sternly. 'I know no one of that name.'

'Basil says you do,' Frida responded. 'Basil.'

Basil stepped from amongst the menagerie.

Again, the Font looked visibly shaken. 'Basil?' she said, glancing at Thyme. 'Two Basils? I don't understand.'

'No, just the one,' said Frida. 'But so alike they could be twin brothers.'

'But…' The Font was struggling to understand just what it was she was seeing. And why.

Frida continued. 'Two peas in a pod who shared the same aim,' she said. 'To destroy the evil.'

The Font collected herself at the mention of the evil. 'Well,' she said. 'If that is true, then this Thyme person, who I repeat, I do not know, wanted what we wanted. To destroy the evil. Apart from not knowing him, I don't see what the problem is.' She again glanced past Frida at the menagerie. 'And, by the look of things, we succeeded. We should be celebrating.'

'But the problem we have,' said Frida, 'is that the evil you sent us to destroy wasn't evil. Quite the opposite.'

'If we had destroyed it,' said Percy, 'we would have destroyed imagination forever.'

'And that's what you wanted,' said Frida. 'You are the one who was trying to destroy imagination.'

'That's absurd,' snapped the Font.

'Twinkle,' said Frida, 'can you bring Thyme over here please?'

248

'With pleasure,' said Twinkle.

Thyme was dragged before the Font and asked if he knew her. He denied knowing her. True.

'See,' said the Font, beginning to lose her patience. 'He doesn't know me, and I most certainly don't know him.' The Font stood taller.

'But I know the voice,' said Thyme, surprising the Font and everyone else. 'It's usually a bit deeper, but it's the same.'

'What?' said the Font.

'And you do know him,' said Basil, suddenly drawing on courage he didn't know he had. And as he did it, he knew he could say goodbye to that television he had always wanted, forever. 'It's one of the names you call me.'

'Have you quite finished?' The Font demanded.

'No,' said Basil, surprising her. In for a penny, he was thinking. 'I thought it was because you forgot my name sometimes, but I don't think that's true anymore. I think it's because you kept getting us mixed up.'

'Again,' said the Font, 'I don't know him. It's stuff and nonsense.'

'You say,' said Frida, now not caring if the Font knew Thyme or not. 'And who cares what you say? At the end of the day, you were foiled, and imagination was saved despite you and your plans.'

The murmurs and occasional gasps uttered here and there at Frida's words now grew.

And as it grew, the Font's patience shortened. Shortened further. She was nearing breaking point. She had never been treated like this before. At breaking point. Cracks were appearing. How dare they! How dare they come here and accuse me? Me, the Font. The cracks grew larger. Who do they think they are? How dare they! HOW DARE THEY! The cracks suddenly became chasms. Joined to become one. And from it emerged... HOW DARE THEY ACCUSE ME? ACCUSE THE MASTER!

'HOW DARE YOU!' roared the Master in the Font's voice, only much deeper now.

Gasps went up. Steps were taken back. Frida, Basil and Percy among them.

'Flipping heck,' stammered Twinkle, 'the Font's turned into a geezer.'

249

'She's two people,' said Danrite. 'Like Salor and Mister Power.' The Font had split her son into two, good and evil. Salor and Mister Power. She had then put them back together again when her plan had ended.

Salor shivered at the thought of his supposed brother.

'Ay caramba,' said Jose, 'you could not be writing this.'

But Thyme had stayed where he was. The Font he had not known. The Master he did. But what had just happened? A thought carried through the room by many at that moment.

The Master's head snapped towards Thyme. 'Why didn't you destroy it?' he snarled. Thyme shrank away. The whole room now shrank back. 'I should have done it myself.' He cast a terrifying glance across the hall. 'I should have destroyed it as I am going to destroy all of you.'

'Keep back,' shouted Percy, now standing his ground, reasoning that as he was a ghost, he could not be hurt.

Vlad stepped beside Percy. What he could do, he didn't know, but at least, like Percy, he doubted he could be hurt.

The Master raised his arms.

Frida stepped forward, her tazer raised.

Danrite had removed his sword and held it out before him as he joined her.

Jose showed teeth that were way too big for his mouth.

Twinkle clenched her fists. She wouldn't let her friends go down without her.

Salor, his staff poised, had joined them. They were family.

And those that could also took a step forward. Stepped up.

The others as one.

The other others as many.

Even Basil.

Seeing this, the Master, screaming a spine-chilling roar of pure venom, aimed and let loose a fearsome and terrifying bolt of energy from his fingertips towards them. To rend. To destroy. To...

To bounce harmlessly off the tip of Danrite's sword.

'Wow,' said Danrite, eyes wide. 'What just happened?'

'I don't know,' said Frida, staring at the Master, who just stood there, arms in the air, like a statue. He looked asleep.

As they then were.

Then, they did know.

And then they weren't.

But the Master still was.

Thanks to the nightmares.

CHAPTER 124

It was over.

The Master had been stopped.

Imagination had been saved.

CHAPTER 125

'Do you think they can hold him?' said Danrite.

'I hope so,' said Frida.

'It'll be easier once they separate him from the Font,' said Percy.

They were the nightmares.

Nightmares, called by thoughts connected to daydreams connected to dreams connected to nightmares, who had been busy sharing imagination with the dreams who had passed it on until it settled in the thoughts, had acted quickly when they got the news. The link alerting the nightmares to the mischief the Master had in mind.

It had taken quite a few nightmares to stop the Master, who, thankfully, had had quite a lot of them. One of which, and proved to be the key nightmare, was about losing his power.

As for the Font, it turned out she was telling the truth about Thyme. She knew nothing of him or the Master, the alter-ego existing inside her that had slowly grown stronger over time. Living only in the night. And she had thought that Thaw really was the evil they had to destroy. The Master playing no small part in that. Diverting everyone away from the real evil wanting to destroy imagination onto the very thing that could save it. A brilliant plan. But a plan doomed in the end by a dream, that had turned to a nightmare. And in turn to many nightmares. The Font would, in time, regain complete control of her mind. She would never find out where the Master had come from. Or she never said.

Basil and Thyme, it turned out, *were* brothers. But in the cloning sense. The size of the castle and the amount of wings it had meant their paths never crossed. That, and them working at different times. Thyme night. Basil day. As for the slipping of the tongue regarding the calling of wrong names, it was down to the Font's mind being slightly smaller than the castle, so the crossing of paths between her and the Master, rare as that was, did happen on occasion. Usually during a headache.

And once the daggers were put away, they found they had much in common. Both liked wanting to watch television, Basil more so, his life revolved around it, but something they both dreamed of. So imagine their delight when, as a reward, the Font told them they would be allowed out on occasion to peep through people's windows to watch it.

Thankfully, Danrite had a whip-round and raised enough cash to buy each of them a portable television. Unknown people living in the area would be unknowingly grateful to him for that.

The others and the other others? They said their goodbyes and returned to the Otherworlds they called home. Promises were made to keep in touch. Numbers and addresses were exchanged. Hopefully, they would be remembered.

'Well,' said Twinkle, giving Vlad a nudge and a wink, 'did you get her contact details?'

'Maybe,' said Vlad, blushing an invisible one.

'I did,' said Salor.

'Did you?' said Twinkle and Vlad, giving him surprised looks.

Salor looked puzzled for a moment, then realised what he had said. 'Oh, no,' he said. 'I meant, I got Wazzocks. We might look at some ties together sometime.' His turn to redden. 'But I don't know. Not looking like this.' He gestured to his face where the cheap mascara was running.

Frida frowned at his remark. It wasn't fair that her friends hadn't changed back. She had seen Twinkle give Wrinkle an envious look once or twice, and she just knew that Vlad wished he could be seen by his Countess properly. Frida decided to speak with Percy about it and see if he had any idea why they hadn't changed. She left the others chatting and went to talk to him.

'What about you, Jose,' said Danrite, 'you keeping in touch with Pablo?'

'Sí,' said Jose, a toothy grin on his face, 'I am being with the touching of him.'

'That's nice,' said Danrite, making a face. He thought he would leave it there, and seeing Frida talking to Percy, he went to join them.

'Just the nephew,' said Percy as Danrite approached.

Danrite smiled but still wasn't sure how he felt having a ghost as an uncle. Just as weird as the living one, he suspected. Time would tell.

'Percy has something to tell you,' said Frida. Her chat with Percy had been better than she could have ever imagined. He had been going to tell everyone when he had the chance, but prompted by Frida, the chance might as well be now. Danrite frowned. 'Well, everyone, really.' She called their friends over.

'What is it?' asked Danrite as the others gathered around.

Percy gave a polite cough before saying what he had to say. 'The Font wasn't being totally truthful about things,' he said.

'You don't say, Sherlock,' said Twinkle.

Vlad had a titter.

Percy ignored them. 'About a few things,' he continued.

'We gathered that,' said Salor.

Percy ignored him as well. 'Especially about Danrite's, and of course Frida's, parents.'

'Go on,' said Twinkle intrigued.

'And about your changing back to how you were,' said Percy.

'What about our parents?' asked Danrite, looking worried. 'Are they ghosts as well?'

'No,' said Frida, 'Percy thinks they're alive but missing somewhere in the Otherworlds.'

'Where?' said Danrite, trying not to be too hopeful.

'Ah,' said Percy. 'That's just it, we don't know.' Danrite's face fell. 'But what we do know is where they were before they disappeared.'

Twinkle was as excited and pleased about the news as anyone, but how did that help them with changing back? She wanted to know. She asked.

Percy told them what he knew. For some reason, they would stay as they were until Danrite and Frida's parents were found.

'We can't change until Danrite and Frida's parents are found?' said Vlad.

'Why?' asked Salor.

'Who told you that?' demanded Twinkle.

'A nightmare,' said Percy.

'You had a nightmare about them?' said Danrite.

'No. It was when they arrived to foil the Master. While we were under,' said Percy, knowing it sounded crazy. 'One of them reached out to me with what they knew through my nightmare. It was just a message. I don't know who sent it, but my nightmare thought the information was good.'

'And you tell us now?' said Twinkle.

'Things happened,' said Percy.

'Fair enough,' said Twinkle, thinking he wasn't wrong.

'I'm hoping you'll help us find them,' said Percy.

'But why like this?' said Vlad. 'Surely it would be better if we were ourselves?'

'Sí,' said Jose. 'I am being bigger and more with the fierce then.'

'I don't know,' said Percy. 'The nightmare didn't know.' He gave them a helpless look and shrugged. 'What can I say? There's a connection somewhere. Which I suppose will be revealed when we find them.'

'So, what do you all think?' said Frida. 'Will you help us find our parents?'

There followed a quick discussion. A very quick discussion. How else were they going to change back to how they were? But more importantly, Danrite and Frida needed their help. They were friends. Family.

'Count me in,' said Vlad, not meaning to be funny.

'Sí, and me,' said Jose. 'I am being counted too. It is what is being friends.'

'For friends,' said Twinkle.

'Yes,' said Salor, a tear in his eye. The mascara?

'For family,' said Percy.

'When do we go?' said Twinkle.

'No time like the present,' said Percy.

Danrite looked at Frida, and Frida looked at Danrite. They were going to look for their parents.

AUTHORS THOUGHT

It had worked. The magic in the stick, when it touched the yellow of the snowman.

Or had it?

Was there magic in the stick? In a world where no magic existed?

Or had the other others imagined it? The sparks. Blue in a world of no colour?

Or was it just the idea of it working that had made it work? No one will ever really know.

I don't.

Something had worked, though.

Something had made the last bit of colour in that Otherworld of diminishing imagination erupt into life, helped it expand, spreading colour into every dark corner of the land once more. But what?

Imagination is a powerful thing. With imagination, you can do anything. Be anything. See anything.

Is that what had happened? Had imagination won the day?

Well, we can only imagine, can't we?